TREACHEROUS SEAS

Acclaim for Radclyﬀe's Fiction

"*Dangerous Waters* is a bumpy ride through a devastating time with powerful events and resolute characters. Radclyffe gives us the strong, dedicated women we love to read in a story that keeps us turning pages until the end."—*Lambda Literary Review*

"Radclyffe's *Dangerous Waters* has the feel of a tense television drama, as the narrative interchanges between hurricane trackers and first responders. Sawyer and Dara butt heads in the beginning as each moves for some level of control during the storm's approach, and the interference of a lovely television reporter adds an engaging love triangle threat to the sexual tension brewing between them."—*RT Book Reviews*

"*Love After Hours*, the fourth in Radclyffe's Rivers Community series, evokes the sense of a continuing drama as Gina and Carrie's slow-burning romance intertwines with details of other Rivers residents. They become part of a greater picture where friends and family support each other in personal and recreational endeavors. Vivid settings and characters draw in the reader…"—*RT Book Reviews*

Secret Hearts "delivers exactly what it says on the tin: poignant story, sweet romance, great characters, chemistry and hot sex scenes. Radclyffe knows how to pen a good lesbian romance."—*LezReviewBooks Blog*

Wild Shores "will hook you early. Radclyffe weaves a chance encounter into all-out steamy romance. These strong, dynamic women have great conversations, and fantastic chemistry."—*The Romantic Reader Blog*

In **2016 RWA/OCC Book Buyers Best award winner for suspense and mystery with romantic elements** *Price of Honor* "Radclyffe is master of the action-thriller series…The old familiar characters are there, but enough new blood is introduced to give it a fresh feel and open new avenues for intrigue."—*Curve Magazine*

In **Benjamin Franklin Award finalist** *Desire by Starlight* "Radclyffe writes romance with such heart and her down-to-earth characters not only come to life but leap off the page until you feel like you know them. What Jenna and Gard feel for each other is not only a spark but an inferno and, as a reader, you will be washed away in this tumultuous romance until you can do nothing but succumb to it."—*Queer Magazine Online*

Lambda Literary Award winner *Stolen Moments* "is a collection of steamy stories about women who just couldn't wait. It's sex when desire overrides reason, and it's incredibly hot!"—*On Our Backs*

Lambda Literary Award winner *Distant Shores, Silent Thunder* "weaves an intricate tapestry about passion and commitment between lovers. The story explores the fragile nature of trust and the sanctuary provided by loving relationships."—*Sapphic Reader*

Lambda Literary Award Finalist *Justice Served* delivers a "crisply written, fast-paced story with twists and turns and keeps us guessing until the final explosive ending."—*Independent Gay Writer*

Lambda Literary Award finalist *Turn Back Time* "is filled with wonderful love scenes, which are both tender and hot."—*MegaScene*

Applause for L.L. Raand's Midnight Hunters Series

The Midnight Hunt
RWA 2012 VCRW Laurel Wreath winner *Blood Hunt*
Night Hunt
The Lone Hunt

"Raand has built a complex world inhabited by werewolves, vampires, and other paranormal beings…Raand has given her readers a complex plot filled with wonderful characters as well as insight into the hierarchy of Sylvan's pack and vampire clans. There are many plot twists and turns, as well as erotic sex scenes in this riveting novel that keep the pages flying until its satisfying conclusion."—*Just About Write*

"Once again, I am amazed at the storytelling ability of L.L. Raand aka Radclyffe. In *Blood Hunt*, she mixes high levels of sheer eroticism that will leave you squirming in your seat with an impeccable multi-character storyline all streaming together to form one great read." —*Queer Magazine Online*

"*The Midnight Hunt* has a gripping story to tell, and while there are also some truly erotic sex scenes, the story always takes precedence. This is a great read which is not easily put down nor easily forgotten."—*Just About Write*

"Are you sick of the same old hetero vampire/werewolf story plastered in every bookstore and at every movie theater? Well, I've got the cure to your werewolf fever. *The Midnight Hunt* is first in, what I hope is, a long-running series of fantasy erotica for L.L. Raand (aka Radclyffe)."—*Queer Magazine Online*

"Any reader familiar with Radclyffe's writing will recognize the author's style within *The Midnight Hunt*, yet at the same time it is most definitely a new direction. The author delivers an excellent story here, one that is engrossing from the very beginning. Raand has pieced together an intricate world, and provided just enough details for the reader to become enmeshed in the new world. The action moves quickly throughout the book and it's hard to put down."—*Three Dollar Bill Reviews*

By Radcly*ff*e

The Provincetown Tales

Safe Harbor

Beyond the Breakwater

Distant Shores, Silent Thunder

Storms of Change

Winds of Fortune

Returning Tides

Sheltering Dunes

Treacherous Seas

PMC Hospitals Romances

Passion's Bright Fury (prequel)

Fated Love

Night Call

Crossroads

Passionate Rivals

Rivers Community Romances

Against Doctor's Orders

Prescription for Love

Love on Call

Love After Hours

Love to the Rescue

Love on the Night Shift

Honor Series

Above All, Honor

Honor Bound

Love & Honor

Honor Guards

Honor Reclaimed

Honor Under Siege

Word of Honor

Oath of Honor
(First Responders)

Code of Honor

Price of Honor

Cost of Honor

Justice Series

A Matter of Trust (prequel)

Shield of Justice

In Pursuit of Justice

Justice in the Shadows

Justice Served

Justice for All

First Responders Novels

Trauma Alert
Firestorm
Taking Fire

Wild Shores
Heart Stop
Dangerous Waters

Romances

Innocent Hearts
Promising Hearts
Love's Melody Lost
Love's Tender Warriors
Tomorrow's Promise
Love's Masquerade
shadowland
Turn Back Time

When Dreams Tremble
The Lonely Hearts Club
Secrets in the Stone
Desire by Starlight
Homestead
The Color of Love
Secret Hearts

Short Fiction

Collected Stories by Radclyffe
Erotic Interludes: *Change Of Pace*
Radical Encounters

Stacia Seaman and Radclyffe, eds.:
Erotic Interludes Vol. 2–5
Romantic Interludes Vol. 1–2
Breathless: *Tales of Celebration*
Women of the Dark Streets
Amor and More: Love Everafter
Myth & Magic: Queer Fairy Tales

Writing As L.L. Raand
Midnight Hunters

The Midnight Hunt
Blood Hunt
Night Hunt

The Lone Hunt
The Magic Hunt
Shadow Hunt

Visit us at www.boldstrokesbooks.com

TREACHEROUS SEAS

by

RADCLY*f*FE

2020

TREACHEROUS SEAS
© 2020 BY RADCLYFFE. ALL RIGHTS RESERVED.

ISBN 13: 978-1-63555-778-7

THIS TRADE PAPERBACK ORIGINAL IS PUBLISHED BY
BOLD STROKES BOOKS, INC.
P.O. BOX 249
VALLEY FALLS, NY 12185

FIRST EDITION: NOVEMBER 2020

CREDITS
EDITORS: RUTH STERNGLANTZ AND STACIA SEAMAN
PRODUCTION DESIGN: STACIA SEAMAN
COVER DESIGN BY TAMMY SEIDICK

Acknowledgments

Thank you to all the readers who have never given up on this series (or given up asking for more). *Safe Harbor*—the first in the series—was my first published book (although not the first one I wrote), and that book and the village that inspired it hold special places in my heart. As soon as I started writing, I felt like I was coming home. I loved introducing a new couple to the mix and spending time with characters I have known for decades. This is most of all a book about the power of community, friendship, trust, and bravery in the face of uncertainty.

This book is better for all the help I've had while writing it: Sandy Lowe for encouragement, belief in my stories, and keeping all the BSB wheels turning; Stacia Seaman and Ruth Sternglantz for editorial expertise; Paula and Eva for the always timely and insightful first reads; and Lee for being there through all the challenges.

Radclyffe, 2020

To all the essentials who keep our lives going,
despite the personal costs

CHAPTER ONE

A ndy Champlain loved warm summer nights, when the sultry heat of the day still lingered like a soft breath against her skin. Tonight the hint of cotton candy mixed with fresh salt air brought images of long-ago trips to the Atlantic City boardwalk, of dodging in and out of the surf and racing down the crowded sidewalks to her favorite ice cream stand, determined to get there ahead of her fleeter older brother. The memories, viewed through the sepia lens of time, carried a familiar patina of sadness, and she pushed the past away.

Walking a beat on the night shift in Provincetown was a whole new kind of special, and after six weeks, she still wasn't used to the way a breeze off the water would catch her unawares and leave her exhilarated and unaccountably content. As she passed through the intersection at Standish and Commercial, maneuvering her way through the crowd spilling out of the ice cream shop on the corner, she scanned down the wharf to the harbor. Past the blinking lights on the fishing trawlers moored along the dock, in the darkness at the far reaches of the bay, pinpoints of light dotted the inky water, as if the sky had turned upside down and dumped the stars atop the waves. Farther out toward Long Point, the rhythmic pulse of the lighthouse beacon beat in counterpoint to the lowing of the foghorn, while here on the street winding along the harbor's edge, at just before one in the morning, life bustled as if sleep was a forgotten pastime. Many of the stores clustered along Commercial Street in the center of town had closed at sundown, but the bars and clubs were open, as was the Mediterranean place across from Town Hall, the cookie and candy place next to it, and of course, Spiritus Pizza, the final congregating point for partygoers before everyone finally disappeared into the condos, bed-and-breakfasts, and rare motels.

Being on foot, after riding in a patrol car during her month-long training period, suited her fine. She relished the chance to feel the night tingling on her skin, to get close to the life that seethed along the main thoroughfare and up the narrow alleys, to breathe in the fragrances of pizza and steak and the occasional whiff of a tantalizing scent as someone brushed past her, smelling like sin. She'd smile in appreciation, then keep her eyes forward and keep walking. The week leading up to the Fourth of July holiday had seen ten thousand more people crowding into the two-by-three-mile town on the very tip of Cape Cod. What had been pleasant throngs before was a crush now, day and night. Tour buses arrived first thing in the morning and disgorged hundreds of travelers who descended on the funky shops and restaurants in a frenzy. The ferry brought scores of day-trippers over from Boston, and the more people there were, the more business for the small Provincetown police force. And Andy loved it. The more action the better. Movement, adrenaline, and danger kept her fed as surely as any food.

Her radio crackled just as she passed in front of the Unitarian church.

"3-Baker-15. Report of a 4-4 at the Alehouse," Ralph White, the dispatcher at the station, reported.

A disturbance—a bar fight, most likely, or one about to erupt—was practically a nightly occurrence. At closing time, the occasional rumpus wasn't unusual, not with a few hundred sexed-up, usually liquored-up bodies jousting for a hookup, or realizing that the person they'd come with had already hooked up elsewhere. Usually, just walking into the place quieted things down. At least, in her six weeks' experience policing in the town, that had been the case. Andy's pulse kicked up a notch.

"10-4," Andy replied. "I'm a minute away."

"Adam-101 en route. Three minutes out," Ralph White added.

"Copy," Andy said, breaking into an easy jog. She was right around the corner from the bar, a popular place on a side street halfway between Commercial and Bradford. Mostly a guy bar, but not exclusively. Known for its leather clientele, but again, not exclusively.

She reached the place a good two minutes before her backup. Bri Parker, who'd been her training officer the month before, would have trouble getting through town in her patrol car, even if she put her lights on. People just couldn't move out of the way in the narrow one-way street, even if they wanted to, and most of the time the pedestrians played chicken with vehicles just to register their displeasure at being inconvenienced while out on a stroll. And really, what was the point of waiting while whatever was going on inside heated up? She was already there. The longer she waited, the more chance things would escalate. She might be new to town, but not to the job.

She gave it another thirty seconds, until a clutch of people burst out of the doors, one of them yelling, "That maniac's got a knife."

Andy jumped the three steps to the narrow porch running the length of the building and pushed her way through the clot of customers all trying to get through the single, narrow front door, keying her shoulder radio as she went. "3-Baker-44. Reports of an armed civilian. Entering premises."

"10-4. Advising backup."

The interior of the long, narrow room was about as dark as the night had been, and fortunately, Andy could see fairly well. She'd never been inside, but the layout was uncomplicated. A bar ran down the entire right-hand side with the usual mirrored wall behind rows of liquor bottles. The barstools were buried behind patrons, six deep, who surged toward the exit in a sluggish jumble of arms and legs. A red strobe, angled in the back corner above an empty ten-foot-square stage, illuminated more people—the ones who weren't shoving toward the door—jostling in a loose circle, facing into the center of the room, which was populated with small tables and chairs pushed askew. Whatever the action was, it was there.

"Police," Andy said tersely, shouldering her way forward through the ring of onlookers. "Break it up. Police."

People tried to move aside, crowding out any clear pathway, and Andy reflexively covered her holstered weapon with one hand as she pressed her way between the mostly male bodies, shoulder leading like a battering ram.

A male voice, gone high with anxiety, shouted, "For God's sake, Max, put it down."

Andy finally managed to push her way between two burly men, one in a tight black tank top with arms the size of tree limbs—big trees—and the other with backless chaps exposing a fleshy bare ass, and got a look at the action. In the center of the ring of onlookers, three men, two in various combinations of leather and denim and the other one, incongruously, in a polo shirt and khaki pants, occupied a small circle of light beneath an overhead spot. The taller of the two leather guys was shirtless with a leather harness strapped over his chest, a big steel ring in the very center, and blue jeans so tight and threadbare Andy could count the veins on his dick if she'd cared to. She didn't, especially not while he brandished a nine-inch blade, slim and narrowed to a nasty point. *Switchblade.* He flicked it in the face of the preppy-looking guy in the khakis, shouting, "Let's see how quick you are to go after someone else's husband next time, you little cocksucker."

The guy in the polo, looking as pale as white flour, even in the dim light, held both hands up in front of his face, palms out. "No way, man. I didn't know—he never said he was with anyone."

The knife wielder glanced sideways at the muscleman. "Oh, is that right. Maybe you're the one who needs the lesson."

With the assailant's attention diverted for an instant, Andy pushed in front of the guy in the khakis, shoved him back with one hand, and shouted, "Police. Put the knife down. Put it down *now.*"

His head snapped around, and the dark eyes that glared at her were wild, just short of outright crazy. Or maybe already there. "Fuck you."

"Put it down," Andy repeated. She kept her eyes on his face, her gaze meeting his, but the knife hand was clear in her peripheral vision. His pupils danced, and she settled her stance, sliding her left foot slightly forward, and centered her weight evenly on both legs. Readied herself. Watchful awareness. Calm and quiet. Slow even breaths.

Not even a second passed.

A flicker of hesitation passed over his face, and then his lids opened wide and he lunged, knife stabbing for her chest.

She pivoted, right shoulder forward, hips square to him, and the knife hand passed by her left side. As it did, before he could pull back for a side-handed swipe or another lunge, she snaked her left arm around and under his knife arm, pinning it to her side, and drove her hip into his midsection. As he lost his balance, she caught him under the chin with her right hand, forcing him off his feet, and took him down with a hip throw. He landed hard, stunned, and she flipped him onto his belly, one knee on his back and the other on his knife arm. She reached forward, pulled the knife away and down by her side beyond his reach, and yanked her cuffs free with the other hand. From behind her, she heard shouts of, "Police. *Move. Move.*"

Backup. Just in time to mop up. Smiling to herself, she clamped her cuff onto one wrist and reached to secure the other. A bolt of pain shot from her jaw into the back of her head, and she was falling.

❖

Reese Conlon grabbed her cell phone on the second ring and rolled away from her wife, hoping that was enough to keep from waking Tory.

"Conlon," she said quietly.

"Sorry, Chief," Ralph White said, "but we've got a situation."

Reese slipped out from beneath the thin sheet, padded across to the bathroom, went in, and closed the door behind her. "What's going on?"

"Officer assaulted—needs medical attention."

Reese's stomach tightened. "Who? Where?"

"Champlain, happened at the Alehouse. Bri's there—just called it in."

"How bad?"

"Not sure. Champlain took a kick to the head, looks like, but she's awake. A little groggy, Bri says."

Reese let out a long breath. No one was dead. "Is the assailant in custody?"

"Oh yeah." Ralph, a sixty-year-old who'd retired to the Cape after a long and lucrative career as a financial advisor in Manhattan, had been the night dispatcher for a decade. He was unflappable in an emergency and could always be trusted to keep everyone else calm, relaying critical intel while keeping an eye on the details that might get missed when adrenaline was high. "Subdued and awaiting transport to lockup."

"Is the scene secure? Crowd under control?"

"Tremont and Ramos are on their way. Should be there…about now. Parker requests clearance to transport Champlain to the clinic."

"Okay. Contact whoever's on call out there. Tell them it's an emergency."

"Done."

Reese said, "I'm headed to the clinic. Have Tremont report when she gets the guy in lockup."

"10-4."

Reese set the phone aside, splashed her face with cold water, swirled a little mouthwash, and eased back into the bedroom for the clothes she always left on the chair by the hall door.

"What is it?" Tory asked from the stillness of the bed.

"One of my summer officers, Andy Champlain, is on the way to the clinic. Doesn't sound real serious, but I'm not sure yet." Reese chucked the T-shirt she'd been wearing onto the bench at the end of the bed.

Tory sat up. "I'll get dressed."

"No, you won't," Reese said, pulling on her uniform pants. "You're not on call anymore, remember?"

Tory laughed softly and switched on the bedside lamp. She pushed her auburn hair, tinged ever so slightly with fine wisps of gray, away from her face with one hand, a gesture Reese had always found quintessentially female and excruciatingly sexy. Now, seriously pregnant, Tory was even more beautiful. The wave of love and not inconsiderable lust must have shown, because Tory gave her one of those smiles that promised Reese would be very happy—whenever she managed to get home again.

"Tor," Reese said, shrugging into her shirt and filing the smile away to be replayed on the ride back home, "no more night call. Less than three weeks now, and the critters will be out of there."

Tory smiled and pressed a hand to her rotund belly. "Three weeks feels like about thirty years. And for the record, *two* is a lot more work than one, even now."

Buttoning her shirt, Reese walked over and kissed her. "I know. Well, I don't *know*, but I can only imagine. I'm really, really glad it's you."

Tory laughed, draped an arm around her neck, and kissed her again. "All right, but I want you to call me or have..." She paused. "Laurel's on call tonight. Have her call me after she sees Andy. I want to know what the situation is. I'm pregnant, not infirm. I'm perfectly capable of taking care of patients."

"Yes, and that's why you're still going in half days. But holding clinic hours just means moving from your desk to the treatment rooms. Not dragging around in the middle of the night." Reese put her hand on Tory's belly and waited for a few seconds. The kick came, and the wild joy that surged through her was just as exhilarating as the first time she'd felt it. "Or dragging *them* around."

Tory laced her fingers through Reese's on her belly. "You need to get out of here. But you know, we're going to have to decide on names pretty soon. We can't keep calling them the critters."

"I'll think on it." Reese lifted their joined hands, rubbed Tory's fingers against her cheek, and kissed them. "Go back to sleep."

"Call me," Tory said as Reese softly closed the bedroom door.

Reese eased down the hall toward her daughter's room. Reggie was, thank God, the world's soundest sleeper. Considering how many calls she or Tory got every night, if the almost three-year-old was a light sleeper, they'd all be in trouble. She peeked in the half-open door, saw Reggie sound asleep in the faint light of the Bugs Bunny night-light plugged in near her big-girl bed, and hurried downstairs. The family was safe. Now what mattered were her officers.

Outside, she jumped into the Jeep and, once clear of the house, set the emergency light on the dash and sped away.

CHAPTER TWO

L aurel Winter took a deep breath, unlocked the clinic front doors, reached in, and turned on the light switch. The waiting area just inside held three rows of chairs on either side of a center aisle and a long counter where, during the day, Randy, the office manager/receptionist, managed intake and kept the patients flowing into the examining rooms in the rear. Less than a week on the new job, and the place was already starting to feel familiar. The butterflies in her stomach were an unwelcome addition, but this was her first time taking call alone. Like, totally alone.

"You can do this," she muttered under her breath. Of course she could. She trusted her training. She'd handled emergencies, hundreds of them, in the ER, and on ride-alongs with the ambulance crews, and during her rotations on the hospital floors. She had backup. Nita was a phone call away. A phone call and five minutes away. She'd be fine.

A siren's rhythmic wail, an uncommon sound here though it had been a steady background noise in Philadelphia, grew louder. The cases she'd see in this small clinic on the tip of Cape Cod were a far cry from the constant high-level trauma and medical disasters she'd been exposed to in training, but she expected a busy summer and looked forward to the perfect chance to get her feet wet before she decided what she was going to do with the rest of her life. Her professional life, at least. As far as her personal life was concerned...well, that was up for grabs and definitely on the back burner.

Dr. King—she still couldn't quite get used to thinking of her as Tory—and Nita, who she'd known all her life and practically thought of as a cousin, had explained to her that in season they handled routine medical care for the townspeople plus all kinds of emergencies that cropped up among the tourists—minor injuries, falls and breaks, asthma attacks, heart attacks, animal bites, the occasional snakebite, and sometimes, multiple trauma from auto accidents if the local EMS crews needed backup. All of it had sounded doable, exciting, and now...here she was.

Alone. At almost two in the morning, in an empty clinic where all her self-doubt could echo off the walls and come back to grin at her, finger waving and reminding her that this was what she wanted.

What she wanted, what she *chose*, and what she would do.

No room for self-doubt now, she walked through the clinic, switching on lights as she went, and opened the door to the treatment room. The table in the center of the room was surrounded by anything she might need to handle a serious medical emergency. Cardioverters, monitors, an oxygen tank, and cut down trays on the counter; IV fluids in a cabinet on the right side—no, left side—of the sink. Catheters, suture trays. The only thing missing was someone else in charge. She took a deep breath. She was ready.

From down the hall, the front door banged open. Laurel hurried back to the front of the clinic.

A female officer in a short-sleeved black shirt with a triangular black patch on the shoulder proclaiming *Provincetown Police* in blue block letters, and black uniform pants, burst through the door. Still in her twenties, it looked like, with short black hair, blazing blue eyes, and a look of fierce concentration on her face. A name tag above her right breast read *Bri Parker*. "She's in the cruiser. Head injury. She's awake, but I don't think she can walk in."

"I don't want her to. I'll get a wheelchair." Laurel turned around. She should've thought of that before. Damn it. She couldn't automatically expect patients to arrive on a gurney here, the way she'd been used to in the ER. In seconds, she pulled a chair from the supply closet and pushed it out through the front door. Three steps led from the narrow landing, and off to the side, a ramp for wheelchairs and stretchers ran down to the gravel parking lot. Pushing the chair ahead of her down the ramp, steering haphazardly, she rounded the corner onto the gravel as Officer Parker pulled open the rear door of the patrol car.

The loose stones grabbed at the chair's wheels, slowing her progress and threatening to tip the chair over, but Laurel muscled it up to the cruiser and slammed it open.

Parker leaned into the back seat and murmured, "Andy, can you slide out?"

"Yeah," came a slow, muttered reply. "I'm okay. I'm okay."

"Right," the young officer said. "But we're going to check you out anyway."

"Let me," Laurel said. "Steady the chair."

Parker turned to grip the handles.

A pair of short black boots followed by legs clad in the same black trousers as Parker wore edged out of the patrol car. Laurel leaned into the back seat and slid an arm around a narrow waist. "I'm Laurel Winter, a physician assistant here at the clinic. We're going to get you inside and take care of you."

The rear of the vehicle was in shadow, but Laurel had the impression of a long, lean muscular body as she helped the officer get her feet on the ground. The officer's heavy equipment belt, laden with cop paraphernalia, pressed uncomfortably into Laurel's hip, like a stranger appearing out of nowhere at a party—curious and dangerous.

"The chair's right here," Laurel said calmly. "Just lean on me, swing a little to your left, and sit back. Can you do that?"

"I'm okay, I'm okay."

Her speech was a little slurred, and the repetition was worrisome.

In the light from the open clinic door, Laurel made out a too bold to be called pretty, definitely striking face beneath a shock of unruly dark brown hair, chalk-pale skin under what was probably a healthy summer tan, and a hematoma the size of a lemon at the angle of her jaw. She was young—younger than Bri Parker appeared to be. Were all the police here barely out of high school?

Parker grasped the patient's arm, and between the two of them, they got her settled. Laurel moved to grab the handles of the chair, but Parker, deftly maneuvering Laurel out of the way, said, "I've got it."

Laurel stepped aside. "The treatment room is all the way down the hall toward—"

"I've been there," Parker said, the fierce look still on her face.

"Right. Go ahead. I'll meet you there." Laurel recognized that expression—worry and fear straining at the steel doors of control that went with the kind of job where the difference between life and death often depended on the skill and courage of one's colleagues.

In less than a minute, Parker had pushed the wheelchair into the treatment room and over to the table in the center of the room. Laurel bent down until she was at eye level with the injured officer and slid a BP cuff over her arm. As she inflated it for a reading, she asked, "Can you tell me your name?"

Deep brown eyes, the pupils so wide they appeared almost black, slid to her face, met her gaze, focused blearily. "Laurel...nice name."

Laurel smiled and glanced at the readout on the Omni portable BP machine. Normal BP, normal pulse. "Thank you. Can you tell me yours?"

"Right. Yes. Andrea. Andy. It's Andy." The dark-haired cop reached for her jaw. "Fuck, that hurts."

"I imagine it does," Laurel said, gently catching Andy's wrist and diverting it from her face. "Andy what?"

Andrea frowned. "Andy. It's just Andy."

"Okay. Andy. What's your last name?"

Laurel glanced up when another police officer, this one taller, closer to her age, and a little more muscled than the others hurried into the room.

"Reese Conlon, Chief of Police." Deep blue eyes narrowed on Andy. "Sorry to interrupt."

She didn't sound at all sorry. She sounded like she'd come to claim what was hers. Bri Parker straightened perceptibly, coming to attention. Her jaw tightened even further. Conlon glanced at her briefly, nodded sharply, and lasered back to Andy. "How is she?"

Laurel knew who Chief Conlon was. Victoria King's wife. Nita had mentioned her when she'd called Laurel to tell her about the opening at the clinic for the summer and gave her the details of the job and a little info about the town. "Stable, but I just started the exam."

"I'm fine, Chief," Andy said.

Reese Conlon's eyebrow rose. "Yeah, I can tell." She stepped back, shot Laurel an almost contrite look. "Didn't mean to get in your road here."

"It's all right. I understand." Laurel'd seen this before too. The closure of ranks around injured firefighters, police, and first responders of all kinds. Team members who were closer than family in some cases. The fierce protectiveness was admirable, if occasionally a little irritating. She turned back to Andy. "Did you come up with your last name, Andy?"

Andy's eyes had sharpened, and her color was two shades closer to normal. "You know, like the lake."

A little worried, Laurel looked at Parker and said, "Lake?"

"Not a New Englander, are you," Parker said, finally smiling.

Laurel shook her head.

"Champlain," Andy said.

Parker added, "It's a huge lake in upstate New York that runs into Canada."

"Ah, okay then." As she talked, Laurel flicked her penlight into Andy's eyes, first the left, then the right. Her pupils constricted briskly. She covered one eye, shone the light into the opposite eye, checked the consensual reflexes, and looked for any problems with eye movement. All normal. Some of the tension in her belly began to uncoil. "Andy, can you tell me what happened?"

Andy hesitated, blinked, and fingered her jaw again. "Sucker-punched."

Parker snorted. "Sucker-*kicked*, you mean."

Laurel glanced up at Bri again. Conlon moved a step closer, a glint in her eye that suggested suppressed anger. "Did you witness it?"

"No, I got there maybe ten seconds too late." Parker grimaced. "This one was on her back, her cuffs still gripped in her hand, one end around the assailant's wrist. He was down too. A couple of the bar patrons told me she'd gotten kicked in the head by a bystander, but they weren't sure who."

"Was she unconscious?"

Bri shook her head. "I don't think so. I was there within seconds, and she was moving, trying to get up. I called her name, and I'm pretty sure she recognized me."

"Okay, good." Still half kneeling in front of the chair, Laurel took both of Andy's hands, one in each of hers. "Squeeze my fingers."

Andy did, firmly and evenly on both sides.

Easing back to give her a little room, Laurel asked, "Can you raise your right leg?"

Again, a positive response. Same on the left. So far the neuro exam was normal, and the injuries appeared localized.

"Andy," Laurel said, "do you have any numbness anywhere in your body?"

"No. Wish I did," Andy muttered.

Laurel laughed. "All right, do you hurt anywhere besides your jaw?"

"Headache. Big one."

"Ringing in the ears?"

"No."

"Double vision?"

"No."

"Can you close your teeth together?"

Andy grimaced and nodded.

"Do your teeth feel like they're in the right place? Like they all meet the way they used to?"

"Yeah, but they hurt."

"Okay. I'm going to look inside your mouth. Don't bite me."

"I usually don't bite. Not unless you ask me to."

Parker made a sound that started as a snicker and turned into a cough. Laurel's face flushed. Okay then. Back to business. "Can you open a little? If I hit a spot that hurts more than the others, make a sound."

She first checked with her light and the tongue blade, and then very gently ran her finger over the inside of Andy's cheek and down along the mandible, searching for any obvious step-off or especially tender spot.

Andy, as promised, did not bite her.

She sat back on her heels. "I don't think it's broken, but we won't be able to tell for certain without an X-ray. First, let's get you up on the table so I can examine the rest of you."

Rising, she gestured to Officer Parker to take Andy's right arm. Chief Conlon quickly slipped her arm under Andy's left, and together, they helped her stand.

"Uh-oh," Andy groaned. "I think I'm gonna throw up."

"Here," Laurel said, grabbing a blue plastic basin off a nearby shelf. When Parker and Conlon got Andy on the table, she set it on Andy's lap. "Use this if you need to."

Andy took a couple of deep, shuddering breaths. "Okay now. Just...dizzy."

Laurel cranked the head of the table up thirty degrees. "Lean back. Take some deep breaths."

Andy sighed. "Better."

"I'll take a look at the rest of you."

Andy closed her eyes. "Be my guest."

Laurel finished a quick exam—listening to her heart and lungs, palpating her belly, running a hand over all four extremities—to make sure she wasn't missing some other injury. She palpated Andy's cervical spine with one hand cupped behind her head, gently feeling each vertebra. No pain anywhere.

She straightened. "It looks like the blow to your jaw is the only injury. We ought to get an X-ray of it, but that can wait until tomorrow when your stomach—and your head—are feeling a little bit more settled." She glanced at Bri. "Do you know if she has anyone at home? A roommate, or..."

Laurel realized she'd been about to say *girlfriend* and fought off another blush. Really, she had no reason to think that, just because Andy was so...attractive. To her anyway. *Aaand* that was enough of that.

"Not that I know of." Bri leaned down to Andy. "Hey, Champlain, are you seeing anybody who might be able to come over tonight, or some other friend in town?"

"Nobody," Andy said.

Chief Conlon said, "She can come to my place. We've got a sofa we can put her on. I'll watch her tonight."

"All right," Laurel said. "Just give me one minute to clear this with the on-call doc. You can help her to the chair while I call her."

She stepped out into the hall, pulled out her cell phone, and thumbed in Nita's number.

Nita answered on the second ring. "Dr. Burgoyne."

"Nita, it's Laurel. I'm sorry to wake you, but I've got a police officer just brought in with localized blunt trauma to the jaw. Neuro exam is normal other than some dizziness and mild nausea. No obvious fracture, but she's going to need a facial series to be sure. I figured that could wait until the morning when she'll be a bit more comfortable."

"Who is it?" Nita asked with absolute calm.

"Andy Champlain."

"Must be a new hire. I don't know her," Nita said. "Any history of loss of consciousness?"

"Not prolonged—the actual impact wasn't witnessed, but she was alert within seconds." Laurel rubbed her eyes. The adrenaline rush was ebbing. "Chief Conlon is going to take her to her place for the rest of the night."

"She ought to be fine there. Go ahead and let her go. Reese will know who to call if there's a problem."

"Thanks." Laurel ended the call and returned to the exam room. Andy was back in the wheelchair, looking tired but alert. "You're good to go. I'll see you back here in the morning at nine, and we'll get those X-rays done." She scribbled her cell number on a piece of paper and handed it to Chief Conlon. "Any change at all, here's my cell number. Call me."

The chief said, "Absolutely."

Andy grabbed Laurel's hand, her grip warm and comfortably strong. Her gaze, clearer now and unsettlingly intense, caught Laurel's. "Thank you."

"You're quite welcome," Laurel said, heat rising in her chest as Andy Champlain's remarkably beautiful eyes seemed to search for something in her face. Andy's fingers slid up to her wrist, lingered there for an instant, then fell away with a soft brush of fingertips.

Andy eased back in the chair and closed her eyes.

The two officers pushed Andy out of the room in the wheelchair, and Laurel leaned against the treatment table, heart pounding and skin hot. What was *that*?

Nothing. Nothing at all.

She'd read too much into that brief exchange. Of course she had. After all, this was her first *real* solo run, and she was super keyed up and oversensitized to everything. That explained her totally unprofessional reaction to a fleeting glance. She'd never once looked at a patient with anything other than complete objectivity before.

Giving herself a pass for the momentary mental lapse, if she could call it that, she basked a little in the pleasure of a good night's work. And, she thought with a rueful laugh, she hadn't even gotten bitten.

CHAPTER THREE

L et me know if the turns are bothering you," Reese said, pulling out onto the darkened highway. "I'll take it slow."

Andy leaned back in the passenger seat of the chief's Jeep and closed her eyes. Her stomach felt a lot better when she did that. The position didn't help her headache any, but at least she wasn't about to humiliate herself by vomiting in the chief's car. It was embarrassing enough that Reese had leaned across the front seat and latched her safety belt for her. What a way to make an impression. Good thing she wasn't looking for a long-term job.

"I'm good, Chief."

She must've been, because when she opened her eyes again the car wasn't moving anymore. They were parked in the drive behind a mostly dark, big single-family house. She couldn't make out too much of it without swiveling her head—still not a good idea—but the light over the garage door on the lower level illuminated the three stories of a classic Cape Cod, from the weathered shingle siding to the wide wraparound porch that extended all the way down one side and across the back. If she turned and looked out the side window she'd probably be able to see the harbor past the circle of trees she could make out in her peripheral vision, but she didn't really want to move her head that much. In fact, if she could figure out a way to suggest she sleep in the Jeep, she would have tried that already.

"I'll come around and give you a hand getting out," Reese said.

"Right." Andy unlatched her own seat belt at least and slowly raised her head until she was sitting upright. No urge to vomit. The pounding in her jaw was about the same as it had been—vicious—but the stabbing pain shooting through her head seemed a little duller. The door opened, and she swung her legs out.

"Take it easy," Reese said. "You might get a little dizzy when you stand up."

"Sorry about this." Like totally disgraced that she'd been blindsided by a civilian who probably worked as an accountant at his day job. On her first week working solo too.

"So am I. I don't like anyone beating up on my officers." Reese slid an arm around Andy's waist as she braced herself on the door and stepped out onto a crushed-seashell covered drive. After a second, the wave of dizziness passed and her legs steadied. So far so good. Reese shoved the Jeep's door closed, and together they made a slow trek up the rear stairs, across the porch, and into a big kitchen. Lights from the various appliances—microwave, stove, coffee maker—lit the room enough for her to spot the long, heavy wood table with seating enough for eight taking up half the center of the room. The scattering of mail and magazines in the middle and a place setting with a Lego toy of some kind suggested it was a place made for living. Nice.

"Come on," Reese said quietly. "Living room is this way."

Thankfully, the chief let her walk on her own, and she slowly followed her down a wide hall with darkened doorways opening along the way. Another large room, visible through an archway opposite a staircase climbing to the next floor, took up the front of the house.

"We've got a guest bedroom upstairs, but the sofa's pretty comfy too." Reese paused just inside the room. This one held two long, overstuffed sofas at right angles facing a fireplace, a thick square carpet with some kind of pattern Andy couldn't make out in the half-light of the moon, a couple of end tables by the sofas, and double French doors leading out to the porch she'd seen from the rear. "The kitchen is far enough away you probably won't hear the chaos when my daughter gets up along with the roosters. Powder room right there under the stairs if you need it."

"Tell you the truth, I'd rather sleep down here," Andy said. Then maybe she wouldn't feel quite so awkward about imposing on her boss.

"I'd probably want to myself." Reese grinned. "Grab a sofa, and I'll get a pillow and some blankets for you."

"Thanks, Chief. I…uh…thanks."

"So," Reese said, pausing on her way to the stairs, "you know the drill. I'm going to have to come down and ask you some boring repetitive questions every hour or so."

Andy winced. Oh, *that* wouldn't be the least bit awkward, would it. "I don't want to keep you up. I'm really okay."

"You wouldn't be here if I didn't think you were medically okay," Reese said, "but Laurel made it pretty clear you need neuro checks. Besides, if I don't do it, my wife will, and I'd rather she get a little more sleep."

"Sorry about this," Andy muttered, sounding like a broken record.

"Didn't mean it that way," Reese said with what sounded like a smile in her voice. "I just want Tory to get as much rest as she can. That's not so easy for her right now."

"Oh yeah," Andy said, fighting the urge to lie down and go to sleep. "I heard she was pregnant."

"Very," Reese said, her grin as bright as the moon. "Twins, and soon."

"That's great. Congrats." Andy gave in and sat on the nearest sofa. Sinking into the deep, firm cushions, she let out a long sigh.

"Be back in a minute," Reese said.

When Reese came back downstairs, Andy was asleep sitting up. Reese lifted her legs onto the sofa and gently laid her back on the pillow. Andy muttered a little bit, and Reese covered her with a light quilt that would double as sheet and blanket. Her breathing was regular, and she looked pretty comfortable, so Reese headed back upstairs.

"Is she all right?" Tory asked.

"Yeah, I think so," Reese said, sliding into bed in a T-shirt and briefs. "She'll have a sore head for a few days, but if there's no concussion, she ought to be fine in a few days."

"I can check her—"

"Nope," Reese said, shifting closer to Tory, who slept on her side most of the time now to make her breathing a little easier. "I was there when Laurel examined her. Andy's okay other than a nasty lump on her jaw."

Tory snuggled closer, rested her head on Reese's shoulder, and threaded an arm around her waist. "Tired?"

Reese kissed Tory's temple. "Keyed up, really. But you should try to sleep."

"I will." Tory kissed her neck and slipped a hand underneath her T-shirt. "But first, I thought maybe I'd get lucky."

Reese went from keyed up to ready in a heartbeat. "Baby, anything you want. Anytime. You don't even have to *try* to get lucky."

"Mm. I sort of figured that, but I still like thinking about the lead-up to lucky."

Tory played her fingertips down the center of Reese's abdomen and she tensed. She was about to get *very* lucky. "Any chance there's more than thinking going to go on?"

Tory laughed. "If you're very good."

She slid her hand lower, and Reese closed her eyes.

❖

Laurel drove the quick five minutes home to the apartment she'd rented in a converted garage squeezed into the narrow backyard behind a home owned by two gay guys who ran a restaurant in town. Their house was dark, but she'd left a light on in the kitchenette, and she smiled when she walked in and was greeted by the sight of her new home.

All hers. What a change. She hadn't lived in a space so small since she'd been in college. She had a Murphy bed of all things, which she loved, more for the concept than anything else, although it was pretty comfortable when it was pulled down from the wall and made up with her favorite quilt. She didn't have a TV, but she never watched it anyway. The internet was reliable, for which she was eternally grateful. The single narrow-ish room offered a kitchenette with a two-burner stove, which she hadn't even known existed until she saw it, an under the counter refrigerator with a freezer big enough for a pint of ice cream—the only essential—and a nice deep sink where it was easy to wash the few dishes she accumulated. The nicest thing about the place, other than the fact that she'd chosen it herself and furnished it with her few meaningful salvaged items, was the open ceiling. The old garage had been expanded up into the peaked attic area, so although small, it still felt spacious. And private. She loved every single thing about it.

She filled the teakettle and put it on one of the burners, pulled down a mug from the single hanging cabinet, added a decaf tea bag because she probably should try to get a little more sleep, and when the water boiled a few minutes later, made herself a cup of tea. Going on three thirty. She could easily get another couple of hours of sleep, manage an early morning walk through town, and still be at work by eight. She carried the tea over to the bed, stripped off her clothes, and slid under the sheets. Propping a pillow behind her back, she ignored what all the experts said about not reading a screen if you were trying to go to sleep and opened her iPad to the book she was in the middle of reading. She was, after all, an adult, who did not need to justify herself to anyone.

She read a few sentences, sipped her tea, and thought about her first night on call as a full-fledged PA. Mentally cataloging Andy's injuries, she reviewed everything she'd done, assuring herself she hadn't missed anything on the exam and that waiting on X-rays was the better part of patient care. If Andy's jaw was fractured, the break was definitely going to be a hairline, and she wouldn't've done anything about it tonight anyhow. Moving her around, sitting her up and down, and turning her head would only have made her more uncomfortable.

Satisfied about her diagnosis and treatment, she settled back with her book, only to put it down a minute later. She wasn't thinking about the case now. She was thinking about Andy Champlain. The woman herself. As she'd first surmised, she was young. Not yet twenty-three. She'd also downplayed her symptoms, her attitude just shy of cavalier, and if she hadn't been shaking and pale as plaster, Laurel might have underestimated her pain.

She wasn't all that surprised by Andy's attempt to downplay her injury. She'd gotten to know a lot of the first responders from her ER rotations during training. The EMTs, paramedics, firefighters, and police officers all seemed to have been stamped from a similar mold—loyal, capable, intense, and, often, a little bit of the adrenaline junkie. She liked them all and admitted, in secret, to finding something attractive about their swaggering self-confidence. Even injured, Andy Champlain gave off a little bit of that. The other two officers, Parker and Conlon, might've been bookends. Handsome and forceful and radiating unstudied sex appeal. Interesting women, all of them.

And not her type.

Okay, she might not have a type—she'd need a lot more experience to say *that*—but intensity was not something she was looking for.

Easygoing, laid-back, soft even—that would work. She'd had all the drama in her life she could possibly need. That train of thought led down the road to the life she'd left behind, and she wasn't going there. She didn't ever have to go there again. Smiling, she went back to her book, sipped her tea, and put dark-haired, dark-eyed, intense women out of her mind.

❖

Laurel's alarm went off at six thirty, and she woke up remarkably untired. Leftover adrenaline, no doubt, added to the still-new excitement of facing a new day in her new life at her new job. New, new, new. And hers to make or break. But she'd make it. No other option. She'd walked out of her life and burned all her bridges. Now she was making new ones.

She showered quickly, pulled on dark jeans, a pale green short-sleeved shirt, and boat shoes, and headed into town. Her little place was just one block off Bradford, and Bradford just one block off Commercial. At the end of the cross street where her street joined Commercial stood Joe's Coffee House. She loved the place. It opened at six every day, proving there most assuredly was a God, at least in Provincetown, and they had great pastries. If she took a two-mile walk out around the West End of town after the coffee and pastry, the calories didn't count—at least she hoped they didn't.

The young woman behind the counter, the same one who'd greeted her every day for the last three days, wore a plain white tank that showed off her muscled arms, the colorful unicorn tattoo on her smooth left shoulder, and small uplifted breasts. Laurel shifted her gaze from those breasts in time to catch a welcoming smile.

"Morning," the barista said, tilting her head contemplatively. "Medium black eye with room for a little almond milk."

Statement, not a question.

"That would be correct." She probably remembered every repeater's order, but Laurel still felt a little charge of pleasure at the attention. She wouldn't think too hard about why that was.

"I've got muffins coming out in about one minute, and, extra special today, chocolate croissants, raspberry Danish, and spinach-feta croissants, all from Connie's Bakery."

Laurel hesitated. "Well, I should probably have the spinach and cheese croissant, because that sort of sounds like a meal, but…"

The barista grinned, and her gaze slowly morphed into one of interested appraisal. "Let me see," she said musingly and after a second announced, "raspberry Danish."

"You're right." Laurel laughed.

"Coming up." The barista paused. "I'm Evelyn. Evie."

"Hi, Evie." Laurel stretched a hand across the counter. "Laurel Winter."

"Here for the Fourth?" Evie asked casually, ratcheting the espresso handle into place.

"No, I live here. New in town."

Evie's eyebrows rose and her appraising look turned definitely more interested. "Not a tourist, then."

"No. I'm temping at the clinic. I'm a physician assistant."

"Summer gig?" Evie asked as she brewed the coffee.

"Yes," Laurel said, "while Dr. King is out on maternity leave."

Evie's smile widened. "That might be a while. Twins." She rolled her eyes. "That's gonna be fun."

Laurel wasn't surprised that Evie knew Tory King was having twins. The year-round population was pretty small, and everyone pretty much knew everyone else. "Well, my schedule's totally flexible, so whatever she needs."

Evie handed Laurel the coffee and a raspberry Danish on a paper plate. "No place you have to get back to after that?"

"No. My time is my own." Laurel paid and added a two-dollar tip. "So, I'll see you tomorrow."

"I'll be here. Six to six." Evie smiled again before turning to the next customer.

Laurel grabbed a couple of napkins and sat outside at one of the wrought iron tables. She sipped the coffee and tried not to eat her raspberry Danish in three bites. She managed probably half a dozen while watching an enormous cruise ship maneuver its way into the harbor. Something that size had to hold a thousand tourists or more. She'd better get her walk in before they disembarked and the streets filled up. After wiping her hands on a paper napkin, she headed west on Commercial Street to finish her drink and burn the extra calories.

She hadn't given any thought to the fall or where she'd be then. She'd only just begun this life. An unusual circumstance for someone who'd thought she'd already had her life planned out not that long ago, but she'd worry about what came next when it came.

CHAPTER FOUR

Andy woke with warm breath, smelling vaguely of peppermint and something else she couldn't identify, wafting across her cheek. She lay with her eyes closed, pretty sure she'd imagined the breath since she wasn't accustomed to waking with anyone. But the peppermint smell lingered. Eyes still closed, she turned her head, cataloging the incremental increase in pain. Not too bad. The pounding was mostly focused in the left side of her jaw now, with just a dull throb marking time in the base of her skull. More importantly, the hollow ache in her midsection registered hunger and nothing more. If she could get something to eat and a shower, she'd be good to go.

Through her closed lids, she registered faint light. Morning, had to be really early still. She opened her eyes.

"Whoa."

A dog with a head the size of a basketball gazed at her from a few inches away, dark eyes remarkably intelligent, or they seemed that way, as they studied her. It opened its mouth in a friendly—she really hoped friendly—peppermint-scented doggie grin and panted.

From the doorway, a woman said in a vibrant, melodic voice, "Oh, I'm so sorry. He's totally friendly, really."

Clearly everyone who laid eyes on the dog—a mastiff the size of a not-so-small pony, now that Andy got a look at the body that went along with the head—had the same reaction. *Run!*

"Glad to hear it. Are there any more of the candy canes he's been eating?"

The woman in the doorway laughed. "That's doggie tooth spray. He loves it. And so do we."

"Me too at the moment."

"I'm Tory King, Reese's wife."

The chief's wife was as pregnant as anyone Andy had ever seen, not that she made a habit of inspecting every pregnant woman she passed. She would have looked twice at Tory King anytime, though. The short-sleeved white shirt that draped her body to just below her hips and her black pants were unspectacular enough, but a little bit of sunlight angled through the front windows and illuminated her there in the frame of the doorway, and for just an instant, Andy had the wild impression she was looking at a painting. Tory's face glowed, highlighted by lush waves of auburn hair in a wild mixture of browns and reds and maybe even a strand of silver here or there. She was... beautiful.

Remembering who Tory was, and where *she* was, Andy pushed aside the quilt after mentally checking that she was clothed in all the essential areas, braced an arm on the sofa, and slowly pushed upright. "I'm Andy Champlain. Uh—Officer Champlain—I work for the chief. Sorry to barge in like this. It's good to meet you."

Tory smiled. "You too. Do you mind if I do my doctor thing—I run the medical clinic here in town—and ask you a few questions?"

"Sure," Andy said.

"How are you feeling in general?"

"Not as bad as last night," Andy said. "Actually, not much worse than if I'd taken a hard tumble off a mountain bike on a steep run."

"Sounds like you've been there."

Relaxing a little, Andy said, "A time or two."

"Any dizziness or double vision?"

"I never had any vision problems. I feel a lot better today." Andy *really* wished she'd awakened somewhere else. Anywhere else, as long as it was alone. Having anyone, especially a stranger who just happened to be her boss's wife, witness her in less than tip-top shape was the ultimate in embarrassment. The only people she could imagine being worse than Tory King were the chief herself...or her father. She winced inwardly, remembering when she'd come to in the ER after being knocked out in a karate tournament when she was fourteen. He'd stared at her from across the cubicle, his arms folded on his chest, his expression flat and cold. He hadn't asked how she felt. He'd asked, *So how did you fuck up?*

Andy sucked in a breath. "Thank you for everything. I should just get going. I've already inconvenienced you enough."

"You haven't inconvenienced me at all," Tory said. "I'm headed into the clinic in an hour or so. Reese told me you're on for a re-exam and X-rays first thing today."

The clinic. Andy pictured the lights and the paper gowns and the people looking at her with sympathy or pity, and a little surge of panic rippled down her spine. Andy sucked in a breath. "I could just go home and shower and get over there on my own."

And maybe she could figure out a way to avoid it.

Tory regarded her for a moment. She hadn't let her nerves show in her voice, had she?

"Are you hungry?" Tory asked.

Andy hesitated. Tory King was watching her, still. Okay, she was overreacting. So what if some strangers she'd never see again saw her at her not so best. "A bit, yeah. I usually eat right after shift..." She looked at her watch. 7:10. "I'd be getting ready for breakfast right about now. I'm not sure I'm up for my usual fare, though."

"I think we can find something that will work. Maybe some tea."

Andy must've grimaced, because Tory laughed. "Ah. I forgot I was dealing with a police officer. All right, coffee then. And be careful chewing."

And that was that. Discussion over.

Andy slowly stood, and the dog padded over to Tory. The dog's head came up to Tory's hip when it was standing, and Tory absently stroked it.

"Okay?" Tory asked.

"Yeah," Andy said, eternally grateful that she was mostly solid. "But I feel like I ran a marathon yesterday."

"Have you ever done that?"

"Actually, I have. Boston, three years ago."

"I'm impressed. Come on, kitchen's back this way."

Andy followed her back to the big room she'd walked through while half-asleep the night before. The chief sat at the oak table next to a little girl with reddish-brown curls and Tory King's eyes who was eating little squares of French toast with her fingers. The scene was so unexpected, Andy halted in the doorway.

Reese looked over, an expression on her face Andy had never seen before. Relaxed. More than that—content. She hadn't had much one-on-one exposure to the chief after the day she'd interviewed for the position. Day-to-day, Reese Conlon was friendly, but not overly so with her officers. Her command was orderly, direct, and efficient. Andy showed up for work, got her assignments from the sergeant after roll call and briefing, and went to work. When she thought of the chief, which wasn't all that often, she figured Conlon would be like her father and his friends. Which meant all she needed to do was be sure she always came out on top, no matter what the situation. Socializing with the chief and her family, especially under these circumstances, was downright awkward.

"Morning, Chief," Andy muttered, still nailed to the floor in the doorway. She half expected the chief to ask her to explain her fuckup the night before. Her shoulders twitched and she squared them.

"Morning, Champlain." The chief picked a soggy piece of eggy bread off her sleeve and popped it into her mouth. "How's the head?"

"Attached," Andy said.

Reese laughed and indicated a seat across from her. "Good."

Andy hesitated but couldn't figure any way to avoid the order. She sat.

"Want some breakfast?" Reese said. "You could have some of Reggie's French toast."

Reggie made a face at Reese. "Mine."

Reese grinned. "Well, then I guess you better finish it before Officer Champlain does."

"We've got plenty," Tory said, passing a plate to Reese and then Andy. "Stop eating Reggie's. Coffee in a minute."

Andy half rose. "I can help you with that."

From behind Reese's back, Tory rolled her eyes. "Coffee mugs are not heavy, but I appreciate it."

Andy sat back in her seat and glanced at Reese, who raised a brow. Then Reese grinned, and Andy's shoulders relaxed.

Coffee followed, and although she usually drank it black, today she put a little milk in it from a small blue ceramic pitcher that sat in the center of the table. She tried the French toast first, and it settled just fine. Better than fine. She was starving, and when a third piece magically appeared, she mumbled thanks and polished it off. The coffee might've been the best she'd ever tasted.

Tory sat down next to Reggie with her plate and took turns with Reese helping Reggie eat. Reggie babbled, at least Andy thought it was babble, although Reese answered her, so maybe there were really words in there. After a few more minutes, Reese stood and picked Reggie up.

"I'll take her upstairs and start getting her ready."

"Thanks," Tory said. "I'll be up in a few."

"Bye," Reggie said, waving as Reese carried her from the room.

"Bye," Andy called.

"Breakfast doing okay?" Tory asked.

"Totally. I feel a lot better," Andy said, and it was true. With her stomach full and a little bit of caffeine surging in her blood, her headache faded and the pain in her jaw was manageable. She'd been really careful not to chew on the bad side.

"Excellent. I'll be ready in twenty minutes or so. If you feel well enough that you think you can drive, I'm all right with that. I can drop you at home, and you'll have time to clean up before your appointment. It's at nine, by the way."

"That's great," Andy said. "I'm fine, really. Just sore."

Tory rose. "There's more coffee on the counter if you want it."

"Thanks for breakfast," Andy said as Tory smiled and left.

Alone, she leaned back and considered what was next. Now that her head was clear, she thought over the events of the night before, and any way she looked at it, she'd fucked up. No *way* should she have relaxed her guard once she had the guy subdued even though she heard backup just seconds away. She could have kept the guy physically restrained just as she had him until Bri arrived. Then she could've cuffed him without getting kicked in the face. The chief hadn't slapped her down for it, but she would. Bri had probably already filed her report, and no matter how bad it looked, Andy would have to do the same.

Nothing she could say was going to make it look any better.

❖

Laurel walked in a big circle along the two-mile route she'd mapped out the first day she'd arrived in Provincetown—west down

Commercial, around the curve past the breakwater and Long Point, up Six, and finally down Conrad to the clinic. Nita had called her in Philadelphia two weeks before she'd been due to graduate from her PA training program to offer her the summer position at the clinic. She'd said yes in an instant, given a month's notice to her landlord, and packed her bags the day after she was official. Twenty-four hours after that, she was parked in the clinic's gravel lot waiting for Nita to introduce her to Tory King and sign all the paperwork.

Like that day—really only a week earlier?—Nita's car was already in the parking lot when Laurel arrived at seven fifty-five. Clinic hours didn't start until nine, but Laurel liked to arrive early to review the charts of patients she'd be seeing that day, since unlike Nita and Tory, she didn't know them all—or any of them—yet. The schedule generally turned out to be only a loose approximation of what the day would really be like. Most days emergencies popped up all day long—kids with cuts and bruises or broken bones, adults with colds or chronic conditions suddenly getting worse, and tourists with everything from worsening health problems to food poisoning. Their clinic hours always ended up running twice as long as scheduled, but she loved every minute.

Nita had quietly told Laurel they'd need to keep Tory off her feet as much as they could, which might be a challenge. So far they'd been pretty successful shunting the emergencies away from Tory, who mostly did paperwork and only saw some of her regular patients who were too anxious to see anyone else.

"Hey," Laurel said at Nita's office door. "Morning."

"Hey yourself." Nita, a slender Black woman in pale yellow silk shirt and tan slim-cut trousers, turned from the bookcase at the far side of the room with a smile. Her understated makeup was flawless and her dark brown eyes bright, with no hint of the interrupted sleep Laurel had contributed to the night before. "Come on in and tell me about your night."

"Let me get coffee first. You want a refill?"

Nita hefted a ceramic mug with a sailboat above the word *Provincetown* in white script. "I'm good."

A minute later, Laurel settled with her coffee into the chair in front of Nita's plain desk.

"I had a few calls sent through from the answering service. Abe Marsh is coming in this morning to rule out kidney stones. He described pain in his right lower back that wasn't in the area where he usually has pain when he's passing a stone—might just be an unrelated muscle strain, but he ought to have a urine check. Mildred Wu also needs to be seen—says she has a chest cold that just won't quit. Nothing has really changed, so it sounded like she could wait." She sipped the coffee, giving Nita a chance to comment, but she only nodded in agreement. "And I told you about Andy Champlain. She'll be in at nine for a facial series, just to rule out a fracture."

"I see your memory is still eidetic." Nita pursed her lips. "I'll never stop being jealous about that."

Laurel smiled. "Believe me, it's probably the only thing about me that warrants being jealous."

"Hey, none of that. Look at everything you've accomplished in the last three years."

"I know," Laurel said. "Every now and then I just wish…"

No, she wasn't going to moan about what Nita already knew all about—and had helped her get through by never once saying she'd known from the beginning Laurel was making a mistake.

Laurel lifted her chin. "Well, you're right. I'm here now."

"You are." Nita's smile lit up her delicate features. "I never expected it, and it's so cool. One of my best friends working right here with me."

"One of them?" Laurel teased.

Nita laughed. "Okay—besties forever. What were we when we pledged that? Ten?"

"*You* were seven. I was ten, remember?"

"Oh, right—that seemed like such a big thing then, and now"— Nita waved a hand—"it's nothing." She paused, her expression softening. "I'm really glad you're here. And that you're happy. You're happy, right?"

Laurel nodded. "I am. I have everything I want."

"You might change your mind about the everything, given a little more time," Nita said gently.

That was another thing Laurel loved about Nita. She never pushed on the personal front. Never asked her if she was ready to try again—or rather, try the right direction this time—like so many of her happily married friends had done at first. Not so much now.

"I don't think so," Laurel said, just as an image of Evie the barista flashed through her memory. A second later, Andy Champlain's face appeared, obscuring Evie's. Laurel caught her breath. "I *definitely* do not think so."

CHAPTER FIVE

Freshly showered and feeling about ninety percent of her fighting form, Andy stood naked in the middle of her bedroom, staring into the closet, with a cool breeze blowing in off the harbor. Warm sunlight dried the few drops of water clinging to her back. She'd been lucky, scoring this place on short notice, although she felt bad that the owner was dealing with some kind of chronic illness and had to sublet. She'd had her name in with a Realtor, and when the listing popped up, even though it strained her budget to the max, she jumped on it. Right in the center of town, on the top floor of a two unit, on the harbor side of the street. The tiny bedroom had space for a bed and not much else, but it opened through a double archway into the single main room, and with the doors open to a deck that looked out onto the harbor, she woke each morning to the sound of gulls, fishing boats motoring out of the harbor at dawn, and the occasional early dog walker calling for their animals. She had a view of the harbor, the wharf off to her right, and the long stretch to Truro on her left.

Right about now, on an ordinary day, she'd be getting ready to catch a few hours' sleep. But today was different, and without knowing if she'd be headed to work in thirteen hours, she felt unmoored. The station house, the other officers, the role she filled on the streets ordered and defined her life. If someone asked her who she was, she'd say, *I'm a cop.*

Her freshly laundered uniform hung next to her civilian clothes. No one had told her she shouldn't report to work, and she had end of shift reports to finish from the night before. She pulled on her uniform, laced up her black shoes, and strapped on her watch and equipment belt. When she caught her reflection in the narrow mirror on the back of the equally narrow closet door, she saw a cop and recognized herself. The unease roiling in her midsection faded away.

Ten minutes to nine. Maybe she should go by the station first and check in with the duty officer. But Tory King had said her appointment was at nine. Maybe if something held her up at the station, she could reschedule, and by the time she did that she wouldn't need to see anyone at the clinic.

The idea appealed, but that wasn't going to work. No way was she going to get back on the street until she was medically cleared. And what was the big deal about a clinic appointment anyhow? No one who mattered, she hoped, would be there to witness her at less than a hundred percent.

Resolutely, she gripped her car keys and walked the two blocks to the lot where she'd arranged for a month-long parking permit. At precisely nine, she squared her shoulders and pushed into the clinic. A slim blond in a formfitting pale violet shirt smiled as she walked up to the counter.

"Well, let me guess," he said in a soft tenor. "You have got to be Andrea Champlain."

"Andy." She almost grinned and would have, if she hadn't wanted to turn around and walk out. "What gave it away?"

If he found her tone abrupt, he didn't show it. Instead, he tapped a finger to his chest. "Name tag. I'm Randy, by the way. I'll let them know you're here, if you want to have a seat."

"Thanks."

A half dozen people ringed the waiting area: a twentysomething woman with a two-year-old who leaned against her with their thumb in their mouth, eyes big and face wet with tears; an elderly man and woman who sat close together in one corner, her clutching a straw purse adorned with plastic flowers while he flipped through a magazine; and a weather-beaten outdoorsy looking guy with a cane propped against his knee and his arms folded. Andy took a seat with her back to the front wall and a view of the entire area. The guy with the cane glanced her way, nodded once, and went back to staring straight ahead. Andy balanced her hat on her knee and reminded herself not to fidget.

Appearances mattered. Always in control. Even if you weren't quite sure what was coming next, even if it might be a swift swat on the side of the head.

The door behind the counter where Randy sat tapping on a computer opened, and a blonde—midthirties, tanned and athletic-looking in a pale green polo shirt and dark blue jeans—glanced into the waiting area. She focused on Andy and smiled.

"Officer Champlain. Do you want to come back?"

No, she really didn't. Andy recognized her now, through the foggy memory of the night before. She'd looked a little different then. Her hair had been pinned up somehow, hiding the spun-gold highlights in the strawberry-blond waves that framed her sensuous features this morning. The steady, ocean blue eyes were just as large and mesmerizing. Andy's head was a lot clearer now, and that was a face she wouldn't forget.

Andy rose, tucked her hat under her arm, and followed her back. As they walked, the blonde said, "You're looking a lot better this morning. I'm Laurel Winter, a PA here, in case you forgot my name."

"I'm sorry," Andy said. "I wasn't paying attention to much of anything last night."

"I'm not surprised." Laurel opened a door to an examining room. "Let me take a quick look, and then we'll get your X-rays."

"I really feel fine." Andy's stomach tightened as she entered the small space with the white paper covered examining table, the stainless steel sink in one corner, the requisite stool and tiny chair crammed into another. She really didn't want to be in here and watched the door, expecting someone to show up and remind her that only the weak showed pain, or got sick, or failed at anything. But that wasn't going to happen. Even when the chief had shown up last night, she hadn't blamed Andy for getting injured. No one had blamed her—yet.

"Officer Champlain?" Laurel said softly. "Do you want to sit down?"

Andy jerked. "Oh, sorry. Right."

Resolutely, she climbed up onto the table, set her hat carefully by her right side, and tried to relax. She'd be out of there in a few minutes. No unwanted questions, no suspicious doctors or social workers or teachers asking her about her latest injury. She grew up in a family of men, and being tough meant playing rough and sometimes—well, you got roughed up. No big deal.

"How are you feeling this morning?" Laurel set her iPad on the short shelf by the sink. If she hadn't seen the officer, dazed and struggling with pain just a few hours before, she wouldn't have suspected just how much discomfort she had to be in right now. She didn't think it was pain, though, that explained the rigid set of Andy's shoulders and the hand fisted on her thigh. For a few seconds, when she'd first walked into the room, Andy'd actually looked panicked. Laurel stayed a few feet away, giving her time to adjust. She didn't know Andy Champlain at all. Anything could account for her uneasiness right now, and the one thing she didn't want to do was add to it. Some people just didn't like doctors *or* doctors' offices.

"Fine," Andy said curtly.

Laurel sighed inwardly. So it was going to be twenty questions. "How about the pain level, one to ten?"

"Uh…" Andy said, as if she was trying to work out what the right answer would be.

Laurel wanted to tell her it wasn't a test and she wouldn't be graded, or criticized, but she just waited, leaning against the sink, giving her room.

"A one."

"Well, that's great," Laurel said. "Want to grade your headache too?"

"That's gone."

"Any other symptoms? Dizziness, nausea?"

"No," Andy said.

"Okay," Laurel said, noting that Andy didn't shake her head or nod or move it much at all. She probably still had a headache, but clearly she wasn't about to admit it. Since history wasn't going to be terribly reliable, she'd just have to rely on the physical exam and X-rays. "I need to take a quick look inside your mouth and see if there's any swelling or bleeding."

Andy's shoulders stiffened.

Laurel picked up a wooden tongue blade and her penlight and slowly walked forward until she was a foot away from Andy. "Ready?"

Andy obediently opened her mouth, and Laurel did a quick intraoral check. A bruise on the inside of her cheek opposite her left molars corresponded to the bruise beneath her mandible that extended down onto her neck. That was to be expected. No intraoral lacerations or obviously damaged teeth. "I'm going to run my fingers along the edge of your jaw. Let me know if any particular point hurts more than any others. I'll try not to make anything hurt more, but tell me if I do."

"Go ahead. I'm fine."

Of course you are, Laurel thought. She gently palpated from the angle of the jaw down to the chin and beneath the lower rim of the mandible. As with the night before, she didn't feel any irregularities or step-offs, and nothing seemed to be causing Andy any acute pain. "Still looks like soft tissue trauma only, but let's get your X-rays to make sure."

"Then I can go back to work?"

Laurel held the door open. "We'll need to review your X-rays, but if they're normal, I'd say…desk duty in three days, five to seven days to full duty."

Andy's eyes opened wide. "Five days. Why?"

"Because sometimes after a significant blow to the head, delayed symptoms can pop up. You don't want to be on patrol and suddenly have a debilitating headache or some kind of visual symptoms."

"But…"

Laurel moved into the hall. "How about we get the X-rays and start there."

Andy blew out a breath and followed. "Sure."

Walking with a silent and apparently silently fuming officer, Laurel had a feeling that right now, she was the enemy—not in any personal sort of way, just that she was the individual standing in the way of Andy getting back to work. That, she guessed, was probably the most important thing in her life. She'd seen that plenty of times and sympathized, but she'd also seen that drive translate into recklessness, and in Andy's line of work, that could spell disaster. Her job was about more than just diagnosing an injury or prescribing a drug to treat symptoms—she planned to treat the person, even when the person wasn't all that happy about it.

Inwardly sighing, Laurel led her down to the X-ray room in the rear of the building.

"If you'll just lie down on the table there, with your head to the left," Laurel said, arranging the X-ray plates in the slot beneath the head of the table. "I have to position your head. Let me know if it's causing you any discomfort."

Andy was obedient and compliant during the few minutes it took to shoot all the views.

When she'd checked on the computer to see all the films looked adequate, Laurel said, "I'm going to review these with one of the doctors. You can wait in the exam room. It's the third door down."

"I remember." Andy slid off the table, retrieved her hat from a nearby chair, and straightened. "Thank you."

"I'll be back in a few minutes." Laurel checked Nita's office first. Her door was open, but she wasn't there—must be with a patient. Tory King was in her office, and Laurel rapped on the door, saying when Tory looked up, "Got a second?"

Tory quickly put aside the papers she'd been reviewing. Sitting down, she barely appeared pregnant. Laurel had a feeling she'd never look so fresh, composed, and just plain *good* when she was nine months pregnant, but then, not likely anyhow.

"Sure, come on in," Tory said.

"I've got a facial series to clear on the police officer from last night. Andrea Champlain."

"Right, yes, Andy. How is she doing?" Tory pulled her laptop closer and hit a few keys.

"Well, according to her, she's pain-free, has no neuro symptoms, and is ready to go back to work this morning."

"Why am I not surprised?" Tory smiled faintly. "What's your assessment?"

"I think she's doing okay. Her exam is normal, and I took a quick look at the films. They seem okay to me too. But still, while she wasn't unconscious last night, she definitely was dazed, and she showed signs of being mildly concussed. She was alert, but a little sluggish."

"She spent the night—what was left of it—at our place." As she spoke, Tory scanned through the images on her computer. "Andy's got a pretty good bruise on her jaw, which looks clear on the plain films. Some periosteal thickening, though, probably from the hematoma. Got to have been a pretty good blow to give her that."

"I agree. The trauma was significant."

Tory pushed the laptop aside. "So, what did you tell her about work?"

Pleased that Tory was asking for her recommendation, even though Nita had told her she could expect to be a full team member from day one, Laurel said, "I told her she could go back on desk duty in three days, and full duty in five to seven, minimum."

"Good. Have her come in for a recheck, and send a report over to Reese Conlon at the police station."

"Right. Chief Conlon came in last night."

"Mmm," Tory said. "I know."

Laurel laughed. "Of course."

As she turned to go, Randy appeared in the doorway. "Sorry, but a couple of things just came up."

Tory sighed. "What's up?"

"EMTs are bringing in a three-year-old who didn't quite make it to the top of the monkey bars, fell, and cut his lip. The kid is stable but the mom's hysterical. And I've got the harbormaster on the phone. He says the captain of the cruise ship that's parked out in the harbor has requested that we see a couple of his passengers as soon as we can."

"Moored, not parked," Tory said, frowning. "Don't they have ship's doctors who can see their guests?"

"That's what I asked," Randy said. "But apparently a couple of folks have some kind of flu, and their medics are recommending they disembark here. The patients are resisting and demanding another opinion. They want to stay on the cruise."

"I don't know what it is about these people and their cruises," Tory muttered. "Okay, sure. We can see them. Are they going to tender them in this morning?"

"They could be here in half an hour," Randy said, "but Nita's really jammed up until later in the afternoon."

"I can handle the toddler," Laurel said. "I've had plenty of suturing experience in the ER."

"Good. I'm not doing anything," Tory said, pushing the paperwork firmly aside. "At least, nothing that can't wait. I'll see the folks from the cruise ship."

"Super," Randy said and disappeared.

Tory grinned at Laurel. "Welcome to summer in P-town."

Laurel grinned back. "Thanks. Just where I wanted to be."

Andy was standing in the exam room with the door open when Laurel returned. "Your X-rays are clear. I need to see you in three days for a quick recheck. Randy out front can set you up with a time."

Andy's jaw set and her lips thinned. She flipped her hat on and leveled it over her very cool brown eyes. "Right. Okay then."

Laurel stepped side. "Call if you have any problems."

"Thanks," Andy said tersely and walked out.

Laurel blew out a breath, wishing she knew what the real problem was. A minute was all she had to wonder before she hurried off to prepare the treatment room for the next patient.

CHAPTER SIX

A ndy drove straight from the clinic to the station and parked in back, next to the chief's Jeep. A single patrol car and a couple of personal vehicles belonging to the day shift occupied the other spaces. She'd expected most everyone to be out on patrol by now, but she might have to face the scrutiny and speculative looks of the other officers after all. Walking into the station felt a little bit like walking off the mat when she'd lost a match or leaving the field after a hitless game, to find her father or brothers waiting to tell her just how many ways she'd failed. Andy sucked in a breath. She wasn't a teenager now. She could handle whatever came her way and meant to prove it.

Just as she was heading for the side door, Bri walked out, still in her uniform. The patrol car must have been hers. Andy slowed, steeling herself for what was coming.

"You done at the clinic?" Bri said quietly, drawing opposite her. Her blue eyes were a little cloudy that morning, like storm clouds, the ones with gray edges that warned something big was brewing behind them. Andy knew that look. Bri was pissed, probably had just finished writing her up. Not that she didn't deserve it, but hell, Bri had been a great training officer. Friendly but one hundred percent about the job. Easy to work with and forthcoming about all the things Andy needed to know about the town and getting along on the job. She'd sort of been thinking they might end up being friends. Maybe not.

"Yeah, just came from getting X-rays," Andy said. "Nothing's broken."

"Good," Bri said, and just like that, some of the storm clouds faded.

Andy frowned. If Bri wasn't pissed, what was she? Andy wasn't sure what to say. Well, she knew what to say—she just wished she didn't have to. "So, about last night...I fucked up."

Bri grinned a little. "Yeah, kinda. Maybe. I wasn't there, so I couldn't say."

Andy's brows drew together. "Ah, well, you know, that's kinda the point, right? Not waiting for backup and all that?"

"Sometimes situations dictate we can't wait." Bri gave her a long look. "Is that what it was about last night?"

Andy saw a little break in the incoming storm. This was her chance to get herself clear of the whole situation. Maybe this wouldn't be so bad. She was the only one there, right? So no one could contradict her report of events. Bri was watching her, almost like she was reading her mind. Andy hoped she wasn't, because the idea of misrepresenting what she'd done embarrassed her. More than that, made her feel small.

"When I got there, things looked fairly quiet, and I knew you were just a couple minutes away. I was thinking about going in, figuring I'd done it before—settled down a rowdy bunch of drinkers—but I thought you might be pissed if I did."

"Not pissed as much as worried." Bri ran a hand through her hair. She was only a few years older than Andy, but her old man had been the chief of police before Reese Conlon, and Bri, like Andy, had policing in her blood. Andy didn't know what Bri's father was like, maybe like hers, but maybe not. She kept looking for the wariness in her eyes, the caution that came with needing to hide things, and never saw any sign of it.

"I don't follow," Andy muttered.

"Well, if you'd gone in there without me or other backup and got into an altercation that escalated a lot more than what happened last night, you could be a lot worse off this morning. Nobody wants that."

"I entered when I heard shouts that some guy had a knife. I didn't think I could wait."

"And you radioed the situation update." Bri lifted her shoulder. "Judgment call. Nobody would fault that."

Andy blinked. "I guess probably the chief will."

"I couldn't say, but I *can* tell you that the chief is always going to be on your side."

"So *are* you pissed?"

"Right now," Bri said, "no. I was pretty teed off at myself last night for not getting there faster."

"Whoa," Andy said. "None of that's on you."

"Isn't it? How would you feel if you were in my place and you found me…" Bri looked away, her jaws clenched tight.

Andy knew that answer right away. If Bri had been in trouble, and she hadn't gotten there, she would have *wanted* someone to kick her ass. "Yeah, I see what you mean."

"So I guess we understand each other." Bri nodded sharply and poked her finger into Andy's shoulder. She didn't push hard, just a little pressure that under other circumstances might've been a fist bump. "Just watch your back, Champlain. And maybe think a little more about being part of the team."

"It won't happen again," Andy said.

"Good." Bri smiled. "So I promised my girl I'd get home early this morning, and I'm already late." Her eyes glinted. "You don't want to disappoint the ladies."

Andy laughed. They hadn't talked about anything personal, despite the month they rode together. Bri hadn't asked and she hadn't volunteered, but she didn't mind Bri's assumption. Why would she—just because she didn't have a lady in her life, and really never had, not the way Bri did. She kind of liked the assumption that she *might* have. Maybe one of these days, she still might. "I hear you."

Bri waved and walked away.

When Andy went through the side door, Gladys, the day dispatcher, a sixtyish, gray-haired, grandmotherly looking woman with sparklies on her glasses frames and sharp eyes that missed nothing, turned from her console and looked her over. "Well, are you doing all right?"

"Just fine," Andy said.

Gladys tilted her head. "That's a pretty impressive bruise you've got there on your jaw. I bet it hurts."

Andy hesitated. What was she supposed to say? Well, she knew what she was supposed to say, but Gladys was giving her that warm, friendly smile, the same one she always did, and she looked a little worried. Repeating *it's fine* sounded like a lie, even to her. "To tell you the truth, it feels like somebody kicked me."

"Parker says someone did." Gladys laughed. "From the way I hear it, though, you kicked a little butt too."

"Uh, yeah." Andy's stomach tightened. What had everyone heard? She cleared her throat. "Is the chief in?"

"Sure is. If the door's open, just knock on it. If it's closed, wait five minutes, and she'll be off the phone."

Gladys gave her another smile and spun back to her monitors. Andy knew what happened when she fell short of a goal and disappointed people, or she thought she did. This wasn't what she was used to. She felt bad, sure, but not berated or belittled or like the world's biggest failure. The feeling of *not* being scared was...scary. "Right."

The chief's office was down a short hall toward the back of the first floor, opposite the holding area. The door was open, and Andy stopped in the doorway. She rapped once and waited.

The chief looked up. "Champlain, come on in."

Andy walked the ten feet to the front of the chief's desk and came to attention.

Reese waved a hand at the visitor's chair. "Have a seat. I just got your report from the clinic."

"Everything's clear," Andy said, sitting forward in the chair with her feet squared on the floor.

"Yeah, good news," Reese said. "So you'll get a few days off to let your head settle, then we'll put you on the desk for a couple days."

Andy cleared her throat. "It's only a couple of days till the Fourth, Chief. It's going to be busy. You'll need all hands on deck, and I'm fine."

"That's up to the docs," Reese said.

No way Andy wanted to be riding a desk over the busiest weekend of the year during the busiest *month* of the year. "Maybe I could go back to the clinic earlier than scheduled, take a test or something."

"I appreciate you want to get back to work. And believe me, I want you back. But only when it's safe." Reese leaned back in her chair. "So, you want to run through it for me?"

Andy knew what she was talking about.

"Yes, sir."

"Chief is good enough," Reese said.

"Yes, Chief."

Andy went through the call to investigate a disturbance at the bar, point by point, putting in every single thing she'd done, but leaving out the things she'd *considered* doing. If she didn't do it, they didn't count.

When she was done, her stomach felt like a swarm of bees had set up house, including injecting about a million points of skittering pain.

"Well, that fills in the rest of the details along with Bri's report," the chief said, letting out a breath. "No way you could've waited?"

"Not in my opinion, no, sir...Chief."

"What would you have done if someone had run out shouting that someone had a gun?"

Andy reiterated what had been drilled into her in training, and when the chief ran through a few more scenarios, questioning Andy about what she might do, she could tell from the chief's expression she was solid. She hadn't expected this conversation. The chief hadn't reamed her out for screwing up the night before.

"Okay," Reese said after what felt like an eternity. "You ought to go get some rest."

"Can I make another appointment at the clinic tomorrow, or the next day?" Andy said. "I really want to come back to work."

"Go ahead," the chief said. "Do you mind if I give them a call?"

"Nope." Andy swallowed her surprise. "That would be great."

"Just remember, they get the final say in this."

"Got it, Chief."

Andy had her phone out to call the clinic for an appointment before she made it to the exit.

Tory pulled one of the visitor's chairs over, plopped her feet in it, and, leaning back in her desk chair, closed her eyes. She might have drifted a little and was only mildly startled when Reese spoke from the door.

"Are you asleep?"

Tory turned her head and smiled. "Oh no, just taking a break."

Reese came in, pulled the other visitor's chair over, and transferred Tory's feet to her lap. She slipped off Tory's shoes and began massaging her feet.

Tory groaned. "Oh my God. That's as close to heaven as I think I'll ever get."

Laughing, Reese said, "I can think of a couple of other ways to get you there."

"Oh, believe me, I haven't forgotten."

Working carefully around Tory's scar and the tight muscles in her lower leg, Reese said casually, "So, I thought you were on desk duty."

"I am," Tory protested. "Most of the time. I haven't been doing anything strenuous. I just saw a couple of people with colds." She frowned. "Nasty ones too. High fevers and coughs. I'd hoped we were past the flu season before tourist season started, but apparently not."

"And nobody else could see them," Reese said.

"We're pretty slammed."

"I hear you."

"So is this a social call?" Tory said, redirecting. Reese would worry if she was sitting home on the sofa, and she did the best she could not to add to her concerns. However, sitting home wasn't all that good for her, and she wasn't doing anything strenuous by evaluating routine primary care cases.

"Do I need an excuse to visit my wife?"

"Not if you're going to massage my feet every time you show up."

"Baby," Reese murmured. "I'll massage anything you want."

"I am well aware of that. And most appreciative." Tory wiggled her toes. "But I happen to know that you are as busy as I am, so…"

"So," Reese said, working her way up to Tory's calves, "this is mostly a social call. I just wanted to see you. Are you doing all right?"

"I have to tell you, I am beyond done with needing to pee every hour, sausage toes that won't fit in my shoes, and waddling around at about half a mile per hour, but other than that, I'm fine."

"So status quo."

"Exactly." Tory brushed the top of Reese's hand, just to touch her. A simple pleasure she never tired of. "What's the other part of your visit?"

"Andy Champlain."

"Hmm. Are you trying to exert undue influence on our recommendation based on your personal relationship?"

"Oh no, not exactly," Reese said. "Maybe a little. How bad is she?"

"Laurel was supposed to send your report."

"And she did. Clear and concise and—maybe, conservative?"

"You *are* trying to exert undue influence. And we're skirting close to confidentiality limits here."

"Andy said I could talk to you," Reese said, "but I'm not here to change your recommendation. I mostly wanted to talk to you about something else, related."

"All right. Let's hear it. What's bothering you?"

"Andy Champlain has the makings of a good solid officer, and really, she hasn't done anything that I probably didn't do at her stage. She's eager, a little aggressive, and wants to prove herself."

"Pretty much like a first-year resident," Tory said.

"Agreed, and if that's all I was getting, I wouldn't worry too much about it. But there's trying hard, and then there's trying so hard you're going to get yourself into trouble."

"She's a cowboy, do you think?"

"Maybe, I haven't decided yet, but she's desperate about wanting to get back to work, and I know where she's coming from. I'd feel the same in her shoes."

Tory nodded. "And you understand that we can't make an assessment based on the patient's desires."

"Completely. She wants to come back for an earlier re-eval. Will you be okay with that?"

"I didn't see her myself," Tory said. "Hold on a minute."

Tory called Randy on her cell.

"Yes, boss," Randy said.

"Can you find Laurel and ask her to come to my office."

"Sure."

Two minutes later, Laurel appeared. "You need me?"

"Come on in," Tory said. "You know Reese."

"Yes, of course," Laurel said. "Hello, Chief."

"Tell the chief why you think Andy Champlain can't go back to work right away."

Laurel looked startled. "I'm sorry. Did my report not go through?"

"It did," Reese said. "I was just wondering—not complaining—if maybe the time off was a little conservative?"

Laurel glanced at Tory.

"Andy wants to come back sooner for a re-eval," Tory explained. "I was just reminding Reese that we don't make decisions just to keep patients happy."

"I did make a conservative call," Laurel said, "that I felt was warranted."

Tory nodded. "Any reason?"

"I'm not really comfortable discussing a patient without their consent."

"I agree," Tory said. "And I don't want you to reveal any confidences. How about we approach it this way, since Reese already has some of the information in your report. Do you think Officer Champlain is at high risk for a complication?"

Laurel sighed. "Do I *think*? Not really. But I'm also not comfortably convinced she's not. I've only got part of the picture to work with." She stopped as if parsing her next words. "You know the subtle signs of a concussion are often symptoms—not something we'd pick up on an exam."

Reese looked from Laurel to Tory and back again. "Andy says she feels fine. That's the problem, isn't it? She's not a reliable historian because she won't admit if she's got a problem."

Tory smiled. "You sound like a doctor now."

"Married to one. Next best thing."

Laurel said, "We've got the physical exam and the X-rays to go on, but I can't get any handle on how she's feeling. Which means I can't trust some parts of my evaluation. With the injury she has, a concussion is not out of the question, even though Bri Parker said she was there within seconds, and Andy was not unconscious. I'd be concerned letting anyone go back to work in this situation, but someone who works with machines or has to do a lot of driving would worry me more. A police officer who might be in an altercation and need to draw their weapon?" Laurel raised her hands. "I'm erring on the side of conservatism because, frankly, I have to."

"Will you see her sooner than you planned?" Reese said.

"Of course," Laurel said. "But I can't promise I'll change my mind."

"Wouldn't want you to," Reese said. "I want what's best for Andy."

"So do I," Laurel said.

"Thanks, Laurel," Tory said. "Sorry to interrupt you."

Laurel nodded. "No problem."

Reese said after Laurel left, "I like her."

"Me too," Tory said. "She's got a lot of confidence for someone just out of training, and she's right. Your officer didn't make it easy."

"Would it help if I talked to her?"

"You might tell her that doctors are a lot like cops. We're pretty good at telling when people are dissembling."

"No kidding." Reese slipped Tory's shoes on. "Better?"

Tory sighed contentedly. "Much. You think we can make that a regular date?"

"Absolutely." Reese gently set Tory's feet back in the chair, leaned over, and kissed her. "See you later, and don't work too hard."

"Hey, Reese," Tory said as Reese headed for the door.

Reese turned. "Hmm?"

"I love you."

"I know. And that makes my day, every day."

Chapter Seven

A t six o'clock that night, Laurel finished notes on her last patient of the day and logged out of the office laptop. She let out a long sigh and closed her eyes. What a day. She was plenty used to working ten-hour days, all ten hours on her feet, especially when she'd been in the ER where things rarely got quiet, and the PAs, especially the PAs on rotation, pretty much were first call for everything. All the same, there was another level of tension associated with being the one actually standing on the firing line, making the decisions and always being conscious of pulling her own weight. She had ample opportunity to consult with Nita or Tory if she felt the need, but after the first few times she'd grabbed one to sign off on a case, they'd made it really clear that they trusted her judgment and she didn't have to review the routine cases with them. She'd been both pleased and aware of another elevation in her level of pressure.

Bottom line, though? This was what she wanted, and on the whole, she'd had a great day.

Nita ducked her head in the door. "Done?"

Laurel sat forward. "Yep. You need anything?"

Nita shook her head. "No, I'm finished too. I sent Tory home about two hours ago, so if you're leaving, we can close up."

"I'll walk out with you."

Rising, Laurel hooked the strap of her backpack over one shoulder and followed Nita through the clinic, closing doors and shutting off lights as they went. Outside the early evening was as bright as noon, with a cool breeze making its way up from the harbor through the narrow alleys and backyards to cut some of the late-day heat. Still, July weather. Had to be seventy-five still.

"Deo is grilling tonight. You want to come over for dinner?" Nita asked as she stopped by her car.

Laurel smiled. Seeing Nita happily wed to Deo, and getting to know the dashing, doting P-town local who ran a construction business, was another fabulous side benefit of this new start. She'd let too much of her life slip away after she'd gotten married, and reclaiming what, and *who*, mattered felt good. "That would make five days out of the ten or so I've been here that you've fed me. You don't really have to do that, but I appreciate it."

Nita rolled her eyes. "We enjoy your company. And Deo always cooks way too much food, but she's not big on leftovers. There are only so many turkey burgers I can eat in a week."

"I'll tell you what. I love leftovers. If you have too many, and you happen to bring some to the clinic, I could be persuaded to have them for lunch."

"Deal. What do you plan to do tonight?"

Laurel resisted the urge to scuff her toe. She wasn't ten years old anymore, trying to act oh so much more grown-up than the seven-year-old, and she didn't need to hide her uncertainties from her oldest friend now. "It's so beautiful out—I don't feel like being inside just yet. I thought I'd go over to the Piper. Just to, you know, see what it was like."

"You should definitely go then. The tea dance ends pretty soon, but nobody ever leaves when it ends anyhow."

"I thought I'd go home and change first."

"You look great," Nita said.

Laurel gestured to her presentable but not exciting work attire. "Not exactly, you know, party clothes."

"Sweetie," Nita said with a long sigh, "this is a shore town. Your clothes are fine. Besides, you're hot. That's plenty enough to get the looks."

Laurel sucked in a breath. "Hey. That's weird. Don't say that."

Nita's laugh was music on the air, light and lilting and filled with warmth. "Oh, phooey. I've been telling you that since I turned eighteen and tried to drag you out to a bar with me."

"I know, I know. And I told you it was the wrong kind of bar."

Laurel shook her head. "That was my first big mistake—I should have listened."

"Well, to be fair, it probably *was* the wrong one for you at the time. You were going through your boy phase."

"Yeah, and look where that got me." Laurel shook her head. "And we're not going back to discussing Peter, ever again."

"Believe me, that's fine with me."

"Anyhow, thanks for the invitation. And next time, I'll take you up on the meal."

"Next time," Nita repeated firmly, "would be on the Fourth. Cookout, seven p.m., be there."

Laurel laughed. "Okay, okay, it's on my social calendar, which is so very full I'll have to do a lot of serious rearranging."

"Hey, it's Provincetown," Nita said. "Five days from now you might have a very busy social calendar. Heck, we might be dragging you out of some love nest just to see you now and then."

"That is so not likely to be happening, but I appreciate that you think I might be capable of that."

"I don't think you know your own strength," Nita said, "or how se—"

Laurel shot up a hand. "No, *so* no."

Nita grinned. "Just so we understand each other—if it happens, you'll tell, right?"

"Believe me, if it happens, I'll take out an ad in the newspaper."

Nita gave her a quick squeeze. "Better not."

Laurel waved as Nita climbed into her sleek little red Nissan sports car, backed out of the lot, and drove away. She hitched up her backpack and started for home. Regardless of what Nita said, she planned to change her clothes and maybe put on a little makeup. Just so she didn't look like she'd been on her feet for ten hours.

When, a half hour later, she got to the bar at the rear of the building across Commercial Street from Spiritus Pizza, she ordered a draft IPA from the willowy brunette working the bar in a barely there white tee and very short shorts, and threaded her way to the rear deck through the groups of mostly women talking, dancing, and basically doing what people in bars did. The outside space overlooking the short stretch of beach to the harbor extended the entire width of the building and was even more crowded than the interior. The wind came in off the water, brisk and cool, as the tide went out. Laurel carried her beer over to the railing and sipped while she watched the gulls swoop over the surf, making the most of the tide as it receded from shore leaving exposed mussels and clams in the sandy shoals. Despite what Nita had suggested, she wasn't looking for companionship. Well, companionship, yes. A tryst of some kind—although probably *fling* would be the right word, since *tryst* sort of suggested secrecy, and at this point in her life, there wouldn't be any secrecy involved. If she wanted to date a woman, she'd do it in public. Just knowing she could felt like enough. For now.

She turned her back to the railing, leaning her elbows on the wood worn smooth from hundreds of other elbows before hers, holding her beer bottle in one hand, and scanned the crowd. She'd always liked people watching. She liked *people*, which was a big part of why she'd chosen her new career. Talking to them, feeling like she'd made some difference in their lives, while doing work that challenged her mentally and just about every other way. So people watching was a natural instinct. Women of all types gathered in groups or couples or occasionally stood alone, interspersed in the crowd or sequestered at the railing like her—talking, drinking, flirting—all imbued with an aura of joy that came with freedom. The tension of the day drained away as she continued her casual perusal of the group, the warm sun on her face, the cool breeze at her back, until with a start, her gaze landed on a face she recognized. Andy Champlain leaned on the railing just across from her in a lazy, loose-jointed pose, watching her. She'd traded her uniform for jeans and a tight short-sleeved red T-shirt with a motorcycle logo Laurel couldn't quite make out. The T-shirt did nice things for her arms and shoulders. With the wind lifting the shock of dark hair off her forehead and a faint smile on her decidedly good-looking face, she looked pretty nice all over.

When Laurel didn't drop her gaze, Andy nodded and, a few seconds later, headed her way.

"Before you say anything," Andy said, "I know you're not working, and I'm not going to ask you any questions about, you know, the report to my chief."

Laurel smiled. "I hadn't actually thought you would."

She checked out what Andy was drinking, and it looked like club soda, but she supposed there could be vodka or gin or something in it. She wanted to question her about it, but that wasn't her place, either.

Andy was an adult. If she wasn't following the instructions she'd been given about avoiding any kind of drugs or alcohol, that was not Laurel's concern. The little frisson of worry was on her—boundaries were her territory.

"Club soda with lime," Andy said, as if reading Laurel's mind.

"Good to know."

"I don't usually get a chance to come over here," Andy said. "I usually go to the gym when I get up, and then I have breakfast or dinner, whichever my stomach signals it's ready for, before I go on shift later."

"I haven't been to the gym. Is it decent?"

"It's good, if things are a little crowded sometimes," Andy said, wondering why the hell she'd walked over to talk to a perfect stranger. Maybe because she was a perfect stranger herself, and Laurel Winter might be a stranger, but it didn't feel that way. They'd already shared something really personal, in a weird, nonpersonal way. She didn't really know anyone in town except the other officers, and she hadn't made any attempt to meet anyone. But after six weeks of work and the gym and solo Scrabble, and about the worst day and a half she'd had in years, she needed to get out. Somehow, seeing Laurel had made her feel as if she'd seen a friend.

Now she didn't know what to say, because she sure couldn't say any of *that*.

"Have you been in town long?" Laurel asked.

"About a month and a half," Andy said, the worry over how to get a conversation going fading. "But most of that time I was going through the department's mandatory month-long training program, even though, you know, I was totally trained already."

"I know what you mean," Laurel said. "It's not like you get hired for a job until you're done with the training part of things."

"True," Andy said, "but it was decent, getting to see the town the way Bri saw it, and learning the routines and things."

"Bri. That would be Bri Parker, who brought you in last night, right?"

"Yeah. She did." Andy felt the blush and tried to tamp it down. "Look, if it's okay with you, can we not talk about, you know, that business last night?"

"Oh, absolutely," Laurel said. "Subject closed. So—what about you. I take it you aren't local?"

"Me? I'm a summer hire," Andy said, although as she said it she wasn't quite sure that was true—or at least, not for certain. "I'm supposed to have a job waiting for me in Brigantine, New Jersey. But there's been a hiring freeze and..." She raised a shoulder. "It's kinda up in the air."

"Is that where you're from?"

"Yeah. How about you?"

"I actually grew up in the DC area, but I've lived the last fifteen years or so in Philadelphia."

"Almost neighbors."

"Almost." Laurel had never been to the Jersey Shore in all the years she'd lived in Philadelphia, although for many people it was practically a summer pilgrimage. She couldn't even remember the last time she'd had a vacation, anywhere. She came back to the present with a start. Andy was watching her with a quizzical expression. Wonderful. The last thing she wanted was for Andy to think she was uninterested. Even if she wasn't *interested* interested. "And I'm temporary too—at least, I think I am."

"You sound like you're not sure."

"Let's just say my plans are in flux."

Andy cocked her head, still studying her as if trying to decipher a silent conversation. "Not planning on going back to the city for sure?"

"Doubtful," Laurel said. She'd moved there for Peter's career, and that no longer mattered. "I took this job right after I finished the PA program. I got lucky—Nita Burgoyne, one of the clinic docs, is an old friend, and she contacted me about filling in for the summer. I don't have any real reason to go back."

"So you're new on the job too."

"Yep," Laurel said casually. Andy probably assumed, like other people, that she'd been at it a while, given her age. That worked to her advantage most of the time, as patients often had more confidence in older-appearing practitioners. Not that age had anything to do with skill, many times, but it never hurt to be perceived as competent rather than still green.

"So what did you do before this?" Andy asked.

Laurel hesitated. Innocent enough question—nearly impossible to answer without a whole lot of time and a whole lot more trust. "Long story, the short answer being I was married for ten years or so, then

I was divorced, and I needed to support myself." *And get a life.* "I thought about what I wanted to do with the rest of my life, and this was it. How about you? Always wanted to be a police officer?"

Andy looked surprised, as if she'd never been asked that before. "Well, yeah. I guess. We're a cop family. All of us—except my mother." Andy grimaced. "But she wasn't around much after I was born." At Laurel's expression she added quickly, "She didn't die, she walked. I guess she just wanted something...different."

"That must have been hard."

Andy shrugged. "I have five older brothers. I've got plenty of family left."

"That sounds kind of amazing. I'm an only child and always wished I'd had sibs." Laurel tipped her bottle and drained the last few swallows. The way Andy's shoulders had tightened when she'd mentioned her mother said the subject was a touchy one. "Nita is the sister I never had."

"It must be great to be working with her now."

Laurel smiled. "It is."

"Do you want another beer?" Andy asked.

"Oh...no." Laurel tossed her bottle in a nearby recycling bin. "I really need to get something to eat. Long day—lightweight drinker."

"I hear you. I'm ready for dinner myself. You want to grab some pizza or something?"

"Um..."

"Hey, no problem," Andy said quickly. "I just figured—never mind."

"It's not that," Laurel said, although she wasn't exactly sure what *that* was. A dinner invitation didn't necessarily mean anything, so nice going, jumping to conclusions. Still, she had to be clear. "I, well, I'm seeing you professionally, so I can't see you...well, you know."

"Oh." Andy blushed. "I hadn't thought of that. I mean, I hadn't thought about the date part."

"Well, now I'm embarrassed," Laurel said, shaking her head.

"No, wait," Andy said quickly, her brow furrowing. "That came out wrong. I didn't think you'd *want* to date me, so I didn't think about the other thing—the professional thing." She grinned and she still looked young, but definitely not innocent. "I would have thought about the date thing the next time, though."

Laurel's stomach did a subtle flip. Yep. Lightweight drinker.

"I see." Laurel didn't, not really. Andy was quite a bit younger, probably too young, but under other circumstances she might not have ruled out a nice casual dinner date. The patient situation nixed the date part. Still, they were both new in town, and being friendly wasn't against the rules. "How about we have dinner. Now that we have the dating issue cleared up."

Andy smiled. She wasn't going to be a patient much longer, and Laurel hadn't said she *wouldn't* date her, sometime. Maybe. "Yeah, I could do that."

CHAPTER EIGHT

Reese parked across the street from her mother's shoreside cottage, unbuckled her duty belt, and leaned around the seat to secure her weapon in the lockbox set into the floor of the rear compartment. She stepped out, stretched, and went through the gate in the white picket fence. The little garden fronting the small porch was in full bloom—brown-eyed Susans bordered the pickets and stretched through, out onto the sidewalk, islands of annuals—pinks and purples and whites and vivid oranges—made islands of color, and hostas in variegated arrays of green and yellow ringed a blue ceramic birdbath filled with clear water, waiting for its winged visitors. A slender golden-glass hummingbird feeder swayed from a short chain hanging from the porch eaves. The two-story shingled cottage, long and narrow, stretched back toward the harbor, beginning with a small living room furnished with a sofa and chairs covered with multicolored woven throws, and ending at a light-filled eat-in kitchen. An adjoining deck, reached through double sliding glass doors, offered an unobstructed view to the lighthouse at Long Point.

Reese rapped on the screen door and called out, "Kate?"

Instead of her mother's husky alto, she heard a squeal and the thunder of tiny feet. Grinning, she pulled the door open, and Reggie, barefoot in yellow pj's decorated with jungle animals, rocketed into her arms, exclaiming, "Mom!"

Chuckling, Reese hoisted her up onto her shoulder, which brought her red-gold curls to within inches of the ceiling. Reese double-checked that all the fans were off, but her mother made it a habit never to turn them on when Reggie was in the house. All the same, always smart to have backup. Thinking about backup brought Andy Champlain to mind.

Something about her, something in the way she'd looked when Reese was questioning her, raised red flags. She'd had all the answers, and she was confident about them, but she was wary. As if she was waiting for something—bracing herself for something. That look started an itch between Reese's shoulder blades and put Andy on her watch list.

Reggie pulled her hair. "Where's Mommy?"

"Your mommy is at home, sleeping, so the babies can sleep too."

Reggie seemed to consider that for a moment, then gave Reese's hair another tug. "Babies."

Walking back to the kitchen, Reese said, "Yup, two of them, coming soon."

Kate popped out of the kitchen, drying her hands on a favorite hand towel with a faded rooster in the middle. "Hi. Long day."

"Yeah, sorry," Reese said. "I was planning on getting over here a couple hours ago, but Allie called in a fender bender in the parking lot over at Herring Cove that got ugly when one of the guys involved punched the other guy."

"Allie's all right?"

"Oh yeah. She had it pretty much under control when we got there to sort things out. We put the one guy in holding until he cooled off. But the paperwork…" Reese set Reggie down before she lost a handful of hair, and Reggie promptly raced toward the kitchen, exclaiming *Cookies!* Reese raised a brow. "Before bedtime?"

"They're for tomorrow. I told her that. But she's persistent."

Reese grinned. "Yeah, she didn't get that from me."

Kate gave her a fond smile. "Oh, I suspect she got that from both of you. Anyhow, you've got things settled down out there now?"

Reese blew out a breath. "Yeah, it's just the normal summertime stuff."

"You look a little tired."

"I'm okay," Reese said. "Had a call in the middle of the night, so I'm a little short on sleep."

"Well," Kate said threading her arm around Reese's waist and giving her a hug. "That's probably good practice. You're going to be very busy in a few weeks."

"Looking forward to it." Reese tossed an arm around her mother's shoulders and squeezed back. Even after five years, their easy familiarity struck a tender chord in her, and what had started first as a cautious physical connection had transformed into a multilayered intimacy she cherished. Growing up, she'd thought her mother had walked away and never looked back, and then she'd learned otherwise. She'd learned a valuable lesson then too, that the stories we're told are not always true, or at least they may be only a one-sided truth. She tried her best to look at all sides of every situation, and that made her a better cop and, she hoped most importantly, a better partner and parent. "How was Reggie's morning at preschool?"

"Well, we haven't had any more block throwing incidents," Kate said.

"Hey," Reese said, "the way I heard it, Jeremy threw one first."

Kate rolled her eyes. "And of course that makes it all right."

Reese chuckled. "Well, Reggie's aim was better. Can't blame her for that. Plus, the blocks are rubber thingies."

Laughing, Kate shook her head. "She's doing fine. It's all just kid stuff, and they're all working it out. That's why they're there—to learn how to get along. She also drew some pictures this afternoon when she got here, which are now gracing the refrigerator."

"You know we'd be in trouble without you and Jean helping out."

"Reese," Kate said gently, "I thought I'd run out of miracles when you came back into my life. But now? Every day brings a new one. And soon, I'll be a grandmother again in duplicate. We can't wait."

"I think we're going to need the help."

"You'd break our hearts if you didn't."

Reggie came racing out of the kitchen at her normal speed, which tended to be triple-time, and crashed into Reese's legs. Reese scooped her up. "You ready to go home?"

Wordlessly, Reggie settled against her shoulder as if a switch had been turned off. Reese patted her back and glanced at Kate. "I think it's bedtime."

After Kate helped Reese get Reggie's car seat out of the rear of the Jeep and secured in the back seat, Reese strapped her in. Ten minutes later she pulled into the drive behind the house, unstrapped her, and carried her inside. Jedi was waiting inside the door, and she let him out.

"Don't go chasing anything," she whispered. She was pretty sure he pretended not to hear her as he bounded down the stairs, across the drive, and toward the beach.

"Let's be really quiet so we don't wake Mommy," Reese murmured as she carried Reggie upstairs. Since Reggie was still half asleep, Reese pulled down the covers, laid her down, and gently turned out all the lights except for the little night-light beside the door. Edging out into the hall, she left the door open a crack and headed down to hunt for food.

While she had her head in the refrigerator considering what appeared to be limited options, Tory stole up behind her and kissed her on the back of the neck. That little bit of unexpected contact, and the instant reconnection, shot through her like a warm breeze. Food forgotten, she closed the refrigerator door, leaned back against it, and pulled Tory into her arms with Tory's back to her front. They fit better that way now. She nuzzled Tory's neck and kissed below her ear. "You're supposed to be napping."

"I napped." Tory tilted her head back onto Reese's shoulder.

Reese threaded her arms below Tory's breasts, one of her favorite positions, lightly cupped each breast, and went back to kissing Tory's throat.

"You could get in trouble doing that," Tory said.

"Ever hopeful," Reese muttered.

"You're late tonight. Everything okay?"

Reese let the day slip away, immersing herself in Tory's scent and the seductive silkiness of her skin. "Nothing serious. Just the usual."

"Reggie asleep?"

"Yeah." Reese kissed Tory's neck. "She had a good day. No altercations at preschool, and there were cookies."

Tory laughed. "Well, there's progress."

"Did you have dinner?"

"How tired are you?" Tory asked.

"Not very."

"I called the station, but you'd already left. Do you love me enough to go back out for Chinese? We could eat in bed." Tory shifted sideways and cupped Reese's face to kiss her. "I could make it worth your while."

"Bribery is not necessary, but I'll take it." Reese grinned. "Call them. Tell them I'll be there in ten minutes."

Tory kissed her. "I just did that."

Laughing, Reese muttered, "Pretty sure of yourself."

"I know the way to your heart." She stroked Reese's stomach and then tugged at her belt buckle. "Don't I."

❖

Sitting across from Andy at a round table for two in a surprisingly open and airy Chinese restaurant on the lower level of a building in the center of town, Laurel said, "I don't know how long it would've taken me to figure out this place was here. One of the things I miss about living in the city is the takeout. I don't cook all that much, and I love seafood, but you know, after a while a little variety is welcome."

Andy sipped her green tea. Hadn't been her first choice, but she'd thought better of ordering a Tsingtao since she wasn't supposed to have alcohol. "I know what you mean. Bri pointed it out the first day. It's the only Chinese place in town, and it's good."

Laurel drenched one of the fried wontons in duck sauce and munched it. "I'd probably be happy with mediocre at this point, so I'll be thrilled with good."

They'd already ordered after choosing several dishes they wanted to share. Laurel relaxed and sipped her tea. She wasn't much of a beer drinker and had learned the painful lesson that in most places the house wine was not worth the effort. "So, what was it like growing up with five brothers?"

Andy's face blanked for a second, and Laurel wondered if she'd misstepped somehow. Curious, she just waited.

"Um." Andy fidgeted with her napkin. "I learned a lot about fitting in, I guess."

"How so?"

Again the pause. So careful—at least with her thoughts. Considering what had brought her to the clinic at three a.m., hopefully with her actions too. Laurel didn't really have the details of what had happened, other than how Andy'd gotten injured—and that wasn't her business. Still, she hoped Andy *was* cautious on the job. She'd seen what could happen to officers in the line of duty, and thinking of Andy being injured again put a knot in her middle.

Andy sat back in her chair, her gaze distant. "If I wanted to be part of things, I had to be good at what everyone else thought was important." She twisted a smile. "That mostly meant sports—football, baseball, soccer, ice hockey. At least one of my brothers was into something."

"So what was your favorite sport of all those?"

"Actually, none of them. Being the youngest, the smallest, and not a boy, I learned pretty fast I needed to be strong. And I wanted to be able to defend myself."

Interesting choice of words, Laurel thought. "And?"

"Ju jitsu," Andy said. "I started training when I was four and was a junior black belt by the time I was thirteen. I competed through high school. I still really love it."

"Well, that's one way of distinguishing yourself," Laurel said. "You picked a sport that no one else could come close to you at."

"Yeah, I did." Andy grinned. "I never thought about that, but it's true."

"There's a dojo in town, you know. Mixed discipline, I think. That's something I hadn't expected, but I saw it when I was walking down Bradford."

"I know," Andy said. "I keep meaning to go in, but well, the chief and Bri are instructors there. It might be weird."

"How do you figure?" Laurel asked.

"I might be a little rusty, and you know, I haven't trained in a while, and I might not perform well."

There it was again, performance. Measuring up. That mattered to Andy, a lot. Laurel wondered what Andy expected to happen if she didn't measure up to someone else's possibly impossible standards. Nothing about her said she lacked confidence, but she obviously set the bar high for herself. Nothing wrong with that, of course, as long as the goal was to do her best for herself. Laurel knew way too well how soul-draining it could be to try to be someone other than herself to make someone else happy. She mentally shook off the melancholy and the anger. Done and dusted. Over. New page.

She smiled at Andy. "Well, I was giving some thought to trying it out myself. They have beginners classes. Basically I need to do something physical. I walk every morning, but I tend to let my schedule get away from me. If I have a set time and place, I do better."

"Really?" Andy waited as the server slid steaming platters onto the table. "That sounds like a great idea."

"You really think so?" Laurel scooped fried rice onto a plate. "I was just a little concerned that I might not be able to keep up, even in a beginners class."

"Why?"

Laurel laughed. "I'm not exactly the jock type, and I'm not twenty anymore."

"You don't have to be a jock, and age isn't a factor." Andy shoveled sweet-and-sour chicken onto her plate and then looked directly into Laurel's eyes. "In anything."

Laurel's heart gave the faintest flip again. Oh. That little addendum couldn't really be misinterpreted, and neither could her reaction. She'd made a promise to herself when she'd left Peter—no, well before that, when she'd *decided* to leave him—that she was done lying to herself. And pretending she wasn't interested, or that she didn't like *Andy's* interest, would be a big fat giant lie.

"I'm thirty-six, almost thirty-seven," Laurel said.

Andy paused with her chopsticks in midair, tilted her head, and gave her a long look.

Her eyes were brown, which Laurel knew. They also had little tiny green and gold flecks around the rim of the iris that she hadn't noticed in the bright sunlight on the deck. They were gorgeous, and so were her long sandy lashes. Another little heart flip.

"I'm almost twenty-three." Andy speared a hunk of sweet-and-sour chicken. "I'm also a cop. I'm responsible, like you, for other people's lives, and I take it really seriously. Age isn't a factor in any of that."

"No, it isn't," Laurel said, dipping her spring roll into the spicy mustard. "Professionally, that is."

"What else is there?" Andy asked.

Laurel gave a start. Well, that was putting things in perspective. She'd headed off in a way different direction all on her own here. Feeling foolish for thinking that Andy had been flirting, she grinned ruefully. "Not a thing."

"You were the one who said this wasn't a date," Andy said, watching Laurel take a precise nibble off the corner of her spring roll.

Her cheeks were slightly flushed pink, probably from the sun out on the deck. When Andy'd spied Laurel leaning against the railing, the first thing she'd noticed was how she tilted her head up a little, as if waiting for a kiss, or to taste the breeze that had her blond hair swirling around her face, and the way the sunlight struck the side of her face, highlighting the graceful arch of her cheek and the pale length of her neck. Other women stood nearby, but none of them stood out the way Laurel did in her simple tailored pants and the open-collared sleeveless shirt that exposed her lean arms. Laurel looked solitary, and exceptional. Andy hadn't ever seen anyone quite so beautiful.

Here, up close, even in the dim light of the restaurant, the impact was even greater. She heard the warning in Laurel's voice, the warning off. And she shrugged it off.

One thing she'd learned growing up was never to quit. When you quit, you never made back the ground. She couldn't afford to lose ground then, and she didn't intend to lose any now. Persistence was her secret weapon.

"But I wasn't necessarily talking about just professionally," Andy said.

"No," Laurel murmured. "Neither was I."

CHAPTER NINE

Laurel carefully lined her chopsticks up in a neat parallel row next to her dinner plate while frantically gathering her runaway thoughts. And keeping her runaway mouth firmly closed. The anticipated, safe dinner conversation had somehow detoured in a totally unexpected direction. Correction. *She* had taken it from the casual to the way-not-so casual. She'd been the one to talk about their age difference, and to bring up the professional barriers, and to open the door to the theoretical dating. All Andy had done was ask her if she wanted to grab something to eat.

For all she knew, Andy might not even be interested in women, let alone her. Of course, if she was reading Andy's eyes right, especially the way Andy'd smiled when she'd said age didn't matter in anything, the liking women part wasn't in question. Still, she wasn't usually the one—make that never—to initiate dates. Considering none of her encounters could actually be considered dates in the regular sort of way, thinking of her initiating *anything* was a stretch as well. The whole chain of events since Andy walked over to her on the back deck of a lesbian bar was a stretch for her.

"You look awfully serious," Andy said. "Did something I said bother you?"

Laurel smiled ruefully. "No, as a matter of fact it didn't. That's what I was thinking about. And the fact that I seem to behave strangely around you."

Andy's brow quirked. "Strangely. Huh. That sounds…kind of interesting."

"Okay. So we might as well go from strange to even stranger. I don't have a lot of experience with—Oh, boy…I don't—Are you sure you even want to hear this?" She let out a long breath.

"I do," Andy said. "You've made me curious. To know more." Andy grinned, a flash of white teeth and full lips, over in a second, but the afterimage fixed in Laurel's brain. "About you."

"That's…new," Laurel murmured.

Andy watched her, her expression calm and easy and, there it was again, *interested*. Laurel, except when she was talking to her friends—okay, *friend*, singular—wasn't all that used to being the focus of interest. Hadn't been in longer than she could remember. And she felt it, like a buzz of excitement deep inside. Something new and fresh and intriguing. Quickly, before she could change her mind, she said, "I don't have a lot of experience with women."

"I guess when you said you were married, you didn't mean to a woman?" Andy said.

"Sadly, no." Laurel tried to keep the bite out of her voice and failed. "I was always aware of an attraction, and I can't really say why I didn't act on it when I was much younger, but I met someone who swept me off my feet." She shook her head. "Or that's what I thought. Let's just say I misinterpreted his interest in having someone interested in him as interest in me."

"You know," Andy said, still with that calm expression on her face, "you don't have to tell me this if you don't want to. But I'm good with hearing it too."

"I don't talk about it a lot," Laurel said. "It's embarrassing."

"Why?"

"Because I feel like an idiot. Because I lived with someone for years, trying my damnedest to make things work, when the entire time I was giving up little pieces of myself along the way to be what they wanted, what *they* needed, and that just makes me feel weak and pathetic."

Andy leaned back in her chair. "Wow. That's being a little harsh on yourself. Sounds to me like you were working really hard to save something, and there must've been something there at the beginning because you don't strike me as weak or pathetic or as someone who would be desperate for anyone's attention."

"How come you sound so smart—and kind, by the way—when I was so damn dumb when I was your age?"

"If this is confession time," Andy said, "I should own up to the fact that I don't have much relationship experience either. As to being smart?" She grimaced. "When you spend a lot of time figuring out what other people are thinking, or trying to figure out what they want, or what they might do next, you get good at reading people. So my read on you is that you mistook self-absorption and subtle manipulation for something else."

"I'd really like to think that," Laurel said, pushing aside her plate. "I don't quite know how this happened, me talking to you about this. I don't ever talk about it. I don't actually like to think about it."

"Then you don't have to," Andy said. "We can start from tonight, no pasts, if that works better."

"Could you do that?" Laurel asked. "Leave your past behind? Not that I imagine someone your age has much of a past."

"Oh, you'd be surprised." Andy looked away for an instant, the usually sharp focus in her eyes growing distant and, somehow, making her look so much older than Laurel knew her to be.

"I'm sorry," Laurel said quickly. "That was unfair. You're right. The numbers don't say as much about us as what we've lived through getting to that age. And maybe what we've learned along the way too. Forgive me?"

Andy's eyes snapped back. "Nothing to forgive. And to answer your question, probably not. Dump the past, I mean. I don't think you can really walk away from the things that make you who you are, but you don't have to drag all the bad stuff around with you forever. At least I hope not."

"You and me both." Laurel laughed. "So getting back to the women part, which is much more interesting. Do *you* have a girlfriend?"

"Me?" Andy sounded as if that was an impossibility. "No. If I did, I wouldn't have asked you out to dinner."

"Oh?" Laurel teased just a little. "I thought this was just a friendly shared meal."

"Well yeah, mostly." Andy shrugged, the grin appearing again. "Except when I asked you, I wasn't thinking about anything beyond you looked hot and I liked talking to you."

Laurel managed not to embarrass herself by blushing. "Thank you."

"You're welcome." Andy lifted a hand. "So, no girlfriend for you now either?"

"Never have had, not long-term or anything really close," Laurel said after a second. "No time, really. I left a marriage and went right into trying to make a new life. I haven't had time for much of anything except that."

"Sounds familiar." Andy leaned forward, close enough all Laurel could see was her face. Not that she wanted to look anywhere else. Andy was very easy to look at. Easy to talk to—easy to open up to. How...new. And how exciting.

"So," Andy said quietly, "I guess we've got a lot more in common than you thought."

"I guess we do."

Andy's eyes flickered away, tracking past Laurel to the far side of the room, and she stiffened.

Laurel followed her gaze. Reese Conlon saw them as she came through the door and veered in their direction. Andy looked as if she was about to stand up, and Conlon waved her down with a smile. "Hi, Laurel. Champlain."

"Evening, Chief," Andy murmured.

"Good to see you again," Laurel said, trying to figure out if Andy was uncomfortable because her boss had seen them together or for some other reason.

"I'm on a mission here," Reese said. "Dinner for four. Me, Tory, and the crit—babies. Sorry if I rush by."

"Totally understandable." Laurel laughed. "Have a good night."

Reese looked from Andy to Laurel. "You too."

"'Night," Andy muttered, her jaw tightening. The bruise on her neck, still in the purple stage, stood out like a shadow streaking toward her collarbone.

"If you do that," Laurel said gently, "it's going to hurt. Stop."

Andy sucked in a breath and let it out slowly, not even bothering to argue. "You're right, it did."

Taking a chance, Laurel pulled her folded cash from her back pocket and said, "How about we settle up and walk off dinner?"

"Yeah. Okay. That'd be good," Andy said.

They dumped cash next to the bill the staff person had left and hurried out. Couples pushing strollers through groups of scantily clad, celebratory men and women, and entertainers passing out promos for the evening's events, jammed Commercial Street.

"Is she a tough boss?" Laurel asked as they twisted through the throngs toward the center of town.

"No, why?" Andy asked.

"I thought you looked tense. I'm sorry if I'm pushing too much."

Andy grabbed her arm and pulled her out of the path of a bicycler speeding in and out between the pedestrians. "No, you're not. I'm just not used to cops like her."

Andy'd mentioned her entire family were cops, and Laurel didn't think Andy was talking about just any cops. Laurel gave a little time for the statement to settle, thrown off track by Andy's fingers, still curled around her forearm. For a fleeting second, she had the urge to clasp Andy's hand. Before she could make a mistake, Andy released her, and wasn't that just lucky for her? Andy seemed to have a far better sense of the appropriate boundaries than she did, even though she'd been the one to set them in the first place. Andy—who was too young for her and, considering she was only there for the summer, probably more interested in something light and easy, which did not describe Laurel, and oh, by the way, she was a patient. How many more *Do Not Enter* signs did she need?

Still, Laurel couldn't quench the need to know more about the silences that echoed beneath so many things Andy said. Or didn't say. "She's different from other cops?"

"Yeah, well, I think so. Bri says she's always there for the officers and puts herself on the line as much as she puts anyone else out there. That she's fair and tough and smart."

"Sounds like what you want a cop to be."

"It's what I want to be," Andy said with vehemence.

"So what *isn't* she like?"

"I kinda messed up last night, maybe," Andy said, answering with a non-answer. Laurel was getting used to that.

"Really? How so?"

Andy told her a little bit about what had happened and didn't skip over the part where she went in without backup. Laurel liked that about her—she didn't make any excuses.

"I think it was justified, and the chief seemed to think so today," Andy went on, "but she could have reamed me out for it, put me on probation, put a note in my file, or just torn a strip off me. But she didn't do any of those things."

"Sounds like she listened to your explanation and was fair about it," Laurel said, slowing at the intersection of Standish and Commercial. The line to the ice cream place was out the door, but she didn't mind waiting. The sun had set, the sea breezes were chasing the heat from the streets, and she liked walking and talking with Andy. A lot.

"Yeah. That's what I mean."

That seemed sad, more than sad, that Andy should find it unusual when someone treated her fairly. A little ache of sorrow circled around Laurel's heart, and she tried not to let it show. Andy wasn't asking for pity, and she would probably hate it. The other side of tough was vulnerable, and Laurel valued defenses too much to try to break Andy's. Before she could stop herself, she squeezed Andy's hand. Andy's fingers clasped hers in the brief second before Laurel let go.

"How about I treat you to a sundae for dessert?" Laurel said softly.

Andy pursed her lips. "Make that a banana split, and I'm there."

"You're on." Laurel's heart did that flip thing again when the clouds in Andy's eyes lifted ever so slightly. She'd buy her ice cream every day—or hold her hand, maybe—if she could put that look there again.

They shared the cost of the outrageously decadent desserts and, ice cream in hand, walked down MacMillan Wharf until they found a free spot along the wall above the harbor. Legs dangling over the side, her shoulder touching Andy's, Laurel said, "I kind of feel like I'm in a theme park. Like maybe all of this will simply disappear. Like it's not real—the partying, the shows, the crowds, and the huge percentage of people who seem to be queer and show it."

"A lot of it does disappear at the end of the summer season, I bet," Andy said, spearing a chunk of banana covered in sinful toppings. "If it's like most shore towns, it will get awfully quiet come fall." She shrugged. "But that's not such a bad deal. I always liked the shore in the winter. It's beautiful, and the quiet is a nice break sometimes from all the traffic and people."

"And crime, I would imagine," Laurel said, scraping the last of the hot fudge out of her paper container.

"That too," Andy said, setting her empty dish aside. "But there's always crime, and sometimes in these small towns where a lot of people are only employed seasonally, you see different kinds of crimes in winter than you do during the season. Too many people not working, having a hard time financially, and just maybe feeling trapped in a life they can't see any way out of."

Laurel shifted to the side, her knee still pressed against Andy's, so she could see her face. "You know, you're a little scary."

Andy huffed, smiling. "Yeah, I think we established that earlier. What'd I do this time?"

"You're very intuitive. Perceptive. I know it shouldn't be an age thing, but it usually is. Until you've lived a little, you don't always see what motivates people the way you seem to."

"Maybe we can put the age thing to rest. And just agree that it's experience, and not years. Then maybe you'll stop worrying about whatever you're worrying about."

As she spoke, Andy leaned a little closer, and Laurel sensed the world sliding away. They were cocooned in the dark, the nearest light coming from a lamppost down the wharf twenty feet away. People passed by, outside their island, but everyone was locked into their own little world of excitement. No one was paying any attention to them. Laurel had the feeling she was about to be kissed, or that she *wanted* to be kissed. Or that she might actually be doing the kissing if Andy got another millimeter closer.

Laurel pushed away, making some space between them. "You know, you're right. I'm prejudging, and I hate doing that. And I wish I didn't have to say this, but I should get home."

Andy straightened. Laurel's body language was clear enough. The wall had just dropped between them again. She shouldn't have been surprised, and Laurel wasn't wrong if she'd guessed she was about to be kissed and that's what had her moving away. She was right. Andy hadn't even thought about it, she'd just moved, pulled to Laurel like the tide carrying her out to sea. One minute safe on shore, the next in deep waters. Laurel was riptide, powerful and seductive underneath the quiet surface. Andy would've gone, gladly. She still wanted to kiss her. She never felt that way around women. Even the couple of times when she knew kissing was going to be involved, she hadn't felt that magically lethal tug in her vitals. She cleared her throat. "Where are you living?"

Laurel told her.

"I'm down that way myself. Come on, I'll walk you back."

Laurel smiled. "You know you don't have to."

"How about I'd like to?"

Laurel stood and dusted off the seat of her pants. She needed to stand up, or she was going to reach for Andy's hand again. She'd never been so compelled by the physical presence of another person. Even when she'd thought she was in love, she hadn't felt the physical compulsion she felt with Andy. It wasn't lust, either. She knew what that felt like now, and this wasn't it. This was something different. Something tender and powerful that made her ache. And she'd already, too damn many times, told herself why that was a bad idea.

"If you walk me home, then you have to walk home by yourself," Laurel pointed out.

Andy gave her an incredulous look. "Um, cop here."

Laurel rolled her eyes. "Grown-up here."

Andy leaned close again, didn't touch her, but the air between them vibrated as if they were touching. "I don't care. I'm walking you back."

Laurel swallowed and, for a moment, didn't think she would be able to look away. Even in the barely there moonlight, Andy was gorgeous. Intense, focused on her, unmovable. When had anyone ever looked at her that way?

"Okay, this time," Laurel said.

"Thank you."

When they reached the narrow little alley that led back to Laurel's house, she wished for five more minutes. Instead, she said, "This is it."

Andy craned her neck and squinted at the cottage. "No roommate?"

"Nope." This was the time to ask her in. Like that wouldn't be obvious. Laurel kept her lips firmly pressed together.

"Looks very cool."

"You'll have to come around and see it…sometime," Laurel said. That was friendly, right? Not anything too suggestive.

"I will." Andy took a step back, her hands in her back pockets. "After I'm off the injured list. I'll call you."

"Andy," Laurel said before Andy could turn and walk away. "When you come to the clinic, you'll probably see one of the other practitioners."

"Why is that?" Andy asked quietly.

"Because I don't want any suggestion that I'm not being objective."

"And why would that be?" Andy said even more softly.

"I don't know, but I'd like to figure that out."

Andy nodded once. "Me too. Good night, Laurel."

Laurel sensed Andy watching until she reached her door, and when she unlocked it and turned back to look down toward the street, Andy was still there. Laurel waved, and with a lift of her hand, Andy disappeared into the dark.

CHAPTER TEN

By the time Reese paid and collected her takeout, Andy and Laurel had left the restaurant. She'd been surprised to see them there together, and Andy was clearly uncomfortable seeing her. They'd beaten a hasty retreat. She wasn't bothered by them being out together. Far from it, really.

Both adults and all that. Maybe what Andy needed was a friend—or more—outside the force, someone with a different perspective on... everything, probably. Life, people, duty.

She'd needed that and never known it until Tory. Growing up a Marine, literally, living with her Marine father on Marine bases and knowing that she'd be a Marine from the time she could understand, she'd had a slanted view of the world. A strict moral code, which had stood her well, she had to admit, but also a narrow view. And forget about personal stuff. There hadn't been any. No lover, not even casual. And she hadn't known she'd needed that either.

She might not know the exact circumstances but saw a lot of who she'd been in Andy.

Tory had opened up the world for her. Given her a new life, a family, and love. This pregnancy of Tory's scared the hell out of her, just like the first time. Not that she didn't want it, didn't want the kids, didn't think it was a miracle, but still, nothing made her feel more powerless and generally useless. She could hunt and gather, and that's what she did. But she couldn't bear the burden, she couldn't take the risk, and she couldn't do a damn thing to keep Tory safe.

Reese settled the food on the floor of the Jeep and climbed in. Thinking about what she couldn't do was an exercise in futility *and* self-indulgent. Tory was fit and strong and smart. She knew how to take care of herself and their kids, and her. And just about everybody else in the town. Tory was a goddamn miracle worker. And she was hers.

Smiling to herself, Reese drove up to Bradford and out toward Beach Point and home. Twenty minutes after she'd left, she was back. She came in quietly, not wanting to wake the baby—who was a baby no more, but she still thought of her that way. Tory, with Jedi beside her, curled in the corner of the living room sofa with the sliding glass doors open and a little bit of moonlight slanting across the floor. The only other illumination came from the soft glow of the undercounter lights in the adjacent kitchen area. Reese set the bag on the low coffee table in front of Tory, leaned over, and kissed her. "I'll get some paper plates. Chopsticks?"

Tory curved an arm around her neck, held her in place, and kissed her back. The kiss was slow and hot.

Reese straightened and let out a breath. "Whoa. What did I do?"

"You brought food."

"I could go out for dessert."

"Believe me, you might have to." Tory patted the sofa beside her. "Get the plates and let's eat."

While Reese got the paper plates, Tory dug out the food, the chopsticks, and the takeaway napkins. Reese dished out food onto their plates and set the open cartons back on the place mat.

"You are my hero," Tory said as she started to eat.

"Try to be," Reese muttered, busy folding her moo shu pork pancake. "How are you feeling?"

"Besides famished?" Tory sipped from the water Reese had brought her. "Good. All quiet on the southern front this evening."

"You think it's time to quit the office?"

Reese tried to sound casual.

"I don't really see why. Walking around here isn't much different than walking around there. The only other thing I do in the office is talk. Besides, with Reggie in preschool and you working, I've got more company there than I do here. So if I need anything, I couldn't be in better company."

Reese paused to consider. "You know, you're right. I hadn't thought of it that way."

"So we're agreed."

"Yep." Reese helped herself to seconds. "Saw Andy and Laurel at the Chinese place."

"Together?"

"Well, they were eating dinner together."

"Huh."

"I thought Andy was going to jump up and salute when I walked in," Reese said.

"You did say she was eager," Tory said.

"You know, there's something there besides eager. She reminds me of a boot who'd been beaten down by a DI, skittish, like she was expecting a smackdown."

Tory set her plate down and shifted to look at Reese. "That really happens?"

"It can. It's not supposed to. Boot camp is supposed to be tough— it needs to be. The Marines, any armed forces division for that matter, isn't for everyone. The training is hard, physically and mentally and emotionally. You don't want someone getting themselves killed or getting someone *else* killed because, in the middle of a crisis, they hesitate...or worse."

"Still, intimidation and mental abuse are no way to condition someone."

Reese lifted a shoulder. "The line between tough and extreme is thin."

"But Andy hasn't been in the service. Is the police academy like that?"

"It can be, but her reaction is unusual for a rookie police officer." Reese considered. All she had was intuition, but she was talking to her wife, and Tory was not only a professional sounding board, she was the one person Reese trusted completely. "I think it's something else."

"Like?"

"Could be as simple as growing up with a strict rulebook, like I did—might be something a little more...personal."

"Does she need counseling, do you think?"

"I can't say yet. But we could all probably use a little, at some point."

Tory laughed, shifted closer, and kissed her. "My, my. Who are you?"

"I was thinking as I was driving back tonight that I'm not the person I was when I met you. That you've changed my life."

Tory drew a long breath. "And that is why I adore you. Because I can always rely on you, lean on you, count on you, and know that you feel the same way about me."

Reese slipped an arm around Tory and edged closer until they touched. "So I'll keep an eye on Andy. Maybe it's just rookie nerves and she'll settle down. If not, I'll talk with her."

"I think that's a good idea. Are you almost done eating?"

Reese gave her a long look. "I could be."

Tory smiled. "Good."

❖

Reese couldn't have been asleep more than a minute when she was wakened by the sound of a cell phone ringing. She fumbled toward her dresser, but Tory muttered, "It's mine."

"What the...?" Reese grumbled, sitting upright. 3:05 a.m. "What the..."

"Shh," Tory said, and then into the phone, "Dr. King...What? All right, call Laurel. You'll probably need the help. And call me back and let me know the situation...It doesn't matter. Wake me."

"What's going on?" Reese asked, awake now. A call in the middle of the night, even a medical emergency, often meant her help was needed too.

Tory set her phone aside. "One of the patients I saw this morning from the cruise ship is critical." She switched on her light, her expression troubled. "That doesn't make any sense. Well, I suppose if something else is going on—an MI or something—it might. But you don't die from the flu that quickly. He was febrile, but otherwise completely stable."

"Was that Nita on the phone?" Reese asked. "I thought the cruise ship had medics."

"They do. The chief medical officer from the cruise ship called the clinic emergency number, requesting backup. Apparently they've got more patients than they can handle."

"So what does it mean?"

"I don't know. They've asked for medical assistance. They've got other sick cruise passengers. It might not even be the flu." Tory rubbed her forehead as her mind churned. "They could have food poisoning or some other kind of toxic situation. Or they could just have a bunch of ordinary flu cases. But they've got a line of people who need to be seen, and they're swamped. Plus, at least one is going to need to be airlifted out."

"Sounds strange." Reese got out of bed. "I'll go down and check in with Howard Jensen. If they're going to be bringing in helicopters, we'll need to clear airspace and maybe arrange for EMT transfers."

"It's probably better to get that in the works just in case." Tory pushed the covers aside. "I'll—"

Reese grabbed her hand. "Nope. You will stay here and try to get some more sleep."

"But—"

"We had a deal, remember?"

Tory sighed. "I'll call you if I hear from Nita."

"I'll call you when I've talked to the harbormaster and the captain of the cruise ship if there's anything you need to know before morning."

"All right. Try to get home and get some sleep if you can."

"Will do," Reese said as she pulled on her pants, pretty certain she'd be missing breakfast.

❖

When the phone rang, Laurel's first barely awake thought was Andy. In the next second as she grasped the phone, she recalled they'd never exchanged numbers. Not Andy. Wouldn't be Andy.

"Laurel Winter."

Nita said, "Laurel, I'm so sorry to get you up. We've got a situation, and I need your assist."

Laurel sat up in bed, wide-awake now. "Of course. Is it Tory?"

"Oh—no. Some kind of emergency on the cruise ship. They're asking for medics. All I know for sure is that they've got a number of people who need to be evaluated, and it sounds like some might be critical. I'm not sure what we're getting into, but I'd rather have more help than not enough when I get out there."

"I can be ready in five minutes. Where should I meet you?"

"I'll swing by and pick you up," Nita said. "That'll be faster than you walking down to the wharf. The harbormaster will have a patrol boat waiting to tender us out to the cruise ship."

"I'll be ready."

Nita rang off and Laurel jumped out of bed. She checked her phone again. 3:12 a.m. How was it that emergencies always seemed to happen between two and four in the morning? Right when you were just hitting that deep sleep—too early to have gotten enough sleep and too late to expect to get any more after handling whatever was happening. She'd be up the rest of the night and all day for sure.

And that was all the time she had to think about her lost night. She'd been through this dozens of times before. She pulled on gray cargo pants, a dark blue polo shirt, and sneakers. She didn't have an emergency kit at home, but Nita probably did, or they'd make do with whatever was available on the ship. Cruise ships were required to have medical facilities and usually carried a number of medical personnel. If they had more patients than they could handle, it had to be some kind of mass contagion or toxin. Food poisoning wasn't all that uncommon.

Laurel stuffed her phone in her pocket, locked her door, and hurried down to the end of the lane. A minute later Nita pulled up in her Nissan. Laurel wasn't exceptionally tall for a woman, maybe a little bit above average, but she still needed to fold herself a little bit to get into the low-slung sports car. Nita was a good five inches shorter, and the car was obviously made for her.

"Do you have any idea what this is about?" Laurel asked as Nita pulled away.

"Not really. Tory saw a couple of people from the cruise ship this morning—yesterday morning now. Didn't sound like it was anything other than mild cases of the flu, but now the husband is worse."

"I remember. They were the ones who didn't want to leave the ship."

"Yes."

Driving through the empty town, Nita reached the wharf within a couple of minutes, drove all the way down past the berths where the fishing trawlers moored at night, and parked opposite the boarding area for the Boston–Provincetown ferry next to a white Ford Explorer with the seal of the Provincetown Harbor Patrol on the side. The red glow of the light bars lit an irregular circle on the pier, and Laurel made out a black Jeep on the opposite side of the Explorer. Reese Conlon stood in front of the vehicles talking to a middle-aged man with close-cropped sandy hair, wearing a short-sleeved khaki shirt with patches matching the seal on the truck. A tag over the right chest pocket indicated he was the harbormaster.

"Dr. Burgoyne," the man with Chief Conlon said in a warm gravelly voice. "Thanks for getting here so quickly."

"Of course," Nita said. "Laurel, this is Howard Jensen, the harbormaster. Howard—Laurel is a new member of our clinic team."

The harbormaster nodded. "Good to meet you."

"You too," Laurel replied.

"I'll take you gals straight out." The harbormaster turned to Reese and added, "I've got all the other boats on standby. They don't have a helipad on the cruise ship, so if we need to evac anyone, we'll either have to take them by ambulance or have the chopper land somewhere in town."

"We'll start clearing the pier as a precaution," Reese said. "Nita— we need a sitrep ASAP if we're going to mobilize the EMTs and call in air evac."

"I'll call you as soon as we get a sense of what we've got out there," Nita said.

"Good. I've put the local fire rescue team on call but didn't want to drag them out unless we needed them."

"Follow me," Howard said.

As they hurried after Howard Jensen onto a ramp leading down to an idling patrol boat, Laurel said to Nita, "How far is the nearest air evac station?"

"The Coast Guard station in Sandwich. They'll evac to Hyannis— that's the closest hospital—or Boston."

The cruise ship looked enormous from the cockpit of the patrol boat as they skimmed across the harbor, and Laurel's stomach tightened. The trip took only a few minutes, and the pilot drew up to a landing platform attached to a steep set of stairs leading to the ship's deck.

"Watch your step there," Howard said, as the boat bobbed on the water next to the docking platform.

One by one they transferred to the platform, and Laurel followed Nita up the steep, narrow metal stairs.

A tall, thin man in a white uniform, gold braid on his hat and shoulders, waited on the deck. "I'm Captain Fernandez. My first officer will take you and your medical team to the med bay."

"Dr. Nita Burgoyne," Nita said, offering her hand.

He waved over another officer. "You'll have all the assistance we can provide."

"Thank you."

Another officer in a crisp white shirt with gold-striped shoulder boards and pleated dark pants joined them, saying, "I'm First Officer Enrico. If you'll follow me, I'll take you to the med bay."

Nita, walking beside him along the passageway, said, "Where did your voyage originate?"

"Brazil, for the guests," Enrico said. "Some of the crew have been aboard since the ship left Hong Kong."

Laurel didn't have a lot of experience with large oceangoing ships, but it seemed they'd walked at least the length of several football fields before climbing an outside metal staircase to another deck, entering a passageway leading to the interior of the ship, and finally wending their way through several open lounge areas toward a passageway ending at a door marked *Medical Center*. Once inside, the area looked much like every emergency room she'd ever been in. The waiting area was carpeted in a neutral green and held ten upholstered gray chairs with curved wood arms, a wall-mounted monitor, now dark, and a central station where presently one markedly handsome young man with thick black hair, wearing a name tag and a white shirt, sat at a computer. All the chairs were occupied by adults who appeared to be in varying degrees of discomfort. All appeared middle-aged or older, most in lounge clothes or sleepwear, several of whom were coughing. Behind the registration desk another closed door evidently led to the treatment areas.

Enrico addressed the man behind the desk. "Please let Dr. Hanlon know the medical team is here."

The young man rose. "I'll take you back."

"Thank you," Nita said. "We'd also like to gown and glove before we get started."

"Of course. Please follow me."

He led them down another hallway to an alcove with a surgical sink and shelves holding stacks of masks, several boxes of caps, and a short stack of disposable yellow paper gowns. "We don't have much call for doing sterile procedures, but we occasionally have to close lacerations or the like. You should be able to find what you need here."

Laurel followed Nita's lead and scrubbed at the sink after donning a disposable cap, finding a mask on the shelf above the sink, and finally putting on one of the nonsterile yellow gowns. Just as they were finishing, a man wearing a white coat over dark blue scrubs entered through another door. He looked to be about fifty, with a neat, close-cut beard, dark eyebrows above intense blue eyes, and thick dark hair cut close on the sides and left a little bit long on the top. He had the athletic build of someone who still kept in shape. His short-sleeved white shirt bore a name tag that read *P. Hanlon, DO.*

"I'm Philip Hanlon, the chief medical officer. Thank you for getting here so quickly."

"Nita Burgoyne," Nita said, "and Laurel Winter. What are we looking at here?"

Hanlon shook his head, looking weary. "I really wish I knew. A little over a week ago, I saw two crew members who looked to have the flu. Classic symptoms. Low-grade fevers, cough, general malaise, nothing out of the ordinary. Prescribed the usual fluids, bed rest, analgesics. The next day I saw a couple more. The day after that, three times as many." He grimaced and blew out a breath. "Then I started to see some of the guests with similar symptoms and concluded we had an outbreak of the flu. When we docked last night—two nights ago now— the first of the guests, a couple, were both running high fevers. Since she was diabetic and he had a history of COPD, I wasn't comfortable with them continuing on with us and recommended that they disembark here. As you know, they weren't happy about that and were seen this morning by Dr. King."

"Yes," Nita said. "She agreed with your assessment."

He nodded. "Since the ship was in port and the couple agreed to stay in their stateroom while they made alternate travel arrangements, they remained on board. The husband showed up back here about two hours ago in severe respiratory distress. I've got him on supplemental oxygen, but his condition is deteriorating quickly. An hour after that, one of the crewmembers arrived febrile to one-oh-four with the acute onset of shortness of breath. I'm not sure what's going on, but we don't have the capacity to deal with this level of illness on board ship."

"Let's take a look at them first," Nita said. "We'll need to see all the charts of everyone you've seen and get them reevaluated. How many medical personnel do you have?"

"Three nurses," Hanlon said.

"Laurel will triage the guests needing to be seen along with your people."

"Fine," he said, looking relieved.

Hanlon took Laurel and Nita into the main part of the med bay, where beds were lined up along one side with curtains in between, and introduced them to the three nurses, one man and two women. The place looked like an intensive care unit, but she doubted it was as well-equipped as one. She could only hope they weren't looking at some kind of significant outbreak, because they'd be hard-pressed to handle it.

CHAPTER ELEVEN

Tory grabbed her phone on the first ring. "Hello."

"Tory, it's Nita. Did I wake you?"

"No, I've been up awhile. I was just getting Reggie breakfast. Where are you?"

"I'm still on the cruise ship," Nita said.

Tory glanced at the clock. 6:15 a.m. "You've been there all night?"

"Yes, and I'm not sure when I'll be done. I left a message on Randy's phone to start calling patients to reschedule if he hadn't heard from me by eight."

"What's happening?"

"That's why I'm calling. I don't really know. Something strange is going on, but we've got a lot of sick people, some of whom are *really* sick." Nita sounded perplexed and worried. Two things she never was.

"Tell me," Tory said just as Reggie decided at that moment to butter her own toast with the little plastic picnic knife Tory had given her for just that reason. Keeping one eye on Reggie, she pulled a pad of paper and a pen off the counter where she kept them to scribble down grocery items when she thought of them.

"There's definitely some kind of outbreak on this ship," Nita said, "and I'd call it the flu except it's not acting that way. The incubation period seems all wrong—and the progress of the symptoms isn't right either."

"How many people seem to be affected?" Tory asked, jotting down notes. "It's late for the flu season but not impossible, especially on a cruise ship that's coming from a different climate. The virus can peak at different times depending on temperature and population factors."

"I know," Nita said, "and that's part of the problem. This is an international cruise with people from all over the world, and with such a brief look at things, I can't see any kind of pattern. The only thing I *can* tell is the first people to get sick were crew members. But anyhow, at least half a dozen are sick enough to be in the hospital—or will be, if their symptoms progress."

"What's the transport situation?"

"Reese has her people working with the local EMTs, who are coordinating with air evac on that. I think we've seen everyone who's affected—or at least everyone who is reporting symptoms right now. Who knows how many more might be incubating something, or how many people might have mild symptoms they're self-treating. I want to be sure we've seen everyone before we leave."

"You're certain it's not something chemical, in the air supply or something?"

"The symptoms don't really fit with that—and if that was the case, I'd at least expect all the affected to be lodging in the same general area of the ship or to have attended the same event or *something*. The patients we've seen, at least, seem random in every way."

"Maybe we're just looking at a virus hitting all at once because these people are all confined together."

"I'm certainly no epidemiologist," Nita said, "but if I saw one of these patients in the office, I would've said flu and not really been all that concerned."

"I know," Tory said. "I saw that couple yesterday."

The silence on the other end of the phone was telling.

"What?" Tory asked.

"The husband, the one with COPD? He's intubated and being air evaced to Hyannis right now. His sats were unbelievably low. The ship's med crew is good, and they jumped on him right away with the supplemental O2."

"Believe me, he had no significant symptoms yesterday, other than an unproductive cough, general malaise, and a moderate temp." Tory frowned, running through all the signs and symptoms she'd registered in the cruise guest less than twenty-four hours earlier. None of them raised red flags then and, even knowing what she knew now, would be hard to distinguish from a common flu today. "Nothing unusual for the flu."

"Well, he's a hundred and four now, labored breathing, and mental confusion along with the desaturation. Whatever kind of variant this is—if it's flu at all—seems to hit some people faster than others."

"What about cultures, blood samples?"

"That's the thing," Nita said. "The med center here is pretty well-equipped for minor traumas, cardiac resuscitation, common variety colds, and whatnot, but it's not an ER. We've managed to culture up some of the sickest patients, but we really don't have the equipment. This could get worse, Tor."

"What are you thinking?" Tory asked.

"I'm worried," Nita said. "If more of these people get sick, or even a few get as sick as some of the people we've seen tonight, the medical facilities here will be overwhelmed. The cruise ship is due to sail out of here at sunset, and they'll be on the open water for another two days before they make port again."

"That doesn't sound like a great idea. Did you talk to the captain?"

"Not yet. I thought I'd better discuss it with you first. We really don't know what we have here."

"Seventeen affected people on a cruise ship, possibly more. *Probably* more," Tory said. "It's not out of the question we could be looking at SARS, or some other kind of Adult Respiratory Syndrome. I think we should call the CDC, tell them what we've got, and at least ask for guidance. They can probably contact one of the local med centers or labs up here to facilitate testing. They might also be able to run interference with the cruise company. Holding a cruise ship is a little bit above our pay grade."

Nita laughed without humor. "You're telling me. I was thinking the same thing. Informing the CDC sounds like the right call—my instincts tell me we're not being alarmists."

"No," Tory said quietly, remembering the couple she'd seen the day before. A man and woman like hundreds she'd seen in the past with an uncomfortable but not dangerous viral infection that would clear up on its own with supportive therapy in a few days. And now one was in a fight for his life. "I don't think we are either."

❖

Andy woke to the sound of gulls and the first hint of dawn coming through her open deck doors. She stretched, rolled over on her back, and, eyes still closed, thought about the night before. Laurel. Whatever Laurel wanted to call it, whatever made her comfortable, was fine with Andy, but she knew what it was. They'd had a date.

Weren't dates about getting to know someone? Not that she'd actually had much in the way of conversational dates. A couple of hookups after a softball game or a party, and that one time when she was in Baltimore for a tournament and bumped into one of the local competitors the first night. What had served as conversation was mostly sports talk, and there hadn't been a whole lot of that. Mostly hormones talking, and that didn't require a lot in the way of revelation. *Revelation.*

There was a word she never would've thought of in regard to herself, but she'd done a fair amount of that the night before. Revealing things she rarely thought about, let alone said out loud. Talking to Laurel was easy. Maybe because when she talked to Laurel, Laurel talked back and told *her* things. Listened to her, trusted her to hear things. And when Laurel smiled, warmth spread through places in Andy's chest she hadn't realized had been cold forever. Her stomach tightened when she thought about the touch of Laurel's hand on her arm, and the way Laurel had rested against her ever so softly while they sat out on the pier. The way Laurel's eyes had widened a little bit when Andy'd leaned toward her, not thinking about kissing her, exactly, but knowing on some level that she wanted to. She'd wanted to. Still wanted to. All she needed was a trip to the clinic, medical clearance, and she could get back to her life. Back on duty, and maybe—no, not maybe, for sure—Laurel. She wanted to see Laurel again on an up-front date, walk through town with her again, touch her. Ask her things. Hear things, maybe things no one else had ever heard.

When the tightness in her belly got distracting, Andy jumped up and pulled on shorts, a plain gray tee, and her running shoes. With her keys and a twenty-dollar bill tucked in the small pocket in her shorts, she left her apartment and headed out to the mostly empty streets. The dog walkers and joggers were about the only people around. She probably shouldn't run, but her head felt okay and she was jittery as hell. Sort of like how she felt on the way to a tournament—a hyped-up adrenaline high. She snorted. Competition didn't usually make her horny, though. Running usually burned that off, but she didn't want to do anything to mess up getting her medical clearance.

Fine. She'd just *walk* off the heavy feeling in the pit of her stomach. She knew what it was and could have dealt with it before she'd set out, but she just didn't feel like it. Well, she *did*, but some weird part of her liked the pent-up sexual frustration. The hot, heavy churning in the pit of her stomach made her feel alive. And she liked that Laurel did that to her. Usually it was reflex. She hardly ever thought about it as pleasure, more like opening a pressure valve automatically. She never really connected the feelings with another person or people. The urge was just there, like a muscle cramp that needed stretching out. She laughed. *This* definitely wasn't *that*. This was something else. She thought the word must be desire. And it had a name.

Laurel.

Still thinking about Laurel and how she'd manage to move their acquaintance in a more personal direction, Andy turned right onto Commercial and half walked, half jogged toward the center of town. A second later, flashing red lights shot into view. Light bars. A lot of them. Trouble. She picked up her speed, and by the time she got to MacMillan Wharf, she was running. Patrol cars, two EMT trucks, and a couple of state police cars blocked the pier. A circle of onlookers, not too big yet considering the early hour, milled around the vehicles, and a few civilians edged past the emergency vehicles and scurried down the pier, phones at the ready.

What the hell. She looked into the sky, expecting to see the reflections of a fire. What else could bring that many first responders out to an emergency? But the sky was clear blue with a few wispy white clouds and the sun just streaking across the water. She threaded her way between the vehicles and headed toward the end of the pier where most of the action seemed to be. She picked Bri out of the clump of officers and hurried over.

"Hey," she said, "what's going on?"

"Hey, Andy," Bri said, pausing to wave a couple of adventurous onlookers back behind the yellow police tape. "Got a medical emergency out on the cruise ship, and a bunch of people have to be evacuated."

"Huh. What is it? Food poisoning or something?"

Bri shook her head. "I dunno. We're not getting a lot of information on that. The chief just wants us to keep the crowds away so the EMT rigs can move in and out."

"I'll head home and get dressed. Where should I report?"

"You better check with the chief—she's around here somewhere," Bri said. "How you feeling?"

Andy grimaced. "I'm good. I should be helping."

"I think we'll have this cleared out in another hour. I'd go with whatever the docs said for now about taking it easy. Might as well save yourself an ass-chewing for not following their recs."

Andy stiffened, her skin reflexively prickling with wariness.

Bri's gaze narrowed. "How'd it go yesterday, when you talked to Reese? Trouble?"

Twenty-four hours before, Andy would've shrugged the question off with her usual *everything's fine* response. Because when everything was fine, or she told herself it was, her fear or pain or anxiety were easier to handle. The less she revealed, the less she admitted, even to herself, the less she felt.

But Bri had never been anything except supportive and helpful. Maybe, like with Laurel, if Andy took a chance, she'd be okay. "It went pretty good. She's tough, though. Made me recite the rulebook—almost all of it."

"Yeah," Bri said with a laugh. "I've been there."

"You have?"

"Oh yeah. First couple times I messed up."

"You mean, *you* messed up?"

Bri gave her a look. "Yo, Andy, everybody messes up. The key is not to get anybody hurt or to get hurt yourself. That's the number one rule, right? You keep people safe. That means you too."

Andy drew in a long breath. She *thought* she knew how to keep herself safe, and she wanted to be a cop so she could do the same for others. But maybe there was more than one way to do it. She shot Bri a grin. "I'm hoping I don't mess up again, because I don't think I know any more of the book."

"Don't worry, the chief will make sure you get it."

Andy scanned the activity on the pier and the patrol boats moving back and forth on the harbor between the pier and the cruise ship. It didn't look like things were going to quiet down for a while. "Okay, look, I'm going to head over to the clinic first thing this morning. I want to get cleared, so I can get back on the street."

"Good luck."

"Thanks," Andy said, for a lot more than she knew how to say.

At loose ends and irritated at being sidelined during an emergency, Andy strode the other way through town until she was standing at the end of the alley that led to Laurel's cottage. The windows were dark. Laurel was probably asleep. Not that she was planning on waking her up anyhow. She didn't even know why she'd gone that way. Well, she did. Part of her insanely hoped that Laurel might head out for coffee, because she'd said she did that every morning before her morning walk. 'Course, she hadn't said what time she did that. And if Laurel walked out and Andy was standing there like some kind of stalker, she'd think that was weird.

All the same, Andy waited a few more minutes, but Laurel never appeared.

Chapter Twelve

Laurel and Nita walked into the clinic a little before ten a.m. Two patients—a man in his midfifties, who sat twisting a faded ball cap in his hands, and a bored-looking teenage girl tapping on a cell phone with a bright pink lacquered nail—waited in the reception area. Laurel didn't recognize either of them.

Quietly, Nita asked Randy, "Have you rescheduled the morning?"

"Everyone except emergencies," he said just as quietly. "Tory wanted to see a few routines, but I put my foot down."

"Good. Give me a few minutes to catch up with Tory, and then I'll let you know about the afternoon. If we double-book a bit, we might get most of the morning's cancellations in."

"What's happening out there?" he asked.

Laurel was conscious of the two patients behind them, who were probably listening. But with the number of townspeople congregated on the pier watching, and the local first responders involved, news and speculation would probably be everywhere by now. At least these two would be hearing it from the source.

"It's a bit of an unknown right now," Nita said. "A contagion of some kind, most likely viral. Possibly just a variant of the good old-fashioned flu, but quite a number of people are pretty sick."

"Wow. Seems like a big fuss for the flu," Randy said.

Nita made a face and sighed. "Ordinarily I would agree with you, but it's rare that we see an outbreak like this in such a closed system. These people have been living in each other's pockets for almost two weeks, which tends to concentrate the exposure and push the spread faster. It's the kind of dynamic you don't see except sometimes in boarding schools or submarines, where the whole population is exposed."

"Neither place I'd like to think about being," Randy said with a little shudder. "Just let me know when you want to start, and I'll make some more calls."

"Thanks," Nita said, heading toward the back.

"Hey, Laurel," Randy said.

Laurel paused. "What's up?"

Randy swiveled in his chair, turning his back to the waiting room, and edged closer. In a near whisper, he said, "A certain really cute police officer was in here about an hour and a half ago asking about you."

No way could she stop the heat from flooding her face. No way. Neither could she pretend she didn't know who Randy was talking about. "I'm guessing you mean Officer Champlain?"

"Well, we do seem to have more than our share of really cute police officers," Randy said, "of all kinds."

"Randy. Short on time here." Laurel rolled her eyes, but she couldn't help smiling. As tired as she was, and as pressed as she felt to get the clinic hours straightened out, the mention of Andy energized her. For a fleeting moment, the fatigue and stress dropped away.

"She wanted to make an appointment for reevaluation," Randy said, all teasing gone, "but I couldn't do it given the circumstances."

"Did she give you a hard time?" Laurel asked, surprised. Andy was eager to get back to work, but she, of all people, would appreciate that emergencies came up and priorities had to be considered.

"Oh no, no, not at all. The soul of politeness. I told her we'd call her back if we could get her in today."

"Good," Laurel said, starting to turn away again. "I'll mention her to Nita when we discuss the schedule."

"But…"

Laurel looked over her shoulder. "Two seconds."

"She asked about you—specifically. If you would be working today. I told her almost definitely. And she smiled." He leaned forward a little bit more. "She looked very happy about that."

"Okay, thanks," Laurel said, heat accompanying the little heart flip this time.

"I got her number if you want to call her."

"No, you should do that." Laurel reached the door to the back offices, paused for a second, then turned around and held out her hand. "Give me the number."

Smiling, he passed her a small slip of paper. "She's cute."

"Thanks for taking care of everything out here." Still smiling a little, Laurel pushed the folded slip of paper into her pants pocket and hurried to the room at the far end of the hall that doubled as their conference area and break room. She'd figured out pretty quickly that Randy might like to tease, but they couldn't run the office without him. Patients loved him, he apparently never missed a day, and he knew how to keep temperamental babies, frantic mothers, and cranky patients calm and feeling cared for. Only the people who actually worked in a medical office, dealing with so many people who were under pressure and scared and not feeling well, could understand just how important that first point of contact could be. She'd known the first moment she walked into the clinic and introduced herself that Randy was one of the precious great ones. And she rather liked being teased about Andy.

After all, Andy was young and hot, and she'd asked about Laurel. Andy was *interested* in her. A little warning bell tolled in the back of her mind. She'd gotten swept away by what she'd mistakenly thought of as interest in her once before, and nearly ruined her life. This was different, of course it was. Still, best not to let her hormones run away with her good sense.

Feet a little more firmly on the ground, Laurel turned into the break room and put Andy Champlain out of her mind. "Sorry. Just checking in with Randy for a minute."

"No problem." Nita held out the coffee mug Laurel used at work. "Thought you might want this."

"Bless you," Laurel said, taking the mug. "Is there milk left? It was my turn to bring some in today, but…"

"Emergency Mini Moo's in the bottom drawer of the fridge," Tory said, seated at the little round table in the middle of the room. A single window looked out on a small copse of evergreens by the side of the parking lot. The rest of the space was taken up by a counter along one wall with a refrigerator underneath and a coffee maker, electric teapot, and small sink above.

"Perfect." Laurel added three of the little shots to her mug and sat down at the table.

Tory pushed a cardboard box toward her. "Sugar and fat."

"Even better." Laurel opened the box and nearly moaned. Croissants and doughnuts. She took a chocolate cake doughnut with pink frosting and sprinkles. Just looking at it made her teeth ache, and she couldn't wait. She took a big bite. Her flagging system immediately perked up.

"Okay," Tory said, "where are we with this?"

Nita took a plain croissant and broke off a corner. If she was ravenous, she was too genteel to show it. She popped it into her mouth, chewed a moment, and swallowed. "Presently, seventeen symptomatic patients, ranging in age from forty-five to seventy-eight. All showing similar symptoms—primarily fever, raspy throat, and a dry, unproductive cough along with systemic malaise. Interestingly, almost none have typical upper respiratory signs, as you would expect with the onset of a URI. Minor sniffles and a few with joint aches and pains."

"So a little bit different than classic flu," Tory said.

"Not just that, but the onset seems different too," Nita said. "We don't have nearly enough information to make even an epidemiological guesstimate, but from what I can gather, the incubation period seems to be fairly long. Several people who share a cabin and presumably would have been exposed at the same time developed symptoms days apart. Some, possibly several *weeks* apart. That doesn't seem to follow the same pattern as the flu either."

Tory frowned. "Seventeen still seems like a small number given the population of the cruise ship. What is it? Eight hundred or so?"

"One thousand fifty-six including crew," Nita said. "And I agree—it wouldn't be all that worrisome. If it wasn't for the fact that the number of people showing up in the last couple of days has escalated, which suggests there will be more. And given that three of those seventeen developed rapid onset pulmonary failure. These people are really sick, Tor. Like, ICU sick."

"Were we able to do any kind of testing?"

Laurel shook her head. "They're just not set up for it. The patients—six who we transferred out for observation or who definitely need hospitalization—will presumably get tested upon arrival. We did a few throat cultures until supplies ran out, but we really need more specific tests and a lab that can handle them."

"All right." Tory rubbed her forehead. "I put a call in to the CDC, and I'm waiting for a call back. The ship isn't due to sail until tonight, correct?"

"That's my understanding," Nita said.

"Well, at this point, it's not going to be our call." Tory propped her feet on the only empty chair at the table. "How do you two feel? Can you see a few patients this morning? Randy's cleared the schedule of everything except emergencies until two this afternoon, but we can postpone most of those patients too. And I can see—"

"I'm fine," Laurel said quickly. She wasn't the one to tell Tory anything at all, especially that she shouldn't be seeing a regular schedule of patients, but she could do her part to take some of the burden. "I need a quick shower and change of clothes, but I was planning to work a full shift."

"I'm fine too," Nita said. "It's not my first all-nighter, and it wasn't even all night." She paused. "Well, I wasn't exactly asleep, but…"

Tory rolled her eyes. "Really? You're going to taunt us now with hints of your fabulous sex life?"

"That was not my intention," Nita said ever so seriously, "although I would never lie to my good friends if questioned. Deo has been out of town on that construction job in Dennis, and she's been staying up there most nights, so she doesn't have to drive back and forth. But she showed up unexpectedly last night."

Happily, Laurel did not blush. Having known Nita practically her whole life, she knew Nita was far from being a prude, despite her apparent reserve, *and* she could sometimes be a terrible tease. If you didn't know her well, her calm, contained, and ultrasophisticated demeanor could be misleading. That was probably the boarding school influence. Laurel had escaped that experience, although the four years when they only saw each other on school vacations and holidays were four of the worst years of her life. She'd met Peter then, and she'd been lonely. As if that was any excuse for ignoring her own misgivings.

And remembering her resolution, Laurel pushed those thoughts aside.

"That's what I mean," Tory said archly. "Taunting us about your hot young lover."

"She's not that much younger." Nita pretended to protest, but her smile said something altogether different.

"No arguing about the hot, though," Tory said. With a sigh, she dropped her feet to the floor. "We better get back to it. I'll let you know what the CDC says."

"I'll ask Randy to rearrange the schedule so we see any urgent ones from this morning as well as the regular afternoon patients." Nita pointed a finger at Tory. "But you do not do any more work. To the office for you."

Tory sighed. "I would argue, but my feet might simply get up and walk away if I did."

Out in the hall, Nita said to Laurel, "You're feeling okay?"

"Really," Laurel said, "I'm probably more used to being up all night than either of you two. I just finished my training, remember?"

"Believe me, I remember, and I've been spoiled. Night call here just isn't that bad."

"Do you think we've seen the worst of whatever's going on out there?" Laurel said quietly.

"I honestly have no idea," Nita said, "and that's what really bothers me."

When Nita went to talk to Randy, Laurel settled in the small office she'd been provided for doing chart work, returning patients' calls, and basically escaping the fray when needed. She fished out the piece of paper with Andy's number on it. She could just as easily have Randy call and set up a time for Andy to return, but she didn't even pretend that was an option. She punched in the number on her phone, her pulse fluttering in her chest.

Andy answered right away.

"Hey," Andy said. "How are you doing? You were out on that ship last night, weren't you?"

"I'm okay. We're back at the clinic. It was a crazy night."

"I know, I was down at the pier early this morning and saw a bit of it."

"We're going to see patients this afternoon, and I can ask Randy to get you in."

"You know," Andy said, "I wouldn't push, but I really do want to get back to work. I think they're probably going to need me. The whole force was up last night, and even if the cruise ship leaves on time, it's the busy season, you know. If something else comes up, it'll be all hands on deck."

"I understand," Laurel said. "How are *you* feeling?"

"I feel…good," Andy said. "Seriously. No headache. My jaw still hurts a little bit, but only right where the injury is. Otherwise, I'm a hundred percent."

"All right. Randy will call you with the time."

"Thanks, Laurel." Andy was silent a moment, then said in a rush, "So, uh, hey—can I see you later? After you're done, I mean."

Laurel should have been thinking of an early night and catching up on sleep, but what registered was the faint uncertainty mixed with anticipation in Andy's voice. And the tremor in her midsection that she finally identified as excitement. "I'd like that. But I don't have any idea how things are going to go here this afternoon. It could be late."

"That's okay. Call me."

Call me. Andy was leaving it all up to her. Her decision. Laurel smiled. "All right. I'll do that."

CHAPTER THIRTEEN

Reese joined Bri next to the yellow crime scene tape that blocked off MacMillan Wharf from the traffic circle at the junction of Commercial and Standish. An EMT van with flashing lights pulled around the corner onto Bradford and disappeared.

"That the last of them?" Reese asked.

"Yep. Unless there's more I don't know about." Bri, as bright-eyed and alert as if she'd just rolled out of bed, kept on the lookout for the adventurous ones among the milling pedestrians who tried ducking under or slipping around the tape and sawhorse barricades they'd hastily erected in the middle of the night. With her legs slightly spread and her hands clasped behind her back, she was the picture of easy confidence and friendly authority. She'd been born with cop in her blood, all right.

"Nope. When Nita and Laurel came ashore, Laurel said those three were the last in line for transfer," Reese said. "The least sick of the bunch, apparently."

"So can we—Yo, Stevie!" Bri pointed at a nine-year-old riding a BMX. "You can't ride your bike down here this morning."

The fair-skinned towhead, already nut brown from the sun in a pair of baggy Nike shorts, high-tops, and red and white striped crew socks, carried a faded canvas bag filled with the free weekly newspaper slung across his narrow chest. He wheeled his bike around, skidded to a stop in front of Bri, and looked up at her, face alight with excitement. "I heard the boat was sinking. Can't I just get down there to take a peek? I won't get in the way or anything."

Bri gave him a look. "Does that thing look like it's sinking to you? It takes a lot to sink ships like that. They're too big to be bothered by almost any size waves, and there's ballast to help stabilize them. They might run aground, but that one hasn't."

"What's ballast?"

"Water in the holds of the ship." Bri poked a finger toward him. "No sightseeing."

"Bummer." His face fell, and he craned his neck as a firetruck rolled down the pier toward another officer who moved the barricade aside to let it pass. "So what are you doing down there, then?"

Bri glanced at Reese for the go-ahead, and Reese nodded slightly.

"Some people on the ship got sick," Bri said, "and they had to be sent to a couple of hospitals up Cape for special care. It's all taken care of now."

"Oh," Stevie said with further disappointment. "So, class still on tonight?"

Bri rested her hands on her hips. "What do you think?"

He grinned. "Yup."

"Right. Go deliver your papers," Bri said.

"See you, Sensei." He hopped on his bike, wheeled around, and pedaled away.

Reese laughed. "You've got your hands full teaching that bunch."

"I like kids that age. They're not delicate, and they're fearless. Plus, they want to learn."

Reese laughed again. "Yeah, I know what you mean about the fearless part."

Bri glanced around, as if checking to see if anyone was near. "So what do you think? Is this it? Is it all over now?"

"I dunno," Reese said. "I hope so, but I got the distinct feeling that whatever's going on out there isn't something routine. Nita and Laurel looked worried."

Bri whooshed out a breath. "So what do *we* do?"

"We consult with the experts, which I'm going to do right now. While I'm at the clinic, I need you to check in with everyone who's been out here all night and make sure we've got enough people to cover the shifts for the rest of the day. As soon as I've talked to Tory, we'll pull everybody who's available into the station for an update."

"Got it."

"Good work last night, Bri." Reese clapped her on the shoulder before she strode over to her patrol car. The turmoil that had been twisting in her midsection the last few hours, as she'd watched stretcher after stretcher carrying patients swaddled in sheets, surrounded by monitors, and hooked up to oxygen tanks, mushroomed as she drove through town, easing her way through the already crowded streets. Two days until the Fourth of July and every available private room, B and B, condo, and campsite was full. Tour buses poured into town at dawn and left at sundown. Thousands of pedestrians and hundreds of vehicles jammed the streets, and she had to police it all with a force full of summer temps, many of whom had never seen anything like this before. And now, a cruise ship with a thousand people sat out in the harbor like a big black box, with something going on inside it that she didn't understand and couldn't influence. Something was coming, she could feel it, and she wanted to form a plan, disperse her troops, and thwart the attack. Except she had no idea how to do that. If a battle was truly coming, she was completely unprepared.

❖

The clinic parking lot was oddly empty for late morning in the beginning of July. Nita's Nissan, Tory's Mazda SUV, and a Ford truck that had to have logged two hundred thousand miles, if the dents and rusted-out fenders were any indication, huddled in the shade under the clump of evergreens at the far end.

The waiting room was completely empty, something Reese had never seen in the hundreds of times she'd been there.

"I guess she's free," Reese said to Randy.

Randy shook his head. "She's on the phone with the CDC."

He whispered as if the waiting room was packed.

Reese's stomach tightened. Tory calling the CDC was akin to her calling for the National Guard. "Okay. So I can wait?"

"'Course," Randy said, trying a smile that didn't look altogether authentic. "Laurel and Nita are in the break room. You know the way. I don't think she'll be too long."

"Thanks."

Reese passed Tory's closed office door on her way back to the break room. Nita and Laurel sat at the single table with cups of coffee, looking weary. "Morning."

"Just barely still," Nita said.

"Here." Laurel pushed a doughnut box toward her. "We saved you one."

"You must be mind-readers."

Nita smiled. "Your wife is."

"True." Reese pulled out a sugar-coated doughnut with purple filling. Blueberry? Raspberry, maybe? Hopefully not grape. She took a bite and got hit with the sugary sweetness and a surprising bit of tangy fruit from the filling. Had to be Connie's. No one else actually made decent doughnuts. After another bite, she got up, found the coffee had boiled down to sludge, and put on a new pot.

She'd just filled her cup when a hand skimmed down the center of her back and Tory said, "Morning."

Reese half turned and kissed her. "Morning."

Tory looked worried. Tory rarely looked worried.

Silently, aware of the atmosphere in the room growing heavier with the weight of everyone's anxiety, Reese asked, "Do you want water, tea, or something?"

"I want a red eye from the Wired Puppy, but since I'm off coffee, I'm good. I just finished tea."

Reese set her coffee on the table and angled the chair she'd been sitting in toward the other empty one and said, "Feet up. No argument."

"None coming." Tory settled and didn't even object when Reese scooped a hand beneath her ankles and lifted her feet. "Thank you."

"Here," Laurel said, rising, "take my chair, Reese. I've had plenty of time for my feet to recover."

"That's okay, thanks." Reese retreated to lean against the counter with coffee in hand. "I'm fine."

Everyone looked at Tory.

"Well," Tory said, "I talked to Roger Tahari, who is the assistant director for the infectious disease rapid response team at the CDC. They agreed that what we seem to have here is not typical in either timing or presentation for known viral outbreaks."

Tory rattled off a few statistics, but Reese was watching Laurel's and Nita's faces as Tory spoke. Both of them grew even more solemn and tense. Something bad was in the wind.

Tory paused and took a deep breath. "They have one other similar outbreak under investigation right now in Southern California. At a resort where half a dozen people who arrived together at the end of a cruise are showing similar symptoms."

"Another cruise? Not this one?" Nita said. "Did their cruise originate in the same place as our cruise ship did?"

"No," Tory said, "I asked that. But apparently the crew or portions of them move from one ship to another depending on their ports of origin, destinations, and work rotations. It's not confirmed yet, but it *is* the same cruise ship line, so it's possible that some of the crew from our ship were also the crew on the first ship."

Laurel asked. "Do we know where that originated? Have they been able to track back to the index case?"

"The first cruise ship"—Tory looked at her phone where she had notes—"the *Princess Diana*, left out of Hong Kong, but as to the passengers? Tracking them gets difficult due to international cooperation, or lack thereof. Not every country of origin is willing to provide travel info—or any info—on its citizens."

"And we're sure it's not SARS?" Laurel straightened. "This is something new?"

"Right now, that's the working hypothesis. The course of this disease doesn't fit with the SARS timetable, and the lab hasn't been able to isolate that virus in the California group. Roger says they expect to isolate this organism very shortly."

Reese asked, "Where does that leave us?"

"The CDC is sending a team," Tory said. "They'll be here this evening."

"Okay," Reese said. "What will they be doing?"

"They're going to want to start on board ship and test everyone. They'll also get contact info from anyone who's ill, or who tests positive without symptoms, and start tracing."

"What about the ship?" Nita asked.

"I got the impression they're going to quarantine everyone for the presumed incubation period," Tory said.

"Which is?" Laurel asked.

"Right now, their best evidence suggests ten to fourteen days."

"Whoa," Reese said. "They can keep a thousand people on that ship for two weeks, what, isolated in their cabins?"

"Apparently, yes." Tory sighed. "That's not all. Once the test reports are back, anyone who tests positive will need to be quarantined ashore."

Reese frowned. "Here?"

"Yes."

"How many people are we talking about?" Reese asked.

Tory shrugged. "I have no idea. It could be twenty. It could be two hundred."

"Tor," Reese said. "The town is full."

"I know," Tory said. "We're going to need a task force—medical, police, harbor patrol, fire rescue—to liaise with the CDC. And I guess we better contact the mayor."

Reese squeezed the bridge of her nose. "The mayor, the town council, the head of the local business association. We're going to have to treat this like a natural disaster crisis."

"It might well be," Tory agreed. "But it's also possible that all we've got is a very limited outbreak, and nothing else will come of it."

"What are the chances of that?" Reese asked.

Tory held Reese's gaze. "Right now, I'd put it at seventy–thirty. Against."

"Yeah, that's what I thought."

"For now," Tory said, "we need to prepare to take care of acute patients, if the CDC team requires more help, and to monitor any patients who need to be quarantined on shore. That means checking our supplies and rescheduling elective nonurgent patients for the next week or so."

Nita said, "I'll handle the scheduling with Randy. He can start calling the urgent ones we need to see today."

Laurel added, "I'll inventory supplies."

"Good. Would you two give Reese and me a minute," Tory said quietly.

"Of course," Nita and Laurel said together and quickly left.

Reese dragged one of the chairs over, sat, and took Tory's hand. "What is it?"

"The chances are slim," Tory said quietly, "but I have been exposed to two of those patients from the ship here in the office."

"Right, the couple that you saw. What does it mean?"

"No one is entirely certain. The mechanism of transmission is not clear, nor is the level of contagiousness apparent at this point. Everyone affected so far has been in close proximity for extended periods of time. I was with those people for a couple of minutes each."

"Okay." Reese summoned every ounce of her control not to squeeze Tory's hand or show her in any way the terror racing through her. "So what do we do?"

Tory smiled softly. "I would like you to take Reggie to Kate's for a little vacation. She loves being there, and you can check on her every day. At least for a week."

"If you've been exposed, I've been exposed," Reese said. "Are we...I don't know, contagious, I guess?"

"You wouldn't be unless I'm actively infected, and we have no indication of that." Tory grimaced. "Right now, we have no idea what much of anything means. But I'm not going to see any more patients. I'm not going to see anyone other than the people I've already seen. All of you, everyone in the office, needs to be tested as soon as the CDC arrives. Then we'll know."

"How quickly?"

"The tests are expensive, and right now only a limited number of laboratories can run them, but the test itself is relatively quick. We'll know in a day, two at the most, but we'll need to be retested once we have a better idea of the incubation period. Or the CDC—or another lab—develops an antibody test."

Reese nodded. The battlefield was becoming clearer. She could site the enemy positions now. She still didn't know what weapons she faced, or how she could protect her family and her town. But she would, no matter what it took. "Do you really think this is a completely new organism? That just, I don't know...popped up?"

Tory smiled. "Every living thing was new once."

"Right." Reese raised Tory's hand and kissed it. "So, let me drive you home."

"I still have some planning to do. Talk to Kate about Reggie and then go back to work."

"You're going to want to talk to the CDC, aren't you."

"You must be a mind-reader," Tory said gently.

"Learned from the best." Reese kissed her. "I'll be back."

"I know. Go, do what you have to do. I'll be here."

Leaving Tory was about the hardest thing Reese had ever done in her life. She wanted to build a wall around her, erect a shield that would deflect every danger, destroy any threat, and protect her from a world filled with meaningless random acts of violence. She couldn't do that. Now more than ever, she was powerless. Fury and fear warred within her, and she reached deep for the calm and the control that she'd learned as a soldier and honed through her training, found her center and her power, and reminded herself that Tory needed her to be steady. That, more than anything else, gave her strength.

❖

Randy magically managed to contact all the patients scheduled for that day and had rescheduled the nonurgent ones and got those who needed to be seen in. Laurel hadn't stopped for three hours, and she'd only made it through half the list on her iPad of patients to be seen. She didn't think about when she might be done, only who was next.

As she opened the door on her way out of the treatment room, she said, "If you have any trouble getting those prescriptions filled, have the pharmacist call me. You should be able to get the generic form covered by your insurance, and your out-of-pocket expense won't be very much. If they tell you they only have the brand name available, *that's* when you tell them to call me."

"Okay, I'll sure do that," the elderly fisherman told her. He probably shouldn't be working anymore at all, but his vertigo wasn't so bad that she thought he was unsafe on deck, and how could she tell him to give up his livelihood when chances were he wouldn't have enough from Social Security, or likely his nonexistent savings, to survive. She saw so many like him, who other under circumstances would be enjoying the retirement they'd worked all their lives for, but who had nothing in the way of savings. Anything they managed to put away from seasonal jobs ended up being used to survive the long cold winters.

"I'll see you in two weeks, or sooner if it gets worse. Deal?"

He grinned at her, his weathered, grizzled face still carrying the hint of the charming lady-killer he'd probably been thirty or forty years before. "You got my word on that. I never lie to a lady."

"Good." Laughing, she stepped out into the hall, glanced down at her tablet to see where she needed to go next, and walked directly into someone. "Oh, sorry."

"Hey, Laurel," Andy said.

Laurel blinked and instantly felt the blush. Was she going to do that every single time she saw her? Blushing had never been her thing. Andy was in jeans and a white T-shirt and looked like she ought to be out on the deck of a sailboat or leaning against the railing at an oceanside bar. Namely, young and drop-dead sexy. "Hey. Are you just coming in?"

"No," Andy said, her eyes bright as she skimmed Laurel's face. "All done. And all clear. Dr. Burgoyne says I'm good to go."

"That's great," Laurel said. "You'll take it easy, though, right?"

Andy grinned as if the idea of Laurel worrying about her was unusual. "Sure."

The hall was empty, but Andy glanced up and down and leaned closer. "So, how are you doing? I got a look at what was going on down at the harbor last night. Looked intense."

"It wasn't what I expected to be doing, that's for sure." Laurel shrugged. "I'm good. We're swamped, but catching up. I think it's going to get busier later. There's a team from the CDC on the way to evaluate the situation."

"Bet that's why the chief wants us all there at change of shift for a briefing." She glanced at her watch. "In like fifteen minutes."

"You should go, then," Laurel said. "We're all going to be here until the CDC arrives."

"Makes sense," Andy said. "Look. Whatever time it is, I'd still like to see you."

Laurel could've written off the stirring in her middle as almost anything—nerves, uncertainty, plain old tiredness—but that wasn't it. The way Andy looked unapologetically straight into her eyes and said exactly what she wanted, no innuendo or clever double entendres, intrigued her. Oh, Andy captured her attention physically, sure—how could she not, considering how downright hot she was—but the anxious, excited *thrill* in her depths was more than chemistry. She couldn't help but feel the intensity in Andy's gaze, and the way she wasn't afraid to say she wanted to see her. From anyone else, that might've been a line, might have been part of the game, but Laurel had a lot of experience with games, plenty enough to tell the difference.

Maybe she *was* misreading what she saw in Andy's eyes, maybe she *wanted* to see it there, and she knew that was a weakness of hers. Wanting to see what she needed to see. But she didn't think so. She'd be careful, just as she'd promised herself she would be the next time, if there ever was a next time, when she'd left Peter.

Carefully, she said, "No matter what happens, I'll let you know when I'm free."

"I'll be waiting." Andy touched two fingers to Laurel's wrist, for no more than a second—not invading her personal space, not anything remotely suggestive, but a touch that said whatever might be between them, Laurel wasn't the only one who felt the spark.

CHAPTER FOURTEEN

A ndy pulled into the station lot just as Bri was getting out of her vehicle. She jogged over to join her with five minutes to spare before the three p.m. briefing.

"How'd it go?" Bri asked.

Andy grinned. "All clear."

Bri thumped her shoulder. "Awesome. Just in time too. It sounds like we might get even busier than usual pretty quick."

"What's happened?" Andy said as they went through the side door and down the hall toward the briefing room. The room next to the chief's office was big enough to accommodate the regular shift numbers, but if everyone was coming in, there'd be standing room only.

"I guess you heard about the CDC, right?" Bri said.

"Yeah, I was talking to Laurel at the clinic. She mentioned they were on their way."

"Well, I guess we'll find out from the chief what that means." Bri paused outside the briefing room. "But knowing Reese, she won't wait for them to catch up. We'll be preparing for any and all eventualities, whether they might happen or not."

"Ever thought of working anywhere else?" Andy grabbed a seat in the second—and last—row next to Bri. The room could only accommodate three seats on each side of the center aisle. Other officers straggled in behind them and leaned against the wall.

Bri snorted. "Not hardly. I grew up here, for one thing. And, well, anything I might need to learn about being a cop, I got from my dad and Reese. Nope. This is where I belong."

Where she belonged. The words hit Andy hard as the shuffling and murmuring in the room began to die down and everyone settled in to wait for Reese. She'd thought she knew where she belonged. Hadn't ever really questioned it. She'd grown up being told exactly where she belonged. What her status was in her family, where she fell in the pecking order, and what her future would look like. She hadn't actually been *ordered* to become a cop, but her father and brothers had made it pretty clear that if she didn't, she'd never be a real part of the family. Lucky for her, she liked law enforcement. Probably someone could argue that she liked it because she'd been taught that she would like it, but she didn't think that was true. She trusted her gut. She knew what it told her. She might not know where she belonged anymore, but she definitely knew what she belonged doing. This was it. As for the rest of her life, she had blanks where she'd never noticed them before. She'd never thought about what a whole life would look like, beyond being a cop and fitting in to her family. She hadn't thought about the other things she might want or need. For an instant, she thought about Laurel. She never considered that a *person* might be as important as what she did or how her family thought of her. She still wasn't sure if she needed someone—wanted someone—who might ask for things she didn't know how to give, but she knew no one had ever made her think about those things before Laurel.

Reese walked to the front of the room and instant silence fell. She stopped directly in the center facing the packed rows of chairs and standing officers, relaxed but giving off that unmistakable air of command that seemed to surround her no matter the circumstances. She scanned the room quickly. Andy straightened in her seat and sensed Bri doing the same beside her. Reese commanded attention—and loyalty and respect too—without brandishing her power like a weapon. Andy wasn't sure how she accomplished that, but she wanted to learn.

Reese said, "Looks like everyone has made it. I appreciate that. Let me tell you what we might be looking at over the next week or so."

Andy listened carefully as Reese detailed the events on the cruise ship the previous night. When she finished with the recap, she said, "At this point, the CDC task force is going to take the lead in determining if there's any ongoing concern and what, if anything, would need to be done about it. That means we'll need to be ready for almost anything, including double shifts and lending whatever kind of support the task force might need. Questions?"

One of the detectives in the front row cleared his throat and raised a hand.

"Jenkins?" Reese said.

"Begging your pardon, Chief, but this sounds like a whole lot of worry and fuss and bother over the flu. People get the flu all the time, and some of them get pretty sick, right? So what's the big deal this time?"

"I'm not a scientist," Reese said, "and from what little information anyone has right now, the problem here is that this bug—most likely a virus—looks to be something new. Because of that, the bug's behavior can't be anticipated—how fast it might spread, if it will spread at all. Plus, there isn't much in the way of effective treatment. Not that you can really treat the flu all that well."

Andy shifted a little in her seat. She didn't think it was much, but Reese must've noticed.

"Champlain?" Reese said.

Every person in the room turned toward her. The scrutiny didn't bother her. She'd been watched all her life—in competition, at the dinner table, at simple backyard pickup games—to see if she measured up. To see if she was good enough. The tightness in her belly was familiar, and she ignored it.

"I'm not a scientist either," Andy said, and a few people chuckled, "but I was wondering, you know...flu shots. That's a vaccine, right? Is there one for this? Because if there is, and it's going to be dispensed in town, that might need some supervision or plan to actually get the stuff to the population."

Reese nodded. "You're absolutely right. Unfortunately, as of this moment, I don't think there's a vaccine. But there *is* a test available to see if someone is infected, and if for some reason there needs to be widespread testing, that's going to require a lot of communication as well as crowd control."

Bri raised a hand.

"Parker?" Reese said.

"What about designating a testing area that's not right in the center of town, so it would be easier to get people in and out, especially if they come with cars. A restaurant or motel parking lot maybe?"

Allie, another officer Andy recognized, shot her hand up. "What about just cordoning off the football field, Chief, you know, with cones, so people could drive through past a station to get tested or whatever. If we needed to do that, mass testing or something, I mean."

"Another good thought," Reese said.

Andy took note of the way Reese let everyone contribute, and speak their minds, even the ones who were skeptical. She'd never been much of a team player. She'd been taught to win at everything. Sometimes, that made you a lousy team player, and she wanted to be one now.

"I have a meeting set up with the mayor next," Reese said, "and we'll talk about using the high school if we need any kind of staging area." Reese pointed to someone in the back of the room. "Carson?"

"This bug, Chief, how contagious is it? Are we going to have to worry about the town getting infected?"

Reese's expression tightened. "Not if I have anything to say about it. Not if there are things that we can do to limit exposure and assist the CDC in containment."

When the questions died down, Reese added, "All of this is speculative right now. We'll know a lot more when the team from the CDC arrives. For now, everyone maintain your regular shift rotations. Make sure the duty officer knows where to contact you if we need you when you're off shift. I'm putting vacation time on hold, but I'll try to make that restriction as short as I possibly can. For right now, your regular time off will continue, but I can't promise you won't get called in. That's all. Dismissed."

The room cleared relatively quickly. As Andy walked out with Bri, Bri said, "I'm going to catch an early dinner with my girl. You want to come?"

"Hey, thanks," Andy said, "I'd like to do that, but I might have plans. I'm waiting for a text."

Bri's brow rose. "Plans. Huh. Like a date type thing?"

"Oh no, just dinner."

"Dinner with a friend or dinner with a maybe date?" Bri pushed, a teasing note in her voice.

"Well, I'm hoping for the date part," Andy said, liking the way it felt to talk about it. Liking having someone to talk about it *with*.

"So, do I know her?"

"Laurel Winter."

"Whoa, the PA at the clinic. Good choice."

Andy grinned. "Yeah, I thought so." Her phone vibrated, and she slipped it out of her pocket to check. Instant buzz in her belly "Hold on a sec. That's Laurel."

Laurel: *Breaking for dinner at five. You free?*

Yes. Where should I meet you? Andy texted.

Laurel: *Takeout at my place?*

Pizza? Andy typed.

Laurel: *Perfect. C U at 5*

"So I guess it's on," Bri said as Andy put her phone away.

"Yeah," Andy said, grinning. "It's on."

She hoped. Even though she wasn't exactly sure what she was hoping for.

❖

Andy parked a few houses from Laurel's and carried the pizza down the narrow lane to her cottage. The pizza place had been jammed, and she was a few minutes later than she'd said she'd be. A light shone through the window next to the door, and she rapped lightly, anticipation welling in her chest. She recognized the feeling, but usually she associated it with that tense, adrenaline-charged energy right before a contest. This was a little bit different than that pre-game high, the edges of her excitement somehow reaching into places that had nothing to do with competition—the pit of her stomach, the hairs on the backs of her arms, the muscles high on the inside of her thighs. Her body was charged, and she was breathing a little fast. Definitely not her pre-match state, when she often sank into watchful awareness— calm, but alert. She didn't feel calm now, but she sure as hell felt revved in every fiber of her being.

The buzz was better than any victory-high she could remember.

The door opened, and Laurel stood on the threshold. For a second, Andy lost her voice. A hazy gold light shone from behind Laurel, filtered through a tinted lampshade somewhere in the room, or maybe a bit of sunlight had been trapped inside and took this chance to escape. Her hair flowed loose around her shoulders, free of the band or clasp or whatever it was she usually wore when she was working, and the little bit of breeze wafting in through the open door made the waves lift and flutter. She'd changed into a sleeveless pale green shirt, a couple of buttons at the top open, and blue jeans that hugged the curve of her thighs and ended at her ankles above soft-looking tan flats. Casual, and beautiful.

"Hi," Laurel said into the silence. Her smile was a bit questioning, and her eyes a little bit amused.

"Oh." That was eloquent. Andy cleared her throat. "Hi. Sorry I'm late. The pizza took a while."

"That's okay, you're here now." Laurel stepped back. "Come on in. I needed a few minutes to pick up, anyway. I hustled out of here in the middle of the night."

"You must be beat," Andy said, saying a little silent prayer that Laurel wasn't going to suggest they postpone their...meal.

"Not too bad." Laurel gestured to a small table adjacent to a window looking out onto a carefully tended flower garden and expanse of lawn. "Have a seat. I'll get us plates and whatnot. I've got juice, beer, hard cider, lemonade, and spring water."

"Water's good." Andy set the pizza box in the center of the round table and its two chairs. The whole cottage was small enough to take in in one glance. Everything you needed was there, but sort of in miniature. Even the table was the kind of little table she saw out on balconies, with scrolly wrought iron legs and a white ceramic top with tiny inlaid blue tiles around the edges. "This place is nice."

Laurel beamed. "Thanks. I loved it the minute I saw it. I was living in a pretty nondescript apartment in the city before I moved up here, not that I was home all that much. But I was still really tired of beige. The walls, the carpets, the appliances, the cabinets. This place was semi-furnished, and I loved pretty much everything in it." Laurel opened the pizza box and Andy sat at the small table across from her. "I only brought the things that really said *me*, you know?"

"You know, I don't," Andy said. "I grew up with guys, and I guess I picked up their habits—or tastes. I didn't have much that wasn't useful for something, and nothing I can think of that said anything about me." She heard how weird that sounded and shrugged. "I like your things."

Laurel smiled at her, not like she'd said something dumb or weak, but something important. "Then I'm extra happy you do."

Andy smiled back and pulled a slice of pizza onto the plate Laurel'd set in front of her. "We might need this. I have a feeling it's going to be a long night."

After taking her first bite, Laurel sighed and half closed her eyes. "God, this is really good pizza. I wouldn't have thought so, since it looks nothing like the kind of pizza I'm used to."

"It's the grease quotient," Andy said, trying not to polish hers off in three bites. "I'm glad you like it, because I have to admit, I'm sort of addicted already."

"I'm good with it—as long as we keep it down to once a week."

Andy paused, the slice halfway to her mouth. "I don't know, that's kinda asking a lot. But if dinner's going to be a regular thing with us, I'm into it."

"I did sorta say that, didn't I?" Laurel shook her head. "You know, I'm not usually so forward with women. Let's make that never. But I like you, and I don't know if that's a problem or not."

Andy leaned back in the chair and placed her half-eaten pizza slice back on the paper plate. "Why is it a problem? I'm single, you're single. I'm healthy, and if you weren't, you would've said something by now."

"'Course," Laurel said.

"And I assumed you hanging out at the lesbian bar said you liked girls at least as much as boys."

Laurel laughed. "Understatement."

"So?" Andy asked quietly. "What am I missing?"

"All right," Laurel said, "this is not exactly the kind of conversation I would expect to have on a first date. Maybe this is the second date, though. Do you think all of our dates will be food related? Not that I'm complaining."

Andy laughed, mostly happy that they'd acknowledged the date thing, finally. And if every date needed to be a meal, she wouldn't care if she weighed a thousand pounds as long as she was getting a chance to spend time with Laurel. "We can probably find some other things to do."

"We can, and I'm stalling," Laurel said. "I don't want to share too much too fast and scare the hell out of you."

"Laurel," Andy said, "I don't scare."

Laurel's brows rose. "Never?"

"Pretty much never."

"How can that be? Don't we all have something we're afraid of?"

"I guess so, but I learned not to be, and after a while, it's habit."

"Why?"

Andy could have pretended she didn't understand the question, but she didn't want to pretend with Laurel. She was good at it, she knew. But *she* knew. "When you're afraid, it's hard to hide it, and when it shows, other people can pick up on it."

"And then what happens?" Laurel asked gently.

"Sometimes you just get chewed out for being a wimp or a wuss, or embarrassed in front of your friends or your coach for not being tough enough."

Laurel nodded, waiting and watching. Patient and warm.

Andy considered for a long time, or what felt like a long time but was probably only a few seconds. "Sometimes you get more than just words."

"I see." Laurel ached to touch her, sadness and anger and tenderness a storm inside her. But Andy didn't need comfort. She needed to be heard. "Well, I, for one, do get scared. And just on the off chance that you ever do, I'm good with that."

"I'll remember," Andy said. "But I think you better tell me what you were going to say, and I'll let you know if it scares me."

"Okay, I'll be as brave as you, then."

Andy snorted. "I don't think I did anything brave."

"Oh, you did, showing me that piece of yourself," Laurel said. "And the fact that you don't even know it makes you even more special."

"Okay," Andy said, "now I *am* scared."

"Why?"

"Because if you think I'm special, you might change your mind, and then I'm gonna lose something I didn't know I wanted."

"It doesn't work that way, not with me," Laurel said. "But we should be careful with one another, deal?"

"Deal."

"All right then," Laurel said on a deep breath. "Back to why I don't have a normal—if that's the right word for it—relationship history with women. You know I was married to a guy."

"Yeah. That's not all that unusual."

"True, and I pretty much had feelings for women before, during, and, well, totally since then. But it took me a while to realize that my marriage was not really working for either one of us, for a lot more reasons than who occupied my fantasies. And to make a long, kind of sordid story short, I'll just say that Peter—the man I was married to—suggested that a little sexual diversity might help us get reconnected."

"Okay," Andy said when Laurel fell silent. She didn't think much of this guy, Peter, if he was interested in any other woman when Laurel was there. Of course, maybe *he* wanted a guy. She didn't really want any of the pictures in her head, mostly because Laurel deserved so much better. Someone who freaking knew how lucky they were just to be with her, let alone touch her. She kept all that to herself. This was Laurel's story, not hers.

"Well, as you probably figured out, I went along with it because…" Laurel raked a hand through her hair and grimaced. "Because I wanted the decision I'd made when I married him to turn out to be a good one. Which it obviously wasn't, but I wasn't ready to admit it. Peter introduced me to another woman, which he thought would work best for us, and he was right." Laurel's laugh carried edges of steel. "In a lot of ways. I was very into her from the first encounter, and she seemed to be very into me. When we started seeing each other *without* Peter, that created problems, as in the end of our marriage. Unfortunately, she wasn't as interested once the triangle and all the drama that went with it disappeared. So there you have it. I am divorced, out, and not very successful with women."

"No regular girlfriend after her?" Andy asked.

"No time. Once I knew I was going to be on my own and needed to make a life of my own, I was totally involved in my training."

"Still not seeing a problem," Andy said.

"I don't have any way to judge what I'm doing," Laurel said, "except this is nothing I've ever done before."

"Same here," Andy said.

"I don't understand."

"Here's what I got," Andy said. "We're having our second date. I think you're totally hot, and I'm hoping that you would like to have another date sometime soon."

"I'm almost fifteen years older than you are."

"Yeah, I know," Andy said, tamping down the exasperation. Like, what did that prove? Or not? Age wasn't an immutable predictor of behavior. "And I've slept with about four more women than you have. So where does that get us?"

Laurel laughed. "Are you trying to say our life experiences mean more than our ages?"

"Maybe. Mostly I'm trying to say that none of that is a deal breaker." Andy reached across the table and took Laurel's hand. "This is what matters. Right now. Right here."

Laurel studied Andy's hand, broader than hers, the fingers heavier, callused on the inside of those fingers. She didn't have to work hard to imagine them moving over her body. "I like your hands."

"Good," Andy said quietly.

Laurel rubbed her thumb over Andy's knuckles and slowly lifted her eyes until she was looking into Andy's. "I happen to think you're enormously attractive. And I like you. It does scare me a little that I seem to be telling you all kinds of things that I didn't really expect to tell anyone."

"I'm very interested in you getting to know my hands better," Andy said, "but I'm a lot more interested in what you have to say."

The fluttering in Laurel's stomach grew until her breath almost floated away. With an unsteady intake, she found her words. "Can we table the sex for a little while."

"I guess we'll find out," Andy said. "I'm not about to push you, but I don't want you to mistake my intentions." She grinned. "Like I said. I have an…interest."

"Interest and intentions noted," Laurel said, her voice still sounding breathy, even to her. She took a deeper breath. "How come no girlfriend for you, then?"

"Didn't have the interest." Andy picked up her pizza and took a bite. After a moment she said, "Come on, you have to help me finish this."

Charmed, and very much interested herself, Laurel let herself enjoy just being with her. When they finished and Laurel carried the remnants of the pizza box and the plates back into the kitchen, she said, "I have to finish up inventorying supplies at the clinic tonight. I don't know if we'll need to meet with the CDC or not."

"You were up most of the night," Andy said. "Do you need to take a nap or something?"

"Not enough time for that." Laurel shrugged. "And I'm too wound up, anyhow. My mind is going a million miles an hour, although my body is starting to complain."

"I'm very good at shoulder rubs," Andy said.

Laurel turned and rested her hips against the counter in the tiny kitchen. "You do know that's a lesbian cliché, right? The back rub?"

"Clichés come from somewhere, usually because they're true."

Laurel grinned. "I wouldn't mind."

Andy gestured to the sofa angled in the corner of the room. "Why don't you stretch out there."

When Laurel kicked off her flats and stretched out on her stomach, Andy edged onto the seat beside her. Leaning over, she put both hands high up on Laurel's back and kneaded her trapezius.

Laurel groaned. "I knew I loved your hands."

Andy kept her word and banished thoughts of Laurel naked while she slowly explored every inch of her—or almost. Her body wasn't as easy to tame, and the heat surged again deep inside.

CHAPTER FIFTEEN

Andy smiled and slid down until she was sitting on the floor with her back against the sofa. She checked her watch. How long did a dinner break last? An hour, maybe. And it hadn't been quite that long, but she wasn't really sure these conditions were exactly the norm, and she *was* sure Laurel would not want to be late getting back to the clinic. She'd give it a full hour, but then she'd have to wake her. Just as she decided, Laurel stirred.

"Oh," Laurel said in a soft, sleepy tone. "Damn. I'm sorry."

"Hey, nothing to be sorry about." Andy twisted around to take her in as Laurel rolled onto her back. Even tousled and a tiny bit rumpled, she looked great. "Back rubs are supposed to make you sleepy."

Laurel chuckled. "I always fall asleep during a massage, that's true, but usually I'm not particularly interested in the massage therapist personally."

"I'll take that as a double compliment, then." Andy eased up onto the sofa until she was sitting next to Laurel's extended legs.

Laurel drew her knees up and half sat to face Andy. "That was great. My back feels awesome. How long did I sleep?"

"Not too long. Fifteen minutes, maybe."

"Good enough for a power nap."

Andy grinned wryly. "I've never been able to do that. Too twitchy, I guess."

"You have to work tonight too, don't you?" Laurel asked.

"Yeah," Andy said, contentment warming her stomach. "I'm all clear for duty, and I've got the eleven to seven."

"And I'm guessing you're not tired." Laurel smiled.

"Nope. That's my regular shift, and I didn't work last night, remember?"

"Because you were recovering, remember?"

Laurel rolled her eyes and Andy laughed. "Oh yeah, that."

"What are you going to do until then?"

"I figured I'd hang around the station house. When the CDC shows up, I might be able to get a seat for the show."

"We don't really know what they're planning for tonight, if anything." Laurel shrugged. "The team is due in at ten, and I imagine they'll contact Dr. King or Chief Conlon. You'll probably hear something when I do. I'll be at the clinic until at least then."

"Maybe I'll catch you later, then," Andy said, rising. "I should get out of here so you can get to work."

Laurel slid off the couch and walked with her to the door. "I'm glad we had a chance to get together."

"So am I." Andy stood a few inches away, and as Laurel reached the door, those few inches disappeared. She didn't think about it. If she had thought about it, she would've done the same thing. She slipped a hand behind Laurel's neck, cupping her nape lightly, and kissed her.

For an instant, Laurel stiffened—surprised more than reluctant, it seemed—and just as quickly, relaxed. The muscles under Andy's fingers were supple and soft and warm, but nowhere near as soft and warm and welcoming as Laurel's mouth. Andy angled her head to kiss her more thoroughly, sealing their breaths, caressing silk over silk. Laurel moved with her, framing Andy's hips with her cupped palms and leaning in until she was pressed against Andy from breasts to thighs.

Cripes, her body was magic. Firm and supple and honest-to-God hot, right through her clothes. Naked, she might be lethal. Andy's breath stopped somewhere down around the bottom of her breastbone, and she slid an arm around Laurel's waist with a groan. Someone's heart tripped erratically against her chest. Might've been hers. Might've been Laurel's—they were that close. She couldn't tell. She was too busy cataloging every amazing sensation, every mind-blowing second— every…every incredible thing that was Laurel.

She could taste a bit of lemon. Lemonade. Laurel had been drinking lemonade. Andy sipped the flavor, the tip of her tongue skating over the surface of Laurel's lower lip. Laurel made a sound low in her throat, a surprised, hungry little sound, and her lips parted. Andy tightened her hold, delved deeper for the sweetness and the heat, and sweat broke out over every inch of her body. Hot, so very hot. She remembered to breathe and managed it as quickly as she could before she sealed the kiss again. Lemons and kisses, Laurel's blazing kisses, were forever written in her bones now.

Laurel's hands gripped her shoulders, her fingertips digging into Andy's muscles, absolutely certain and sure. The certainty burned a white blaze across Andy's brain, searing away reluctance and hesitation. More. She wanted more and now. Now.

"Laurel," she murmured, edging nearer, stroking over the curve of Laurel's hip and along her side to just below her breast. Her thumb brushed the underside, just grazed the heavy curve, and Laurel jerked. Andy froze.

"It's okay," Laurel whispered, backing up one step and leaning against the still-closed door as if she needed the support. "I…it's fine. You're…fine." She laughed unsteadily. "Me, not so much."

"Better than fine, incredible," Andy muttered and pressed into her, sliding her thigh between Laurel's, canting her hips to fuse the curves of their bodies. She kept her hand where it was, almost cradling Laurel's breast. *Easy*, some voice somewhere in her rational brain mumbled while the wild, animal voice shrieked, *More, right now, so good, so amazing, don't fucking stop.*

When Laurel slipped her hand down the front of Andy's chest and traced a line along her collarbone to the little hollow at the base of her throat, the burning feathers of sensation turned Andy's hot skin into goose bumps. Andy whimpered, an altogether helpless sound she'd never made in her life. The need boiling up from somewhere deep down inside her was so exquisite, hurt so damn good, she couldn't help it. Another second of that unbearable pleasure and she was going to be on her knees, pleading for Laurel to let her touch her—everywhere.

Then Laurel planted both palms on her chest, pushing her back a millimeter, two, an inch.

"Time-out," Laurel said in a breath so high Andy could barely hear her.

She swallowed on a groan. Every muscle locked in place. "Right. Okay, right."

"Sorry, I need…I need to stop."

"Okay," Andy muttered, the pounding in her head, in her belly, between her thighs about to make her nuts. She sucked in a breath and eased away. "Better?"

"Oh, it's not bad." Laurel brushed her fingers through Andy's hair, trailed down her cheek. "Just the opposite. I don't believe I've ever been kissed quite like that before."

Laurel's voice sounded husky, the words stilted, as if each one took effort to express.

"That means good, then?" Andy worked on breathing and getting her legs to stop shaking.

"Oh," Laurel said, her laughter breaking like waves on the hot sandy shore, "much better than good. *So* good. So much better than good, I need a minute. No, I need more than a minute."

"All you need," Andy said, "as long as we're good."

Laurel's eyes were wide, the blue Andy remembered almost disappearing as her pupils darkened. Her smile was somewhere between amused and amazed. Incredulous, even. And Andy felt herself growing ten feet tall. Her kiss had done that. And all she wanted was to do it again. Right now, preferably.

"I know," Laurel said, her gaze fixed on Andy's mouth while reading what was written in her eyes. "Me too, but I've got to get back to work with a working brain."

"Right, I know."

"You are a phenomenal kisser," Laurel said.

"No." Andy shook her head, stretching both arms out to the door on either side of Laurel's shoulders, half to support herself and half to keep the heat vibrating between their bodies from disappearing for just a few more minutes. "I'm not. I wasn't even thinking about kissing you. I just...you were so beautiful, and I didn't want to say good night."

"And then what were you thinking about?" Laurel asked, a playful note in her voice.

The thunderstorm building in Andy's belly roared back to life again. "I was thinking about how good you tasted, how I like the sound you make when I tease you with the tip of my tongue."

Laurel's head thumped against the door. "Okay, do not answer any more questions tonight. I can't take any more. You're going to make me certifiably crazy."

"I'm good with that. For now."

Laurel rested her fingertips along the edge of Andy's jaw, her thumb skimming the corner of Andy's mouth. "You have a beautiful mouth. And an amazing body. You're downright gorgeous everywhere. And no matter what you say, a phenomenal kisser."

"Please tell me there's not a *but* coming."

Laurel smiled a little wryly. Andy already understood her better than Peter probably ever had.

"I won't say *but*," Laurel said, "because all of those things are unqualified. They're all true. The *but* isn't about you, Andy."

Andy groaned. "Don't say that either. Don't go the it's-not-you-it's-me route. Even I've been around enough to know about that one."

"I won't say that either." Laurel sighed. "I'll just say I'm not sure about what I want, or maybe a better thing to say is I'm not sure what the hell I'm doing."

"It's a kiss, Laurel. Just a kiss."

"If you say so." She ducked under the frame of Andy's outstretched arms. If she stayed there any longer, she was going to do something she'd regret, like touching her, or kissing her. And she didn't just need to get back to work, she needed the proverbial brakes. A little processing time. A little space.

Andy didn't try to stop her or move in any closer.

Laurel opened the door, and Andy walked out with her. When they reached the street at the end of the path, Laurel stopped. Andy's hair was mussed from her fingers running through it. Her shirt was half-untucked from where she'd pulled it out. Sometime. Sometime when she'd been mindlessly helplessly hopelessly lost in how good she felt. How good Andy made her feel.

Now what was she going to do?

"Good night," Laurel whispered, not knowing what else to say.

"It is," Andy said, leaning forward to kiss her on the cheek. "A great night."

Laurel watched as Andy strode away. What in hell was she going to do?

❖

Kerri Sanchez gripped her briefcase and stared at a nick in the vinyl covering of the seat back in front of her, determinedly not looking out the small oval window inches away on her right...or at the water a few inches below that. Not liking to fly wasn't all that uncommon. What sane person thought it was a good idea to get into a three hundred and fifty ton metal tube propelled by flammable fuel, not to mention being susceptible to crashing from lightning strikes and, for that matter, *bird* strikes, while soaring through the atmosphere six or seven miles above the surface of the earth?

They called humans *bipedal* for a reason—two feet. Which ought to be on the ground at all times. However, she couldn't do her job if she didn't fly, and usually if she had the aisle seat or, worst-case scenario, a middle seat if it couldn't be avoided, she could pretend she was in a bus, which was about as close as she could get to feet on the ground while not locomoting under her own steam. This thing, however, was something out of her worst nightmares. *Surpassed* her worst nightmares.

About the size of a Volkswagen—okay, a Volkswagen on steroids, more like a Volkswagen van, really—it seated ten people in very close proximity, which was barely enough room for her team and the pilot, who looked like he was a year or two out of high school, so fresh-faced she doubted he even shaved. Of course they gave the newbie pilots the short hop from Boston to Cape Cod for the practice, never mind they were flying over an ocean through clouds as thick as Marshmallow Fluff. No, those weren't clouds outside the window she *wasn't* looking through. That was fog. She knew that because in the one mistaken glimpse she'd taken out the window, she'd noticed the thick white layers swirling below the tiny wings with the little teeny tiny propellers and the somewhat rusted rivets that seemed to be holding everything together. Although the way the floor rattled beneath her feet, she wasn't even certain that was going to last.

From across the aisle, a bare three inches away, Ralph Carmody chuckled. A Black man a decade older than Kerri, wearing square, steel-gray framed eyeglasses and looking cool and comfortable in summer weight dark gray trousers and a light blue shirt with cuffs rolled back, he was a poster model for hip scientist, instead of nerdy professor. "Enjoying the ride?"

"Shut up," Kerri said through clenched teeth.

"We'll be there in fifteen minutes, Ker. And these runs have a great safety record."

"You know what they say about statistics," she said, her throat tight and her words pinched. "Odds don't matter if you're that 0.1 percent. You're. Still. Fish. Food."

"Practice your breathing."

"Shut up."

He laughed again.

It was all his fault, anyway, that she was in this thing hurtling through the dark toward—oh my God—was that an actual lighthouse? The nightmare continued. Ralph had been her thesis advisor in grad school, and they'd gotten to be professional friends first and then close personally. She never thought she'd have a guy as a best friend, especially a straight guy, but he was easy to talk to and seemed to understand what it meant to be female in a world that was still primarily male. When he'd moved south from the university to the CDC, she'd gone north to Seattle for her postdoc. But they'd kept in touch, and when she was ready to start her real job, he'd been there with an offer. *Come join me in Atlanta. You'll love it. It's an epidemiologist's dream.*

So here she was, five years later, heading her own team in the field for the first time. That wasn't why she was nervous. Okay, maybe that was part of it, but she knew all the members of the six-person team, professionally, at least. They were ready—so was she. If she lived to reach land.

"The water's getting closer," Kerri muttered.

"We're descending. Remember? Twenty-five minutes from Boston."

Twenty-five minutes. It felt like a million years.

As she'd done a dozen times after she got the call from Roger Tahari at midday, she went over again in her mind what they needed to do once they landed. Somehow, Roger had managed to get them rooms at someplace called the Provincetown Inn. He'd sounded apologetic, explaining that the entire town was completely full, but she really didn't care where she slept. Chances were they wouldn't be there long. Three to four days to get everyone on the cruise ship tested, and then a few more days after that to correlate the results. While they were waiting for the lab work, they'd interview—with the help of the locals, she hoped—the symptomatic individuals and look for common contact sources: where they'd all been before they felt ill, if they'd been anywhere at the same time, where they boarded the cruise, where they were before that. Perhaps they'd all been on the same bus or the same flight at some point, or eaten at the same restaurant.

Outbreaks usually came down to a common location. Food poisoning from a salad bar, cholera from a contaminated drinking well, even smallpox from a herd of infected animals. The investigation, the sorting through of clues, fascinated her. As did the incredible complexity and versatility of the organisms they chased. She was a bug hunter. Her father had been appalled when she'd told him she wasn't going to medical school but was going to get her PhD in public health and epidemiology.

"And do what with that?" he'd asked. "Chase bugs all your life?"

She'd laughed. "Exactly. I'm going to be a bug hunter."

He'd rolled his eyes, shook his head, and got behind her. Because he loved her even if she wasn't going to follow in his shoes. She left that to her younger brother and sister.

The plane thumped and rattled, and she caught her breath, searching for the nonexistent armrests. All she had was a flimsy little lap strap holding her in her seat.

Out the window, the fog blurred the lights from what must be the terminal. A few spots glowed yellow on the ground, the runway signals. The plane made a tight U-turn and seconds later stopped. The pilot turned in his seat, his young face cast in gold from the lights on his instrument panel.

"Your bags will be brought inside in just a minute. Welcome to Provincetown and beautiful Cape Cod."

Kerri unbuckled and stepped out into a steaming night, the air heavy and damp. Surprised it didn't feel all that much different than Atlanta, she said to Ralph as he descended the narrow steps from the plane, briefcase clutched to his chest, "I thought it was supposed to be cooler up here."

"It's still July," Ralph said. "Hot everywhere."

Kerri walked toward the terminal a few feet away to watch their baggage being unloaded from the plane's tiny hold. They'd taken the commercial flight rather than waste any more time waiting for a private plane, which wasn't in the budget anyhow, and they'd been told to pack only enough for overnight to leave room for their equipment. She had only a knapsack with personal items and her computer. The rest of their luggage was coming in the morning on another flight. That was a lot cheaper than chartering a plane.

The cartons of test equipment came off first.

"Here," Ralph said to the woman wearing a blue shirt with an airline logo on the front who was moving their gear from the plane to a short conveyer belt in the terminal's outside wall. "I'll give you a hand."

She didn't object, and while Ralph oversaw the rest of the unloading, Kerri ventured inside with the other two men and two women, who all drifted off toward the restrooms. The terminal was minuscule—a tiny counter with two vacant computer terminals, a gate separating the door to the runways from the seating area that held about ten empty seats, a tiny X-ray machine, and a couple of vending machines. They definitely weren't in Atlanta any longer.

A woman came through the door, young, long blond hair caught back in a loose ponytail by a blue-patterned scarf that fluttered behind her, sleeveless cream linen shirt, tailored celery-green slacks, and stack sandals. She paused, took in Kerri and the rest of her team who'd wandered back, and headed straight for Ralph.

"Dr. Sanchez?" she said brightly.

Ralph gave her a quizzical look and shook his head. "Sorry, no."

"Oh."

Ralph pointed to Kerri.

The woman redirected, her smile never faltering. "Sorry, I didn't get a full name."

"Of course," Kerri said flatly. That was only about the hundredth time someone had mistaken one of the male members of a team as the boss.

"I'm Phoebe Winchester," the blonde went on, "*Boston Chronicle*. I understand there are hundreds of infected people on the cruise ship. Will you be quarantining everyone aboard?"

Kerri managed not to blink. How in the world had the press found out they were coming, and so quickly? Usually, they were the behind-the-scenes team, not the out front, give a press conference team.

"I'm sorry," Kerri said, "but as you can see, we've just arrived, and I have no information. I can give you the name of our liaison in Atlanta, who handles all formal press releases from the Center. I'm sure

Mr. Armod will keep the press appropriately informed, if and when there's anything the public should know."

"Don't you think the public should know that there's a cruise ship in the harbor with infected people who might be contagious and a risk to others?"

Kerri kept a smile on her face, or at least squelched the snarl that threatened to replace it. "As I said, I have no information that any of that is the case. Rumors at this stage are not helpful, as I'm sure you appreciate."

Phoebe Winchester's smile didn't falter either, but her eyes cooled.

"We can help each other, Dr. Sanchez," she said with a flinty emphasis on the title, "probably more than you realize."

"Here you go," Kerri said, pulling a small notepad she habitually carried, much to the amusement of her digital-only colleagues, from the front zippered pocket of her backpack and scribbled down José Armod's name and number. She tore off the tiny piece of lined paper and held it out. "I'm sure all the facts at hand will be made available to you as soon as appropriate."

Winchester all but snatched the piece of paper, and Kerri turned away. It wasn't her job to handle the press, but it was her job to prevent panic, and that's exactly what she intended to do. Ralph and the others had carried their equipment out to the curb, and miracle of miracles, a van not much smaller than the airplane they'd arrived in stood with its back doors open.

Phoebe Winchester hurried past them, jumped into a red Porsche, and zoomed away.

"That was fast," Ralph muttered, looking after her as they loaded their gear into the back of the transport.

"I know. I wonder how she found out."

"It's the internet era," Ralph said. "Could be anybody. Someone on this end, someone in Atlanta, hell, it could even be somebody on the ship."

"Something tells me it's going to be a very long night," Kerri said.

"Let's just hope it's a false alarm and wraps up fast."

She always hoped for that, for a quick solution and quick containment, but something about this, even from the quick sketch the local physicians had been able to put together, warned her otherwise.

CHAPTER SIXTEEN

H ey," Nita said from behind Laurel, who sat on the floor in the clinic supply closet with a clipboard on her knee cataloging supplies. "You're still here."

Laurel glanced over her shoulder. Nita had changed after office hours into svelte black jeans, a scoop-neck lavender top with cap sleeves, and strappy sandals. As always, she radiated quiet confidence and serene beauty. Laurel wished she had the capability of doing that but expected the best she usually managed was wholesome. A word that always reminded her of cows, for some reason.

She laughed at herself, trying to remember the last time she'd actually thought about her appearance other than to be sure she was clean, wearing fresh clothes, and that nothing was on inside out. Now she wondered how others saw her. Specifically, Andy, who'd said some of the most beautiful things to her she'd ever heard. Laurel kept searching for some other message beneath the words, for the game that might be there, for the trap of her own desires opening before her. Peter had been like that, using words that were beautiful, persuasive, and seductive to convince her that following his vision of their life was what she wanted and needed. What she'd wanted all along. A year and a half of therapy had helped her see that, but the memories remained, and so did the fear of old patterns.

"Laurel?" Nita asked. "Everything okay?"

Laurel smiled wryly. "I don't see how that could be possible. We're in the midst of...something...medicine-wise that could turn into something bad. So there's that. And then there's...whatever else I'm doing. Which I wish I knew."

"Uh-huh." Nita settled into that relaxed stance, one hip cocked a little bit, her hands lightly curled at her sides and somehow never looking out of place, even though Laurel rarely knew what to do with hers, with an expression that said she had all the time in the world. "That sentence was extremely convoluted and confusing. I get the uncertainty part about the cruise ship and whatever is going on out there. Believe me, that's on my mind too. But that slightly befuddled, slightly nervous look in your eyes isn't about the cruise ship, is it?"

Laurel blew out a breath, sending aloft a wisp of her hair that had strayed to her cheek. Impatiently, she tucked it behind her ear. She really needed a haircut, although she liked the way Andy had lifted her hair and cradled her neck beneath the length of it, almost like a secret touch. Andy. She glanced up, startled to find Nita regarding her quizzically.

"I'm too old for an adolescent crisis," Laurel said, "and too young for a midlife crisis. Granted, I did ditch my husband of twelve years, acknowledge that I've always been attracted to—*wanted*—women sexually, started a new career, and moved a few hundred miles away from my home territory. I suppose that could be some sort of crisis. Is there a midthirties crisis?"

"I wouldn't call making positive life choices a crisis at all," Nita said, "but the one thing you left out of all of those changes you've listed? A person in your life. Women is a general term, but *woman*—that is specific. And that sort of thing creates turmoil at any age. Are you having turmoil?"

Laughing, Laurel nodded. Nita could somehow put everything in perspective without ever judging, lecturing, or even analyzing. Sort of the Socratic method of friendship, which was a rare talent indeed. "I've had a date. No, two dates. You think blazing kisses are allowed on the second date?"

Nita grinned. "Thinking back, I believe blazing kisses might be indicated *before* you've had a date. That's certainly one way to go about it."

"I don't think you've ever told me that. Is that how things started with you and Deo?"

Nita blew out a breath. "Things started with Deo and me in a blaze of lust, I guess you might say. And I was just as wary of that as you are of that kiss."

"Now you're bragging again."

"You asked." Nita's teasing expression turned gentle and serious. "But what I'm trying to say is there isn't any right way to start a relationship. Some people probably go months just getting to know each other, taking things slow, testing the waters. Other people start out in bed and then figure out if they want anything else. It works differently for every two people, and probably differently for every person, every time."

"God, I hope so," Laurel said, taking a long deep breath. "I don't want to think I'm going to do the same thing I did with Peter every time I get involved with someone for the rest of my life."

"Hey," Nita said, "that's not what I meant at all. You were, what, nineteen? And in a state where you hadn't really stopped questioning what you wanted or what you felt about anyone, man or woman. And then along he comes, a little bit older, handsome—even if he's not my type, accomplished, and he flattered the hell out of you."

Laurel pointed a finger. "There, see? You said it too. He flattered me."

"There's a thin line between flattery and appreciation," Nita said, "and sometimes, if someone is very good with the flattery, they will absolutely make it sound like appreciation. You can't take all the responsibility for everything that happened between the two of you." Nita glowered, an expression that Laurel rarely saw. "Peter is a snake. And he's done and dusted. You need to let him go."

Laurel opened her mouth to argue, then considered Nita's words. *Let him go.* Hadn't she done that? Hadn't she stood up for herself, told him she was done, divorced him, moved out, with no clear plans for the future and everything that was her past jettisoned, she might add. But then, here she was, still second-guessing herself about Peter. "You're right."

"Thank you," Nita said. "Now, back to the important conversation. Second date with who, because I don't remember a first date."

"Well, the first time wasn't actually a date-date at the time, not really. It was just a casual dinner. Tonight was more a date."

Nita made a rolling get-on-with-it motion, and Laurel added, "Andy Champlain."

Nita's brows rose.

Ha, she was surprised.

"Okay," Nita said, sounding a little impressed. "That went from zero to sixty pretty fast. She's adorable."

"She is not adorable," Laurel said. "She is…gorgeous. And hot."

"Well, if you like them young and sexy and handsome as sin, maybe."

Laurel glowered back. "And why shouldn't I?"

Nita grinned. "Can't think of a single reason, actually."

"I hate you."

"No, you don't, you love me. She seems nice. I only spoke with her a few minutes this afternoon, but she was polite, professional, and surprisingly earnest."

"Oh my God," Laurel complained, "you make her sound like a Boy Scout."

"Mm, she does have that air about her. But more than that," Nita mused, "underneath the earnest, she's very intense. Very determined. I can see where under certain circumstances that translates into very sexy."

"I know."

"Yep," Nita said with a nod. "That kind of intensity can be very… pleasant."

Pleasant didn't even come close. Laurel hadn't been able to shake the impact of the kiss in the last three hours. She could barely keep her mind from drifting back to it, or her body from flushing with an uncomfortable pressure between her thighs. From a kiss. She'd had a fair variety of sex in her life, some of it life-changing, especially the first time she'd slept with a woman, but nothing had supercharged every nerve ending in her body the way Andy's kiss had done.

"That good, huh?" Nita probed.

"Outstanding." Laurel sighed. "Honestly, Nita, I'm not sure I'm ready for this. The timing is horrible on multiple levels. And besides, I've never been a fling sort of person, and neither one of us is going to be here three months from now."

"How do you know you've never been a fling kind of person, since you've never actually had one?"

"Well, there was Maranda—"

Nita snorted. "Oh, please, that was not a fling. That was Peter's fantasy. Maranda was an avatar, not a real person."

"Oh, I like that," Laurel said, laughing as the heaviness of memory lifted a little. "An avatar. I'm going to think of her from now on in some sort of leather and chain-mail costume, you know, like in one of those online games. After all, it *was* a real-life game."

"Back to the fling," Nita said, relentlessly keeping her on point. "A casual relationship. There's nothing wrong with a casual relationship between two people who enjoy each other, who respect each other, and who want to share physical pleasure. I don't need to tell you that, do I?"

"No, and I completely agree," Laurel said. "I've just never done it."

Nita lifted her shoulder. "There's a first time for everything, Laurel."

"You know," Laurel said quietly, "you've got a point."

She could do it. She could have a fling. Maybe this was the time and place to do it. Everything here was temporary. Her job, the crowds, the excitement and sexual tension everywhere she looked, even whatever was happening out on that ship, would end. She would move on to wherever she could find a permanent position. Andy would go back to her cop family, stronger, Laurel hoped, and better able to separate herself from what sounded like an oppressive family situation.

If everything was temporary, why couldn't pleasure be the same? She looked up at Nita. "You're right."

❖

Andy arrived at the station fifteen minutes before roll call, dumped her gear in her locker, and found a seat in the middle of the briefing room to wait for the duty officer. Andy, Bri, and another officer had the night shift, her on foot and the two of them in patrol cars. She hadn't heard any word about the CDC or that anything new was happening with the cruise ship. For all she could tell, it was just a regular night.

Only nothing about the night was regular for her, not since kissing Laurel. Tonight had the feel of a change about it—she just couldn't quite figure out how. Since the moment she'd met Laurel— not counting the few minutes she'd been flat on her back after being kicked in the head—she'd been thrust into a new and different arena. A world without games, without rules, without boundaries. She was feeling her way along one step at a time, guided by instinct. And even those instincts were new. Her aptitude for survival was razor sharp—

she knew how to win. But Laurel wasn't a game or a prize. She was far, far more important than that.

And Laurel *had* set one rule, more or less. Go slow.

Andy sighed. Going slow was not her usual MO. Hopefully the night would not be too quiet, and she could work off some of the pent-up adrenaline that still buzzed through her in the wake of that kiss.

Bri came in a few minutes before eleven, sketched her a wave, and dropped into the seat across the aisle. The last officer, Smith, a veteran of the force for ten years or so, tall, skinny as a rake, sandy-haired, clean-shaven, and friendly, nodded to both of them and took his seat in the row in front of them off to the side. The duty officer, a sergeant named Pinero, short, dark-haired, dark-eyed, and brusquely efficient, arrived at the dot of eleven with a tablet in his hand.

He gave them all a quick look, cleared his throat, and said, "Evening shift reports a presumed B and E, possibly linked to the one reported three nights ago, at a guesthouse—the Mulberry, 311 Truscott Place—a little after ten p.m. The owner had come down to the kitchen and hadn't turned the lights on. Heard a commotion on the porch. Flipped on the back lights, saw a figure vault down into the yard and run off. Called it in. Caucasian, slightly above-average-height male or larger female, dark ball cap, dark T-shirt, jeans, running shoes." Pinero looked up. "That makes three guesthouse break-ins in that area in ten days. Patrol cars will shorten their swing cycle through neighborhoods north of Bradford after nine p.m. until further notice."

Pinero went on to note several 911 calls for accidents and other medical emergencies, a couple of fender benders, a dispute over the cost of an ice cream sundae—go figure, two attempted shopliftings, a dog bite, and a domestic. Routine night.

"Any word on the CDC, Sarge?" Bri asked when Pinero finished.

"If I had an update on that, Parker, I would've given it to you."

"Yes, sir," Bri said, sounding totally unperturbed.

Andy wasn't certain, but it looked like the corner of Pinero's mouth twitched.

He pointed toward the hall. "The chief is in her office. I think there might've been a phone call around ten fifteen or so, but no updates yet."

"Thank you, sir," Bri said.

Andy was sure she saw a twitch this time.

Pinero huffed. "That's it, then. Have a safe shift. Keep your eyes open and your heads down. See you at seven."

Andy rose and joined Bri. "You think we'll hear anything about the ship tonight?"

"Probably not, unless they need us for transport or something, like earlier."

"If something happens, you'll let me know, right?"

"Hey, do I look like the duty officer?" Bri said.

Andy grinned, thinking of Pinero, as wide as he was tall, a block of muscle with a head on top. "Yeah, you sorta resemble Pinero a little bit."

Bri rolled her eyes. "You know, you can be on the force and still wear your eyeglasses."

"My eyes are fine," Andy said.

"Speaking of, you know, fine sights, how's Laurel?"

Andy felt the blush. "Hey. She's, uh, good, I think. Fine."

Bri paused in the parking lot in front of her patrol car. "Fine? What does *fine* mean?"

"Well, you know, she's probably working right now, but she was fine when I saw her. When I left, you know."

"What did you do, Andy?" Bri goaded.

"Nothing," Andy said quickly.

"Hey, you're a lousy liar."

"Well, okay. We had dinner, and it was fabulous, and right before I left, I kissed her."

"Okay then. Props for you."

"This is private, right?" Andy said. "Because, you know, it's personal."

"Jeez, Andy. I don't need any other details. I don't think you're breaking any kind of rules mentioning a kiss. It's kind of a generic thing, you know?"

"No, actually, it isn't." Andy thought about that kiss, *again*, as if she hadn't been thinking about it enough yet. On the scale of kisses, it was definitely fifteen out of ten. Maybe twenty out of ten. Maybe ten to the tenth power out of ten.

"Okay, well, now I'm sorry I said I wasn't fishing for details," Bri said. "Anyhow, good for you."

"Yeah," Andy said softly. "True that."

Bri settled her cap low on her forehead. A shock of midnight hair slashed toward her brow. The word *pirate* came to mind. "You want me to drop you off in the center of town?"

"No, I'll walk," Andy said. "See what the streets look like."

"Okay, just remember, I'm five minutes away, less if you need me."

"I know," Andy said.

Bri nodded, hopped into her patrol car, and, a minute later, pulled onto Shank Painter Road and headed left toward Route 6. Andy crossed the gravel lot toward the sidewalk as a red Porsche pulled into the lot, shot to a stop, and a blonde jumped out.

"Excuse me," she called.

Andy turned and the blonde hurried over to her.

"Hi, I'm Phoebe Winchester. *Boston Chronicle*." She held out her hand.

Andy automatically extended hers and returned the handshake. "Andy Champlain."

"I'm covering the story on the cruise ship," Phoebe said. "I wonder if you could tell me what the plans are for evacuating the infected individuals?"

Andy resisted the urge to take a step back. She actually wanted to backpedal but stood her ground. Impressions were important, especially when faced with an unknown, potentially threatening situation. The woman herself wasn't threatening, but the word *reporter* was inexorably associated with danger signs in her brain. She'd grown up listening to her father denigrate the press, railing that they never failed to paint the police in a negative fashion and drum up sympathy for perpetrators. Andy understood now that was not true, but just his particular interpretation and his paranoia, even, but she still knew better than to discuss anything with a reporter. "Sorry, but I don't have any information on that at all."

"Were you there last night, when they moved out the worst cases, in the middle of the night, under cover of darkness?"

"I wasn't part of that."

"But you do agree the evacuations were hurried and planned for a time when they'd draw the least public notice."

"Look, I don't have anything to say about that. I wasn't part of it."

"What about tonight? Is the CDC headed to the cruise ship to start quarantining the passengers?"

"I'm sorry, I can't help you. You'll have to speak to the chief."

Phoebe smiled. "Thanks, Andy. I will. Next time, I'll buy you a coffee."

With that, she strode toward the station house.

Next time?

Andy stared at her retreating form, wondering what the hell had just happened.

CHAPTER SEVENTEEN

Reese's phone vibrated, and she checked the number. Tory. Her heart bumped a little bit. Almost eleven fifteen. Tory should have been asleep by now, for *hours*. Reggie was with Jean and Kate—she'd had dinner with them and put Reggie to bed herself when she'd taken her over for her adventure.

"Hi," Reese said when she answered.

"Are you still at the station?" Tory said.

Reese rubbed her face. "Yeah. When I talked to the mayor earlier, she insisted we notify the town council and the league of business owners about any possible disruption to normal business activities— *just to keep them in the loop* was the way she phrased it. I've been fielding phone calls and squelching rumors ever since."

"That's politics, I guess," Tory said, "and exactly what we don't need right now. I'm sorry."

"No matter—it's the job," Reese said. "What's up? Are you all right?"

"I'm fine. I dozed for a little while earlier. But the CDC has arrived, and their team leader contacted me for a briefing. It became apparent pretty quickly we needed to have a task force meeting right now. Can you come and pick me up?"

"Are you sure, Tory? Can't you hand this off to Nita?"

"I have a feeling Nita is going to be up to her eyeballs with our regular patients and assisting the CDC. They're asking for local help, and that's us. I didn't think I was in quite the right shape to be heading out to the cruise ship."

Reese nearly broke her molars, she clamped down on them so hard. After a second she said, hoping she sounded a lot calmer than she felt, "Fuck no."

Tory chuckled. "All things considered, I think the station house is the best place to set up our communication center, if you agree. We could do it at the clinic, but we really need to have your officers involved, and it seems easier for me to go there than to drag your folks over here."

"Sure, that's fine. We ought to have enough room, if we all get along."

"Hopefully," Tory said quietly, "we won't have to get along for very long."

"I hear you. I'll be there in fifteen minutes. But, Tor, we have to make this short. You can't be staying up all night."

"Yes, Doctor."

Reese snorted. "Right. See you soon."

She stopped at the front desk and told Pinero what was happening.

"I guess that means more coffee," Pinero grumbled.

"Probably wouldn't hurt."

"You think this is going to be a shit storm, Chief?"

Reese sighed. "You know, Tommy, I wish to hell I knew. We might be done with this in a day or two. But then again, maybe not."

"Yeah," Pinero said dourly, "maybe not."

Tory was waiting in a glider on the side porch when Reese pulled into the drive. She parked, left the engine running, and bounded up the steps to kiss her. "Hi."

"Hi." Tory held up her hand and Reese took it.

"Lift," Tory said.

Grinning, Reese gently helped her out of the glider and onto her feet. Tory stretched and pressed a hand to her back. "I'm ex-ing off the days on the calendar now."

"Me too. Come on, let's go get this over with."

"We can only hope."

Reese kept her fingertips lightly on the back of Tory's arm as they descended the stairs to the drive. She would've carried her if she thought Tory wouldn't try to escape.

"Remember when I carried you up the stairs the first time?"

Tory laughed. "I don't think it was these stairs precisely, but I certainly do remember. You made quite an impression."

Reese slid her arm farther around Tory's waist as they walked to the car. "Did I now."

"Oh, you certainly did, all quiet and serious and strong."

"More like stiff and clueless." Reese shook her head. "I'm surprised you even agreed to go out with me."

Tory pressed her hand flat to Reese's chest, lifted onto her toes, and kissed her. "You shouldn't be. I fell a little bit in love with you right then."

Reese opened the passenger side door and waited for Tory to get settled inside, closed it, and came around to get behind the wheel. "I fell in love with you the first time I saw you out on the water in the kayak."

"Aren't I lucky, then."

Reese leaned over, kissed her cheek, and murmured, "I love you."

They rode down Bradford in silence, Tory's hand on Reese's thigh. Ten minutes later Reese pulled into the station house lot next to Nita's little red Nissan.

Six newcomers awaited them in the briefing room. Reese hung back a little and let Tory go in first.

"Dr. Sanchez," Tory said, walking to a slender, dark-haired woman of average height, looking to be in her thirties, wearing a yellow polo shirt and dark washed jeans with white Converses. Her shoelaces were red, a little nod to a sense of humor.

She held out her hand. "Yes. Dr. King?"

"Call me Tory."

"I'm Kerri."

"I see you've already met my colleagues," Tory said, indicating Nita and Laurel on the right side of the aisle across from five other people Reese didn't know.

Sanchez made the rest of the introductions, and Reese made a mental note of their names. She could see Pinero doing the same on his tablet.

"I know it's late," Kerri Sanchez said, "and I apologize for keeping everyone up, but we want to get to the cruise ship the first thing in the morning."

Nita said, "And what time would that be?"

"Five a.m.," Kerri said.

"The harbormaster will need to be informed tonight," Reese said, tilting her head toward Pinero, who nodded back. "We'll handle the arrangements for your transport."

"Yes, thank you," Kerri Sanchez said. "I have been in communication with the chief medical officer out there and advised him of our timetable. He assured me we would be able to begin testing immediately."

"Do you have equipment that will need to be transported?" Reese asked.

"Yes," one of the men with Kerri said. "Approximately four hundred pounds in eight cartons."

"Sergeant Pinero," Reese said.

"Got it, Chief."

Tory said, "How long do you expect it will take to test everyone aboard?"

"A lot depends on how efficiently we can move people through the testing area," Kerri said. "Obviously, even with a ship of that size, the physical layout is not conducive to mass movement of the guests. Usually individuals are scattered throughout the ship, and transit between locations requires lifts or stairs and narrow passageways. Even at mealtimes, individuals make their way through a number of routes to the dining areas, of which there are several. We will essentially need to direct everyone toward a single point, which may require some discussion with the ship's captain and assistance from the onboard crew."

"Unfortunately," Nita said, "some of the crew are ill, and I imagine more will become symptomatic. The infectious agent appears to have been concentrated in the crew initially, if the incubation period is fairly consistent."

"We can't speculate until we identify the agent, of course," Kerri said, "but based upon an outbreak we believe may be related, we seem to be looking at a long incubation, anywhere from two days to ten."

Tory said, "You're presuming it's the same as the one affecting the small group in Southern California?"

"We have evidence to suggest that, yes," Kerri said, sounding cautious. "One of the first things we'll do is send samples to our labs for identification and comparison."

Reese suspected Sanchez's carefully chosen words were an occupational attribute. And she couldn't blame her. They really didn't know what they were dealing with yet. She'd much rather have a calm, cautious investigator in charge than a cowboy who'd charge in and incite a panic.

"What about individuals who may have come in contact with cruise ship personnel or guests here in town?" Reese asked. "How are we going to identify them?"

Silence fell, a sure indicator the question was not only important, but that the answer was uncertain.

Kerri nodded to a middle-aged Black man in a crisp, pale-blue short-sleeved shirt, expensively tailored trousers, and shiny black loafers. "Dr. Carmody is our vector analyst, and an expert at contact transmissions. He will be in charge of our contact tracing efforts. Ralph?"

Carmody remained relaxed and confident looking where he sat with his legs crossed and one arm draped over the back of the metal folding chair.

"The plan is simple: track, test, contain. So our first task will be to determine how many infected individuals actually left the ship and when. From there, we'll trace their movements on shore, identify their contacts, and examine *those* contacts for signs of infection. If we're lucky, we'll be able to isolate those individuals quickly, get any symptomatic contacts tested and isolated, and so on. It's early in the game, so with vigorous testing and tracing, we can shut this down."

"We're talking a matter of days, then?" Reese said.

"Yes," Carmody said.

Tory said, "I saw two of the patients from the cruise ship at the clinic several days ago, as you're aware. I don't have any symptoms, but if the incubation is a long one…"

"We can test you," Kerri said, "but in the absence of symptoms, the likelihood of infection is low."

"Considering the circumstances," Tory said, "I'd prefer being cautious. Obviously, there's some urgency to that."

"Of course," Kerri said, "we can do that tonight."

Pinero shot a look at Reese, and Reese carefully schooled her expression to show none of the surge of panic. Tory didn't want her to worry, as if that wasn't part of her responsibility. If Tory was worried, she shouldn't be worried alone.

A petite redhead in a tight black T-shirt and black jeans, a multicolor tattoo peeking out below the sleeve on her right bicep, spoke up. "Dr. King, if you stop by the Provincetown Inn when we finish here, I'll take care of that for you."

"Thank you, Dr....?" Tory said.

"Gillian McIntyre." The redhead grinned. "You can call me Harley. Everyone does."

Tory smiled. "Thanks, Harley."

"The final item on the agenda," Kerri said, "involves where we'll set up if we need to do land-based testing. For a few contacts, we can test them at their locations or at the clinic, but that's not going to work if we have more than a few identified contacts."

Tory glanced at Reese. "Have the mayor and the town council agreed on a location for a staging center if we need it?"

Reese nodded. "If you can't handle things at the clinic, we'll set up a secondary medical staging area at the high school. There are a few summer classes still being held, but the bulk of the building is empty. I was thinking the gym."

"That's perfect." Kerri glanced at her team. "Anyone have anything else?"

No one did, and Kerri said, "We'd like someone from your team, Dr. King, to accompany us tomorrow, as it will make coordination with any land-based follow-up easier. They can head up the local team under Ralph's direction to track and test once we have identified any contacts."

"Of course." Tory glanced across the room. "Laurel?"

Laurel stood, gave a little wave, and said, "Absolutely. I'm Laurel Winter, a PA from the clinic. Where should I meet everyone?"

Everyone looked at Reese.

"If you want to start at five, you ought to be at the pier on the end of MacMillan Wharf at four thirty. The harbormaster will be in charge of tendering you out. I'll have an officer there to assist." She glanced at Tory. "It might be a good idea to have a few of my officers assisting the contact-tracing team here in town too."

"Good idea," Tory said, and Kerri Sanchez nodded.

"We're set for the time being, then," Kerri said. "Will we be able to get a cab at this hour?"

Pinero said, "No problem. I'll call for you. If I were you, I'd tell the cabbie that you're going to need a ride at four thirty in the morning out at the Inn. They'll come and get you."

"Thank you, that's a great idea," Kerri said.

The CDC team filed out, looking a little rumpled and a little weary.

"Laurel, you better get some sleep," Tory said.

"Right, thanks," Laurel said and disappeared.

"Well, that didn't go too badly," Tory said.

Nita joined Reese and Tory. "It's good they're here. Maybe if we jump on this thing right away, if there's a problem with contagion, we'll keep it on the cruise ship, or contain whatever spread we've got in the village."

Reese put her hands in her pockets. "I'd feel a lot better if we didn't have a town full of transient tourists."

"You're right," Tory said, "but we can only move as quickly as we can get testing and contact information. That has to be our priority."

"Starting with you," Reese said. "Come on, I'll drive you out to the Inn."

Nita walked out with them and drove off.

Reese waited until Tory was settled in the vehicle before she said, "How worried should I be about this virus thing and you?"

Tory sighed. "I don't know why I think you won't notice when I'm worried."

Reese wheeled out onto Shank Painter Road and headed west toward the Provincetown Inn. "I know you're worried, and you're trying not to show it. I'm just gonna worry more if you don't tell me."

"I know that too," Tory said, "and of course I know you can handle anything. I think sometimes I just don't want to say things out loud because *I* don't want to think about them."

Reese reached across and grasped Tory's hand. Out of habit, she stroked the wedding band on Tory's ring finger with her thumb. "I get that, and there's nothing wrong with it. But if you're worrying, sharing helps."

"I don't know how worried to be, and that's the worst part of it." Tory's voice sounded strained, and she gripped Reese's fingers hard.

"This could be nothing more than a variant of the flu, which is no fun, to be sure, but something we've been dealing with for decades."

"But?"

"But it's new—at least that's the direction things seem to be moving in. So there are a lot of question marks. We don't even know the exact presentation or the incubation period, or any of the potential side effects."

"What about the babies?"

"Most viruses aren't particularly threatening for pregnant women, although there are circumstances where they *can* be, especially during early fetal development. And then you have things like measles, which are far more dangerous. The upside is, I'm very near the due date and the babies are all formed. So that's a positive."

Reese pulled into the parking lot at the Provincetown Inn, parked, and stopped. "So the risk there is pretty low."

"As far as we know, yes."

"And you feel fine."

"I do."

"Okay then," Reese said. "We're good for now. We're good."

Tory raised Reese's hand and kissed the backs of her fingers. "Baby, we're always good."

"Then let's get this done." Reese jumped out, came around the car, and walked Tory inside. The redhead with the tattoos was waiting for them in the lobby across from the small reservations counter.

"We're down this way," Harley said. "We've got a bunch of rooms, and we set one up as an impromptu lab."

Reese and Tory followed her down a wide corridor decorated in nautical-themed carpets and wall decorations into a room with windows facing the breakwater and Long Point. The air was stuffy and a little musty, which was pretty typical of seaside rooms, especially in the middle of a sultry summer night. They'd opened the windows and the outside door, and a lazy breeze wandered in.

Harley extracted what look like a long Q-tip from a cylindrical plastic container and said, "This won't take very long, but it's a little uncomfortable."

"That's fine," Tory said.

Reese winced inwardly as the swab seemed to disappear an

inordinately far length into Tory's nose and toward the back of her throat. Tory coughed a little, and then it was over.

Tory rubbed her nose. "Yes, not too much fun. How long before we get an answer?"

"We'll FedEx the first batch out tomorrow morning. There's a lab in Boston waiting to get started. A couple of days, we hope."

"You hope?"

"There's been some…" She looked a little uncomfortable, as if she didn't want to say too much. "I guess Kerri—Dr. Sanchez—can fill you in on that."

"I'm guessing that the labs don't have the reagents manufactured to test for this organism, since it's new."

"Something like that, yeah," Harley said. "But like I said, a couple of days. We hope."

A couple of days felt like twenty years to Reese, but she held her peace.

Tory took her hand. "Let's go home."

Laurel ought to be tired, but instead she was wide awake and just short of jittery. Almost midnight. She needed to be at the wharf in just a few hours. She really ought to go home to sleep. Instead she walked toward town, needing to move. Needing…something.

Commercial Street was as busy at midnight as it was at noon, although the population was distinctly different. Gone were the families with strollers and the senior citizen tourists from the buses. Now the crowd was younger, a mix of couples, gay and straight, and groups moving en masse like mini-pods, while bicyclists weaved their way along impossible routes between pedestrians and vehicles. The sky was clear, the night warm, and the atmosphere jubilant. She passed Spiritus Pizza and thought about the dinner she'd had with Andy. On impulse, she pulled out her phone and texted, *Is this okay?*

Great, came the instant reply.

FYI-CDC headed to cruise ship at 430 a.m.

Got the message 2 where are you

Commercial, Laurel answered.

Buy you a coffee?

Can you?

Can take a break headed your way

Laurel's pulse quickened. The jitteriness transformed into something far more focused, excitement and anticipation. To see Andy. She scanned the crowds as she walked toward the center of town. A minute later, she saw her coming.

Tall, built—God, she really was—and looking formidably sexy in her uniform. Like when had she ever been turned on by women in uniform? But then, everything about Andy was a first.

Andy grinned. "Hi."

"It's really okay?" Laurel asked.

"Sure. I'll take fifteen and grab a coffee and, I think, a doughnut at this point."

"You know," Laurel said, "I think I could do a doughnut."

"Come on, the place down the alley across from Town Hall has great doughnuts."

"How do you know these things?"

"Bri."

"It's clear to me I might need a guide. Maybe I can ask her."

"Hey, you got me," Andy protested.

Andy was definitely a guide of some sort, and at the moment, Laurel was happy to follow. "Lead on, then."

CHAPTER EIGHTEEN

A plate glass window with a view to the harbor fronted the doughnut shop, one big room bisected by a counter above glass cases jammed full with trays of enormous doughnuts in a rainbow of colors. The place was brightly lit and smelled of sugar and vanilla. Six people huddled in front of the shelves, oohing and aahing over the elaborate choices.

"The maple bacon ones are good," Andy said when they got close enough to peruse the selections. "You can sort of pretend it's breakfast. You know, protein and all."

Laurel laughed. "At this hour, I think I'm going to go for something a little simpler."

When they ordered, Andy went for the maple bacon and Laurel a chocolate glazed, the plainest thing on the menu.

"Coffee, officer, madam?" asked the surprisingly cheerful— considering the hour—thin, dark-haired counterman in a pale blue T-shirt emblazoned with a pink-frosted doughnut.

"Yeah, with a shot of espresso," Andy said.

"Hot chocolate for me," Laurel said. "I might actually need to sleep a little bit tonight."

He passed Andy a cardboard tray with a flourish, and they wandered back out toward the harbor, away from the lights toward the sound of the sea. They passed the spot where they'd sat the previous night until they were well down the pier beyond the view of passersby on the streets, where only the moonlight reached.

"I got a call from my duty sergeant to stand by when the CDC heads out to the ship," Andy said as they walked, "so I'll be out there with you tonight."

"I can't imagine there's going to be much interest in the way of spectators," Laurel said. "No flashing lights to attract attention this time."

"Yeah, at that hour, I mostly only see the fishermen heading out on the trawlers, really serious runner types, and the partiers who just got in and remembered to walk their dogs."

"Do you like it, the night shift?" Laurel asked.

"Yeah, I do," Andy said. "Especially here. About halfway through the shift, everything changes. The bars close, the shows are over, the stragglers have all settled in somewhere, and the night gets really quiet. Just the ocean, the stars, and me sometimes. Beautiful."

"I know what you mean," Laurel said. "It happens in the ER that way too. Around about three, everything slows down for a couple hours, and then the morning crush begins again. Seems like a day can't start without at least one trauma alert for an MVA."

Andy nodded. "Here it's locals in trucks coming in to get coffee and breakfast at a couple of the places down here on the wharf, before they all head up Cape or wherever they're going to work for the day. Then at seven the buses arrive, and the town wakes up and the celebration starts again."

"I'll take this kind of craziness," Laurel said, gazing out toward the sea. "Only not with this present situation."

"Bad luck, maybe, that ship putting into port here."

"Maybe," Laurel said quietly, "or maybe not. Wherever it put in there'd be the same problem with the contagion, and not being able to dock on shore prevented a lot of people from going into town."

"Lucky." Andy leaned against one of the lampposts in the shadows opposite the faint circle of light cast by the overhead globe. One side of her face was faintly illuminated, the other shaded, light and dark, handsome and mysterious. Both equally tantalizing.

Laurel swallowed. She made friends, *casual* friends, easily. She'd had quite a few among the people she'd trained and worked with in the last few years. People, men and women, she'd have dinner with after work or grab lunch with in the break room.

Andy was different, an intriguing mix of contrasts—open and

generous and easy to talk to. Easy to open up to. Guarded and not always easy to read, keeping her secrets close. Impossible to take casually, already making Laurel want more. She'd spent years wanting to want less. The freedom of wanting more—on her own terms, so far at least—was exhilarating. And that ought to be enough to make her cautious.

"Text me when you're done tomorrow?" Andy said into the silence.

"You'll be asleep."

Andy shook her head. "Probably not. I'll sleep when I get home this morning, but I tend to do it in bits and pieces. Always have. Besides, I'd rather see you. I'll just walk you home so *you* can go to sleep."

"I'll most likely need to go to work, not bed." Laurel smiled. "Besides, you know it's only a few blocks from here, right?"

Andy grinned, a little flicker at the corner of her mouth, devilish, sexy, that sent a twist of something hot and urgent through Laurel's belly. "You can do a lot in a few blocks."

Laurel laughed. "I think that's supposed to be a few minutes or something like that."

"That too. But, you know, you have to start somewhere."

"I think you've already got a pretty good start," Laurel murmured.

A light sparked in Andy's eyes that might've been a reflection off the water, but Laurel was reminded of the shine from a feline's eyes when the moon hit the prowling animal just right, in the dead of night.

Andy watched her watching, smiled again, and skimmed a finger along the edge of Laurel's jaw. "Unless you say something, I'm going to kiss you right now."

"How about yes," Laurel whispered.

Andy kissed her slowly, thoroughly, in that way she had of smoothly moving from light and easy to firm and commanding. Her kisses were like her, subtle and strong. Laurel gripped Andy's bare arm beneath her short-sleeved uniform shirt. Her skin was warm, the muscles beneath her fingertips hard. That was like Andy too.

The kiss lasted long enough to ignite every nerve in Laurel's body. When Andy moved back, Laurel leaned toward her for an instant until she caught her balance.

"Like I said," Laurel gasped, ridiculously dizzy in a completely pleasant way, "phenomenal kisser."

Andy chuckled, a low, dark satisfied sound that turned the pleasant buzz in Laurel's depths into an insistent pulsing imperative. She wanted another kiss. She wanted more than that. She wanted the heat of Andy's skin against her own. She wanted the hard-muscled body and velvet mouth on her. She shivered.

"My fifteen minutes are up," Andy said. "I'll see you at four thirty."

"Okay."

"And Laurel? Think about tomorrow."

Andy didn't elaborate, leaving the possibility up to Laurel. That was new. That was exciting. That was exactly what Laurel wanted.

"I'll do that."

Andy watched her walk away and smiled to herself. If she wouldn't have felt like an idiot, she would have hummed some asinine happy tune. Laurel had texted her. Made a move. *And* there'd been another kiss. A small one, just a taste, but tonight hadn't been the time or the place for more. Maybe there would be soon. There had to be, because she wasn't going to be able to go slow forever. Not without losing her mind.

❖

Laurel woke just before her alarm at four a.m., a little groggy but feeling better than she expected. Maybe it was the doughnut. Smiling, she showered quickly, pulled on fresh clothes, pushed a twenty-dollar bill into her left front pocket and her phone into the opposite one, and locked the door on her way out. The walk into town took only a few minutes, and the Coffee Pot, where the locals congregated for their morning caffeine, fat, and gossip, was open. She grabbed a double espresso and a warm spinach croissant and headed down the wharf with ten minutes to spare. Andy waited next to the gangplank for the Boston–Provincetown ferry that would be arriving at seven a.m. Laurel slowed, just to take her time perusing her. She carried a cup of coffee as well and looked better than she had the night before, if that was even possible. The fishermen clambering around on the boats moored on the opposite side of the wharf were the only other people around.

"Hi again," Laurel said as she joined Andy, hoping she sounded a little more together than she felt. "How was the rest of your night?"

"Busy enough to keep me from getting bored." Andy sipped from the cardboard cup that steamed into the mercifully cool morning air. "Got a call from someone who'd locked themselves out of their car and needed some expert help getting in right after you left. Then a bartender asked for an assist with a patron who insisted on driving despite being clearly intoxicated—said patron's now sleeping in the holding cell at the station and going to wake up with a really bad hangover—and a lost dog report."

"Like we said last night," Laurel said. "Small-town policing."

Andy nodded. "Fortunately, not a lot in the way of violent crime, but there's some. That's everywhere too."

An unexpected surge of anxiety caught Laurel up short. Andy was a law enforcement officer. And Laurel knew better than most what dangers they faced, even on supposedly quiet, routine shifts. One moment could change lives. "You are careful, right? Because you're right, anything can happen, anytime."

"Hey," Andy said gently, running her hand down Laurel's arm. "You don't have to worry about me. Cop family, remember? Paranoia is practically a family trait."

"Well, there's nothing wrong with healthy paranoia," Laurel said, tamping down the unwarranted fear. Fear could paralyze. She knew that—even though she hadn't lived in the shadow of physical fear, she'd lived with a low-level sense of wrongness for a long time. But that was the past. And she wouldn't let it seep into her present, or her future.

"Speaking of scary things," Andy said quietly, "you're really careful out there on that ship, right? Because like everybody's been saying, this is something unusual. Right?"

"Maybe," Laurel said. "It's outside the norm enough to get the attention of the CDC, so yes, everyone's being careful. But new viruses crop up all the time, everywhere in the world. Even more now than in the past."

"Why is that?" Andy asked.

Laurel raised her shoulder. "I can only give you my slightly informed understanding, but a lot has to do with changes in environmental conditions, mostly, of course, from human activities that alter the balance of just about everything in the world—water, air, foliage. Most viruses start in animals and then mutate to the point where they can infect humans. Most of the time, they're relatively harmless, and we don't even notice." She laughed shortly. "Humans haven't been around this long without developing really good immune responses."

"So you're telling me this isn't an unusual occurrence."

"In one way, that's right." Laurel looked out at the enormous cruise ship, dwarfing all the sailboats and even the large pleasure yachts moored in the harbor. A floating city filled with people living in close proximity, like luxurious tenements. "But the one thing we do know is that humans *do* get infected, and they can get very ill. Maybe only a few of the infected people on that ship are actually ill, but we don't know that yet. That's really what we're trying to find out."

"Right, some people get very ill. Don't be one, okay?"

"I'm careful. Don't worry." Laurel smiled a little. "But it's nice, that you worry."

"Hey, I don't usually—make that never—kiss women I don't care about. And I never kiss them more than once."

"Really."

"Pretty much. I'm kind of a one-night stand sort of person, not by design, just by circumstance. Until now."

"We haven't actually *had* a stand yet," Laurel pointed out playfully.

"Yeah, that didn't come out right at all, did it." Andy glanced at her watch. "We've only got a couple minutes, and then everybody's going to be showing up. So let me just say this. I've never had a relationship. And I don't know all the rules or the right way to go about it or what the timing is. But you're different. Nice different."

"Well, that might be the *nicest* thing anyone's ever said to me," Laurel said. "You're nice different too. And in case you're interested, you'd be a first for me too. Relationship-wise, in the ways that matter."

Car lights drew closer.

"What ways?" Andy asked quickly. "Tell me."

"I'm figuring out what I want, and you're giving me room to do that." Laurel huffed. "That probably doesn't make any sense to you."

"It does. We'll figure it out together, okay?" Andy said.

"I…yes."

A cab pulled down the wharf and stopped beside them. Kerri Sanchez and her team climbed out.

"Hi," Kerri called as several people began emptying cartons out of the rear.

"Morning," Laurel called back.

A door opened in the trailer on the opposite side of the wharf, and the harbormaster exited through the door. He strode toward them and nodded to Laurel.

"You the folks from the CDC?" he asked of the others.

"Yes," Kerri said, walking forward with her hand out. "Kerri Sanchez."

At the same moment, a red Porsche convertible with the top down zoomed down the wharf. Andy stepped forward as it pulled to a stop beside the cab. Laurel and the others turned to watch.

A blonde in a sleeveless dark shirt, tailored white slacks, and short heels, clutching a phone in one hand, jumped out. She brushed strands of hair away from her face with a practiced gesture that highlighted her nearly model-perfect profile.

"Hi, Andy," she said brightly as she strode toward the group.

Andy said, "You can't leave your car here, Ms. Winchester."

Winchester turned, leaned into the open vehicle, and flipped a press card onto the dash. Ignoring Andy, she arrowed directly toward Kerri Sanchez. "Good morning, Dr. Sanchez. I understand you're going aboard the cruise ship. I'd like to go along."

Kerri frowned. "I'm afraid that's impossible."

"Actually," Winchester said with her cheery false smile still in place, "it isn't. I actually have clearance from the captain."

"I don't care if you have clearance from the governor," Kerri said calmly. "You're not going. This is not a situation secured for civilians at this point."

Winchester's face transformed into one of quiet fury. "You seem to think you have more authority than you actually have."

"In this circumstance, I'm afraid I do." Sanchez turned to the harbormaster. "We're ready when you are."

He surveyed the pile of crates they'd unloaded from the cab when they'd arrived.

"We ought to be able to handle all of that in one trip. Four hundred pounds, you say?"

"That's right," Ralph answered.

"I'll get some people to help carry it down to the boat."

Ralph said, "That's not necessary. We're used to hauling it around. Just point us in the right direction."

"We're just down here," the harbormaster said, pointing the way and heading off.

Pointedly ignoring Winchester, everyone on the CDC team grabbed boxes and followed him to a gangplank.

Winchester took a step forward, and Andy intercepted her path. "It seems you don't have clearance for this. I'll have to ask you to move your car now."

"You really don't want to get in my way," she said.

"Actually, you really do want to cooperate, or I'll impound your car and cite you for interfering with government officials in the course of their duty."

"You're joking."

"I don't joke about things like that."

"You win this time," Winchester said, "but that's the last time."

She spun on her heel and marched stiffly away.

Laurel looked after her, then to Andy, as she picked up the last of the boxes. "Friend of yours?"

"Not to speak of," Andy muttered with a shake of her head.

"In that case," Laurel said, "be careful. She looks like she plays to win, at any cost."

Andy shot her a grin, and she didn't look earnest any longer. She looked a little dangerous—and a lot attractive. "So do I."

Laurel thought about that all the way out to the cruise ship.

CHAPTER NINETEEN

Tory woke to the warm familiar comfort of Reese curled against her back. Reese's arm encircled her ever-enlarging middle, her palm pressed just below her navel, her fingers spread, the gesture at once protective and tender. Tory covered Reese's hand with hers, and their fingers automatically entwined.

"What's the news from the hinterland?" Tory murmured.

"Critter number one is very active this morning, while critter number two is content just to stretch now and then."

Tory smiled. "You do realize all that peaceful quiet is going to change very soon."

Reese kissed her between the shoulder blades. "I'm ready when you are."

Tory laughed. "Oh, believe me, you couldn't possibly be as ready."

Reese chuckled.

Tory tightened her grip and lifted Reese's hand, turning it to kiss her palm. "So we should talk."

"Okay." Calm and steady as ever.

"I think you should move in with Kate and Jean for a week or two. Reggie will love it."

"Reggie already loves it. She's totally happy there, and I see her a couple of times a day—minimum. She'll start missing you anytime now, and we'll figure something out then."

"Okay, I didn't think that would work."

"What's this all about, Tor?" Reese asked gently.

"I'm not going to get the test results back for a few days, and even then I'm not entirely certain that the timing is going to be adequate to be sure I'm not infected."

"And what? You're worried about me?" Reese laughed. "Come on, baby."

"Why would that be strange?"

"Considering our present location, that seems kind of moot, doesn't it?"

"Actually, no," Tory said. "I'm not showing any symptoms right now, but possibly I might in a few days or a week and then you'd be at risk. That's the thing about a novel virus—it's *novel* because we don't know anything about it. So the incubation period is just one of the many question marks."

"But a negative test will mean we're okay," Reese said reasonably, "and we'll know that soon."

"That will be comforting, yes, but I'll feel a lot better if I test negative in another week."

"You were only with those folks a few minutes, right?" Reese asked. "Is that really long enough to…I don't know, catch something? You see patients all year round with viruses and other things and you don't get them."

"You're right, and our usual routine—frequent handwashing, et cetera—offers a lot of protection. But some viruses are highly contagious just in the air, whereas others are not, and again with this one, question marks."

"Okay, I see what you're saying," Reese said with a note of finality. "And I'm not going anywhere. If and when your situation changes, then we'll reassess. But you're about ready to deliver these babies, and that could happen anytime. You aren't going to be here alone. I'd stay home from work if I could."

Tory bit her lip for a second, refusing to allow the tears that burned on the undersides of her lids to surface. "That might be a tiny bit extreme."

"Yeah, maybe. But the only way I'm going to be completely happy is if I'm watching you twenty-four hours a day, which would make you crazy."

"Well, we're in complete agreement about that."

"So we compromise." Reese sat up and leaned over so she

could kiss Tory without making Tory move. When she was done, she whispered, "You're my wife, and more than that, you're my life. I'm here, no matter what. Okay?"

Tory wrapped an arm around Reese's neck and turned to kiss her properly. "Okay. I'm going to talk to Kerri later this morning and see if she thinks I should isolate. They'll probably have more information by now."

"What does that mean?"

"That means I stay home."

"Well, I'm all for that."

Tory smiled and stroked her cheek. "Yes, I rather thought you would be."

Reese kissed her one last time and got out of bed. "I have to get to the station. You've got your phone nearby?"

Tory rolled her eyes. "Absolutely."

"Don't wait too long. First contraction, and no timing them. I don't care how far apart they are. I want to know."

"I've got that too."

"All right then. I'll leave you to take care of this part of the family. I'll stop over and see Reggie this morning. I ought to have time to shovel in some oatmeal."

"I love you," Tory said.

"I love you too." Reese shook her head and muttered on her way to get a shower, "Even if you are a little crazy."

Tory's laughter followed her.

❖

"Hey, Andy," Gladys said as Andy walked in at the end of her shift. "The chief wants to see you before you go home."

Andy frowned. "Yeah, okay, sure. Uh, do you know—"

Gladys shook her head. "No idea."

Andy sat through roll call, half listening while the day commander reviewed the events of the night and went over the duty assignments for the day, sorting through everything she'd done the night before. She couldn't think of anything that could've been a problem. Her calls were all routine. She hadn't filed her reports yet, but everyone did that at end of shift before checking out. Couldn't be anything there.

Twenty minutes later, uneasy and trying not to show it, she rapped on the chief's half-open door.

"Come in," the chief called.

"Chief?" Andy stopped two feet from the chief's desk. "You wanted to see me?"

"Have a seat, Champlain." Reese walked to the office door and closed it.

Andy hesitated, uncomfortable sitting in the presence of her commander, but tried to look relaxed as she finally sat.

"So tell me about this reporter, Winchester," Conlon said, returning to her seat behind her desk. Her expression was as smooth and unreadable as marble.

Andy frowned. "I don't know much about her, Chief. She said she's from the *Boston Chronicle*. She seems to have some pretty good information, since she showed up at the wharf last night, the same time as the CDC team. I don't think many people knew that was happening."

"I need to ask—she's not getting it from you, is she?"

Andy blinked. She wasn't often caught off guard, and certainly not when she was being interrogated. The muscles between her shoulder blades tightened. "No, sir. She is not."

"The *sir*'s not necessary," Conlon said quietly. "I didn't think so, but it's my job to be sure."

"I understand." Andy squelched a fiery wave of anger. "Did someone say—"

"No. I wouldn't be talking to you now if Winchester hadn't mentioned you'd suggested she see me for the details of the evacuation the other night."

"That's not quite the way it went down, Chief." Andy consciously unballed her fists. The chief wasn't blaming her—yet. Hadn't found her guilty—yet. The chief was listening to her. Giving her a chance. "She stopped me in the parking lot and had a lot of questions—she already had part of the story and was looking for official confirmation. I told her to see you, that I knew nothing about it."

Reese grunted. "That sounds about right. Here's the situation. She's got an article in the *Boston Chronicle* referencing 'a source close to the emerging crisis' in the police department. And as near as I can tell, I'm the only one who's talked to her other than you, and I didn't tell her anything."

"I did talk to her, like I said," Andy said, "twice. Once outside the station, I think the morning she talked to you, and then early this morning on the wharf. Both times she approached me."

"And you didn't tell her anything."

"Absolutely not. I don't even know anything. *She* seemed to have all the information. This morning she said she'd already talked to the captain of the cruise ship for clearance to board with the CDC team."

"But the CDC shut her down?"

"Tight as a drum," Andy said.

"Okay. What do you think?"

"I think she has a source," Andy said, "but I'm willing to bet it isn't coming from here. First of all, we're all following the CDC's lead, and none of us on the night shift even knew about the plans to go out to the ship when we started our shifts. Plus, we don't have anything to gain from talking to a reporter."

"Some people might think differently about that," Reese said. "Media coverage can occasionally help advance a career."

Andy scoffed and didn't bother hiding her disdain. "Maybe so, but that wouldn't be me."

"Okay. Well, I don't think she's going to go away, because reporters never do. They do have a job to do, and I appreciate that. Sometimes they can be really helpful. So far she hasn't been. If she approaches you again, you know the standard answer."

"I do, and the thing is, Chief, I already gave her that. Twice. You think if I talked to her we might be able to, I don't know, find out something?"

"So far she's been a little annoying but not really any more than most reporters," Reese said. "I wouldn't suggest actively seeking her out, but if she tries for more information from you, I wouldn't be opposed to a little fishing."

"Will do. Wherever her sources, they're good ones." Andy relaxed. They'd talked it out.

"One more thing," Reese said. "I'm assigning you to be our official liaison with the CDC team. They want our assistance in contact tracing, and since they don't know their way around, you can facilitate that, plus assist in transporting test materials and anything else they need locally. Keep me in the loop."

"Yes, Chief." Andy tried not to sound as eager as she felt.

"I'm switching you to days, starting tomorrow. So rest up today." Andy said, "I'm good to work today. This switchover has never bothered me. I'll grab a couple hours this morning and be fine if they want to get started today."

"I appreciate that. There's urgency to this issue, and the faster we jump on it, the faster we secure the village and get a lid on this thing."

"You'll let them know to contact me, then?" Andy said.

Reese smiled. "I was just about to mention that."

Andy felt herself color. "Oh, sorry."

Reese shook her head. "Hey, I've got no complaints with an officer eager to do their job."

"Well, that's everybody on the force, Chief."

Reese nodded. "I know that. Finish your reports and get out of here."

"I'm on it." Andy hurried back to the squad room to file her reports. Something big was happening, and she was part of it.

Andy slept until a little after noon, four solid hours that left her feeling good. She'd just grabbed a breakfast taco from the waterfront takeout stand when her phone vibrated.

Laurel.

are you awake

yes. where are you.

on the pier

be there in three minutes

Andy pocketed her phone, dumped the last few bites of her taco in a trash can, and jogged toward the center of town. Laurel was walking down the pier toward her, her eyes shadowed and her face drawn.

"Hey," Andy said when she reached Laurel. She stifled the urge to kiss her, but she wanted to—a lot. Just seeing her quickened her pulse and electrified every nerve. "How was it?"

Laurel sighed. "Long. The usual chaos when you're trying to get something like that organized. It took us a while to get the logistics right, but Kerri and the others have done this plenty of times. We managed to interview ninety percent of the patients who reported symptoms, at least as far as we know. The problem is, we *don't* know that everyone who has symptoms has reported them."

"Why wouldn't they?" Andy frowned.

"A bunch of reasons—fear of being blamed or ostracized if they're seen as a danger to others, not accepting the seriousness of the situation, general refusal to admit *any* kind of illness. Communication is a big part of the job. We need to convince people of the need for all this without causing alarm."

"Yeah—I can see how anyone who isn't feeling sick would want off that ship."

Laurel nodded. "That's started already. The captain and the crew are doing the best they can, but there are a lot of disgruntled people on that ship who want to leave. They've already been in port for longer than expected, and they've figured out that the cruise is not going to proceed on schedule. Most of those who aren't affected, or who aren't affected *yet*, either want to continue on to the final port ASAP or want to be allowed to leave the ship. I think if they were actually shore docked, they'd be demanding they be allowed to disembark. As it is, that's not an option."

"Sounds like a setup for a lot of unhappy people," Andy said as they walked.

"It's going to get a lot worse if they have to be quarantined for any length of time."

"Is that a possibility?"

"I think at this point it's a probability," Laurel said. "We know there's an outbreak, and we don't know the extent. Basic containment requires that we keep all of the potentially infected people away from uninfected people. Which basically means they can't go ashore until they test negative."

"What about letting them disembark and putting them up in a hotel or something?"

"I suppose that's a possibility, but not here. Literally no room. And transporting them from here to somewhere else is a logistical nightmare." Laurel shook her head. "The other possibility is for the ship to travel to a port of call where they can offload passengers, and that may happen. But not until the ship is released by the CDC."

Andy said, "Can't say I'd be too happy about all of that if I was a passenger."

"I know. Everyone was pretty cooperative today, but tempers are short, and I think they're going to get a lot shorter."

Andy took her hand and squeezed. "I'm sorry. Sounds tough."

When she would've let go, Laurel tightened her grip, and they continued walking hand in hand. Andy would have been happy to walk to Boston if she could keep Laurel's warm hand in hers.

"It's okay," Laurel said. "It's stressful, but you know, that's the thing about medicine—the tough parts are often the most interesting and exciting. Nobody enjoys other people's suffering, but the challenge of figuring out treatment and making a difference, that's the good part."

"I get that. So what's next?"

"The CDC is collating data and crunching the numbers, trying to nail down the timelines, identify the incubation period, catalog the symptomatic period, and determine the mechanism of transmission. All of that's happening all at once, with their people."

"Sounds crazy," Andy said.

"Intense, for sure." Laurel rolled her shoulders and sighed. "By tonight, or tomorrow at the latest, we'll have a starting point for contact tracing, including ashore. I'm going to do that with Harley, and whoever else gets assigned. I'll probably be really busy."

"Me too," Andy said. "The chief assigned me to work with your team."

"Really?" Laurel smiled. "Well, that's a bonus, then."

Andy grinned. Oh yeah.

They'd reached the lane down to Laurel's cottage.

"I've been switched over to days, so I'm actually off tonight," Andy said. "Maybe I can see you later?"

Laurel tilted her head. "Have you eaten?"

"Not really," Andy said, figuring half a taco didn't really count.

Laurel smiled. "Then come on in. I'm starving. Breakfast or lunch?"

"Anything you want," Andy said.

Laurel smiled again, and she didn't look tired any longer. "Now that's a dangerous answer."

CHAPTER TWENTY

"D r. King," Kerri Sanchez said when Tory answered her phone midafternoon.

"Tory, remember? Hi, Kerri."

Kerri gave what sounded like an exhausted sigh. "Yes, hi. Nita's here with me on speaker, so we can conference. It's probably wise for you not to come in until we get the results of your test."

"I've been thinking about that," Tory said. "Reese and our receptionist, Randy, probably should be tested also. Reese, obviously because of me, and Randy because he saw those two patients during the intake process."

"I think the risk is low, but I can't argue with an abundance of caution," Kerri said. "We're at the police station now—I'll have Harley get Chief Conlon taken care of."

Nita added, "I'll do Randy's when I stop by the clinic this afternoon."

"Good." Tory hesitated, almost hating to ask the question. "We've got a three-year-old. What about her?"

"That's hard to say," Kerri said. "So far, we've only seen affected adults. Is she there with you?"

"No, with her grandparents."

"In that case, I would say to wait."

"All right then. How are things looking?"

"We don't have a complete profile at this point," Kerri said, "but I'm fairly certain we're dealing with the same organism causing the outbreak in Southern California. I also just received a report on my way back here of two cases in Florida that may be related. These are two health care professionals, and at this point, there's no clear point of contact."

"I see," Tory said, her chest tightening. "Possibly only brief contact, then."

Nita cut in, "Which doesn't really mean anything, Tory. We don't know yet how infectious this agent might be. It's possible that many more people were exposed on the cruise ship and never developed symptoms."

Nita's point was a good one, and Tory knew she was right. That didn't help the anxiety of not knowing a whole lot. But she couldn't wish for a better group of people to be working to find the answers.

"I understand," Tory said. "So—where does that leave us?"

"Well, for one thing," Kerri said, "I'm going to recommend that Roger advise President Powell and alert the National Institutes of Health. If we're seeing outbreaks at multiple geographic points, we'll need a national health alert to monitor reports of new cases and possibly institute local measures to control community exposure. We'll certainly need vigorous contact tracing of all suspected cases."

"When the Ebola threat hit the US," Tory said, "that was shut down very quickly, wasn't it?"

"Yes," Kerri said, "but patient zero was identified almost immediately, and contact tracing was instantaneous and vigorous. Essentially one exposure point, one entry point, and rapid shutdown. That's what we're going for here—identify, trace, contain."

"Brushfires," Tory murmured. "Before the fire gets too big."

"Exactly," Kerri said. "Right now we've got brushfires, and if we put them out, they won't spread and lead to wildfires. The analogy is imperfect, but it's apt."

"What about the tourists who may have been exposed on shore?" Tory asked. "Some of them must be gone, and even if they're not—how do we notify them?"

"We may get lucky there," Kerri said. "In addition to the individuals you saw, only a few hundred people actually came ashore, and of those, only a small number report symptoms. Hopefully, everyone who's experiencing any kind of symptoms will be identified in the next few days. We will compile exhaustive lists of where they might have gone."

Nita said, "We plan to start contacting everyone who may have been exposed tomorrow morning. So far the risk sites are restaurants and retail stores, so we'll be focusing on staff who might have had prolonged face-to-face contact with someone with the virus. Tourists who were merely in the vicinity of an infected individual are at far less risk." She paused. "We *hope*. Judging by the infection rate we're seeing aboard the cruise ship, we think the actual transmission rate is low."

"How many of the locals are we talking about?" Tory asked.

"A lot," Nita said, "if you consider all the waitstaff in a dozen restaurants and the clerks in another twenty stores."

"Should we make any kind of public announcement?" Tory asked, thinking that Reese would need to know, as would the mayor and town council.

"At this point, I don't think so," Kerri said. "We don't have enough information to be helpful, and we don't have significant recommendations to follow up. As soon as we have a clear picture of how the organism spreads, we'll know who might be at risk, and we'll be able to make sensible recommendations for containment."

The plan made sense to Tory, but the waiting bore down on her like ominous storm clouds over an angry ocean. "All right. I'm sorry I can't be there to assist."

Kerri chuckled. "I think you've got a very good excuse."

Tory settled her hand on her midsection where Reese's hand had been that morning. Funny, she could still feel her there. Maybe the babies could too, because they answered with a few resounding kicks. "You're right, I do."

❖

"How do you feel about spaghetti with fresh tomatoes, and…" Laurel paused and peered into her mini refrigerator. "Broccoli?"

"Sounds like a lot of trouble to me," Andy said. "I could run down to get a pizza."

Laurel looked over her shoulder, still kneeling in front of the undercounter fridge. "I love pizza, and I could probably eat it every day, possibly several times a day, but there's no way I can walk enough to deal with that. I'm cooking."

"Then it sounds fabulous. Uh, what can I do?"

"How about chopping broccoli?"

Andy let out a sigh of relief. "Yeah, that sounds easy."

Laurel set her up on the counter left of the sink with a knife and a cutting board and said, "Have at it."

"This is kind of fun," Andy muttered, wondering if there was a right and a wrong way to slice broccoli. It was only vegetables, right?

"It is," Laurel said, running water into a pot.

Andy paused at something in Laurel's voice, something wistful, sad? She put the knife down and turned. "What's the matter?"

Laurel shut off the water and shook her head, but her eyes gave her away.

"You're upset. Should I go?"

"No," Laurel said, her voice husky. "That's actually the last thing I want you to do."

"So you want to tell me what's bothering you?"

"I was just…" Laurel made a gesture with her hand as if she wasn't quite sure that she had the right words. "Thinking that *nice* is a word that comes up a lot where you're concerned. You're easy to be around."

"So that shouldn't make you sad then, right?"

"I'm not sad. I'm a little leery, I guess, of just how good it *does* feel," Laurel said. "It's new, and I like it, and I think if I'm not careful, I could like it a lot."

"Yeah," Andy said, nodding, "I know what you mean. As I already like it a lot. What are you afraid of?"

Laurel's brows rose. "Well, that's getting to the point."

"Can't see any reason not to."

"Remember when we talked about not having any rules for what we were doing? Well, I wasn't kidding. I don't actually know *how* to have a casual relationship. You know, light and friendly and fun and… nice."

"I don't think nice necessarily implies casual," Andy said carefully. "Casual sounds like take it or leave it to me, and I don't really feel that way at all."

"How do you feel?"

"Like I want a lot of things with you."

"Like what?" Laurel whispered.

"Like starting with this." Andy slipped her arms around Laurel's waist and kissed her. Laurel's arms came around her neck, and their bodies cleaved as if drawn to one another by a magnet. Her pulse jumped from sixty to a hundred in less than twenty seconds, and she groaned. Laurel slipped a hand under the collar of her T-shirt and traced her thumb over the pulse point in her throat. The move was so sexy, Andy's legs weakened.

Laurel's tongue teased between her lips, found hers, and stroked. Thoughts of food fled on a surge of hunger, raw and needy. Andy tugged the back of Laurel's shirt from beneath her waistband, dipped her fingers along the hollow at the base of her spine, and underneath her khakis. She brushed the swell of Laurel's hips, and Laurel surged in her arms.

"Laurel," Andy gasped, "I want to be naked with you. Tell me what you want."

"I...I don't know...too much, everything, God, I don't know."

"Let's find out." Andy grasped Laurel's hand and looked around. "Where the hell is the bed?"

Laurel laughed and pointed to a set of doors Andy had assumed was a closet. "In there."

"Okay, sure," Andy muttered, because she really, *really* didn't care if they had to lie down on the floor, but they needed to do something soon or her head was going to explode. "Why don't you just start and see what you want. Do anything you want. Just—start."

"Just like that?" Laurel said. "Just anything?"

"God, yes."

"Stand right there." Laurel hurried across the room, threw open the enclosure for the Murphy bed, and yanked it down from the wall. When she turned, Andy was right behind her.

"Okay, that's cool." Andy spread her arms, palms up. "All yours. What next?"

"Can I..." Laurel said, scarcely believing what she was doing. "Can I take your clothes off?"

Andy swallowed. "Hell, yes. You want to do it?"

"You have no idea how much."

"You're in charge, Laurel," Andy said, shaking as the lust rode her hard. "Just...please...do it."

"Do you mind if I go slow?" Laurel asked, her voice husky and strained. Her smile flickered, wistful, with that edge of something that could've been sadness and shouldn't be.

Andy brushed her thumb against the corner of Laurel's mouth. Her fingers trembled. "Hey. If you don't want—"

"No," Laurel said instantly. "God, I do. So much. I just…I want to remember everything. It's the first time."

Andy drew a long, staggering breath, absorbing the words the way she absorbed body blows during a contest. The first time. The first of more? The first of something too amazing to take in when her body screamed for release. "I said everything. I meant it. I want you to have me."

"Oh yes." Laurel's hands shook as much as Andy's body trembled. Andy had said anything, and she wanted everything. Ached for it. Had to touch her, now. She gripped the bottom of Andy's shirt and lifted it up, inch by slow inch, exposing her tanned middle, the skin so smooth, so sleek over the indentations and planes of the muscles etched ever so subtly beneath the surface. "So gorgeous."

When she dragged her fingers lightly down Andy's stomach, the muscles twitched and Andy's hips jerked. On Andy's quick intake of breath, Laurel looked up questioningly. "What?"

"When you touch me," Andy said, her voice ragged, "when I just *think* about you touching me, I'm ready to go off like a firecracker."

"You can if you want to." Laurel smiled, no sadness there this time. Satisfaction, a victory smile. "As long as you're not done right away."

Andy's stomach quivered and the muscles in her neck stood out like steel wires stretched taut. "I'm never going to be done."

"Raise your arms," Laurel whispered.

Andy did, her small breasts lifting, the muscles in her arms and shoulders tensing as Laurel drew her shirt up and off.

"No bra."

"Can't stand them," Andy said.

Laurel laughed. "Well then, why wear one."

"Exactly."

"How about underwear," Laurel murmured. "How do you feel about those?"

"That's a function of who's wearing them," Andy said, "and what they look like." She sucked in a breath when Laurel pressed a palm flat to her middle. "Lacy bits can be nice."

"I'm going to disappoint you today," Laurel said. "I'm not dressed for seduction."

"Believe me, you couldn't possibly disappoint." Andy framed

Laurel's face and kissed her. She knew she was supposed to wait, to let Laurel take every step, but she was dying. Laurel was water to her drought-parched soul. Just a taste, just a sip, and then she'd be patient again. Her breasts brushed Laurel's shirt, and her nipples tingled. When Laurel gripped her ass and tugged her even closer, Andy dove for the life-giving spring, drinking in her kisses.

Laurel filled her hands with Andy's taut muscles, squeezing, digging in her fingertips, holding on while Andy plundered. God, she'd never get enough of those kisses. When her head went light and her brain threatened to empty of everything except the need pounding through her, she gripped Andy's hips and pushed her back. "Enough for now."

Andy's chest heaved, her breasts tight and her nipples small hard pebbles, her breath coming in uneven pants. Her brown eyes were stormy and lashing with urgency. "Can we—"

"Wait," Laurel murmured and popped the button on Andy's jeans. Slowly, slowly, she eased down the zipper, holding her breath to curb the pressure to hurry. To touch. To take. Andy's plain black low-cut briefs stretched tight over her pelvis. "I almost expected commando."

"Sometimes," Andy whispered.

"Good."

Laurel hooked her thumbs under the waistband of Andy's jeans, caught her briefs at the same time, and pushed everything down. "Off," she said.

In a rush, Andy toed off her shoes and kicked free of her tangle of clothes. She watched Laurel watch her every move, pleasure coiling between her legs when Laurel's face flushed and her lips parted. She wanted Laurel to want her, needed Laurel to touch her. Soon, before the thin tether on her restraint snapped.

Still clothed, Laurel slipped behind her and pressed up against her back, encircling with both arms to cup both breasts in the palms of her hands. When she squeezed, Andy's stomach convulsed and her clitoris pounded.

Andy's body arched and she warned, "Keep it up and you'll make me come. I can't take much more."

"Mm. Too bad. I've got more." Laurel kissed the back of Andy's neck. She stroked down the middle of her abdomen, brushed along the inner curves of her hipbones, traced the elegant arches with her thumbs, and finally dipped one hand between her thighs.

Andy jerked with a sharp cry.

"See?" Laurel breathed against her neck, kissing her just behind her ear. They were almost the same height, and their bodies fit perfectly. She slipped her fingers lower, catching Andy between the vee of her fingers as she stroked. Andy's ass tightened and pushed back into her, her whole body tightening, boardlike, and she gasped again.

"You're making me come." Andy's jaw clenched and her spine bowed. "Fuck."

"I can't stop," Laurel said. "You're so beautiful."

Andy grabbed on to Laurel's arm, squeezed her wrist to keep her in place, and thrust against her hand.

Satin smooth and so warm. Laurel squeezed and stroked.

Andy came in convulsive thrusts, low groans punctuating each jerk of her hips until she sagged in Laurel's arms.

"Give me a second," Andy gasped. "Just...don't let go."

"Not a chance." Laurel laughed. So light now, amazed, so incredibly free. The bed was only a few feet away, and she tugged Andy with her. They fell together, Andy on her back, Laurel right next to her. She kissed Andy then, thinking this might be the first time she'd ever been the one to kiss her first. Not gentle. Not awestruck. Hard and furious, hunger raging, rising out of someplace within her she'd never known was there. She gripped Andy's wrists, held both hands to the bed, slipped on top of her, and devoured her with kisses.

Andy came alive beneath her, wrapping one leg over hers, sliding the other between Laurel's thighs, hips thrusting upward. An invitation.

Laurel pushed herself up, fumbling at the buttons on her shirt, and finally, frustrated, just tugged the whole thing off. Her bra came next, and Andy's hands were on her pants, opening them, tugging them down. The instant Laurel was naked, she straddled Andy, craving the smooth, hot, tight expanse of her, needing her everywhere. Looking down, she found Andy's eyes—dazed with the orgasm *she'd* torn from her—found her lips, swollen with *her* kisses. Andy had given her everything, and now she wanted, needed, even more.

"Touch me," Laurel urged.

In an instant, Andy's hands closed on her breasts, and she arched, speared by the pleasure arrowing through her belly and into her sex. She rocked on Andy's tight belly, the pressure a teasing torment against her pounding clit. She swung one hand behind her, between Andy's legs, and into the heat again.

Andy's hips lifted, inviting her, and she slid inside.

Andy's neck arched and her lids fluttered. "God, I'm close again."

"Come inside me," Laurel gasped. "Quickly. I'm about to come."

Andy glided her hand between Laurel's thrusting hips, over her engorged clitoris, and inside her. Joining them. Andy filled her, deep and tight, and the pressure built, bursting upward, a rocket explosion of pleasure. Laurel might've screamed aloud, or maybe it was only the primal sound from somewhere deep within her, the sound of need finally answered.

She tumbled onto the bed and pressed against Andy's side, fighting for breath. Andy's arm came around her, and she finally found the strength to sling her leg over Andy's hips.

"I'm destroyed," she muttered.

Andy kissed her forehead. "Close your eyes."

Laurel never wanted to sleep again. All she wanted was to feel this moment never ending. That probably should've terrified her, but right then, in that breathless perfect instant, she didn't care.

CHAPTER TWENTY-ONE

I hate to say this," Laurel said drowsily, "but I should probably get some sleep tonight. I'm supposed to meet the CDC team at six thirty."

"Yeah," Andy muttered, fascinated by the smooth curves of Laurel's breasts and the way her nipples puckered when she lightly brushed the surface with her thumb.

Laurel arched. "God, on the other hand…"

Chuckling, Andy continued exploring, kissing her way down the center of Laurel's abdomen, circling her hips, and gently nudging her legs apart.

"Andy," Laurel breathed, "I don't know if I can again."

"You don't have to do anything. Just let me do." Andy settled herself comfortably in the vee of Laurel's thighs. Who knew a fold-down bed would turn out to be the best place she'd ever been. She took her time, needing to sate herself with every impression—the softness, the sweetness, the heat, and ambrosia of taste and scent. Distantly, she registered the soft moans and the imperceptible tremors growing stronger, coalescing beneath her hands and her mouth. Heat rose from her loins, the tingling pressure rapidly awakening her desire.

Laurel's fingers in her hair, restless and urgent, choreographed her pace, now quicker, now slow, now soft, now deep and firm. Andy's heart beat faster, her stomach clenched. Laurel's thighs tightened, her hips lifted, and Andy followed her lead. Finally, when the tension threatened to wash over them both, she filled her. Laurel's cry triggered the coiled tension deep in Andy's belly, and she thrust against her free hand, coming hard when Laurel came.

With a low, satisfied groan, she pillowed her cheek on Laurel's lower abdomen. "You're amazing. Who needs to sleep when you can do that all night?"

Laughing shakily, Laurel tugged at Andy's hair. "*You* might not need anything else for sustenance, but I do. Come up here."

Grinning, Andy roused herself and stretched out beside Laurel, propping her head on her elbow. She kissed her and went back to stroking.

Laurel covered Andy's hand. "Stop."

"Really?"

In the pale gold reflection from the undercounter lights in the little kitchen across the room, Laurel's face grew somber. Andy frowned.

"What?"

"I'm not even sure what to say."

"Don't think, just talk," Andy said.

"You're not like anyone—anything—I've ever encountered." Laurel sighed. "I don't seem to have any brakes where you're concerned. You know, the kind that you use to slow down a runaway train. Because that's how I feel. You're the train and I don't want to get off. I just want to ride and ride."

Andy grinned. "You know, those are really cool metaphors. We could just stick with that."

Laurel couldn't help herself. She laughed. "It's probably because the rest of my brain has been burned out and only the sex centers remain."

"That sounds good to me." Andy liked when Laurel smiled, was glad to see it, but she saw the worry in her eyes still. "What would make you not worry that we're having fabulous sex that we both like really a lot?"

"I think feeling this good and getting used to how much I like the way you look at me is going to take some time."

Andy traced the arch of Laurel's collarbone. That seemed like a safe place to touch. Laurel shivered. "I guess one day at a time doesn't really work for you?"

"I know it should—in fact, I want it to—but I'm not quite there yet."

"So what are you saying?"

"I just don't want to overshoot our headlights, you know? I mean, go so fast that we end up in the dark somewhere, not sure what's happening."

"Does that mean no more sex?"

Laurel caught her hand and held it curled between her breasts. "Would it sound horribly callous if I said sex with no strings?"

"You mean you only want me for my body?"

"God, no," Laurel said, frustrated at her own uncertainty. "I love your body. It's awesome. Gorgeous. I'd be happy looking at you naked twenty-four hours a day. And your hands—they're magic. And I won't even get started on your mouth."

"Okay, you're doing a good job there. If you don't want my hands and my mouth on you right now, you better stop, though." Andy spread her fingers over Laurel's breast, on the spot where her heart beat. "I don't want to stop touching you. If you tell me to, I'm not sure I can."

"I don't think I can be around you without wanting you to touch me." Laurel smiled a little wryly. "Just, no expectations, okay? We'll just—"

"Light and casual. I get that. I'm good with that." Andy wasn't, not really, because light and casual didn't even come close to what she was feeling when she looked at Laurel, but she was where she wanted to be, in bed with a gorgeous woman who fascinated and intrigued and satisfied her. A woman she could talk to. A woman who listened to her. A woman who made every other experience in her life seem a little smaller, because the moments she spent with her touched so much more of her. Whatever that was, she wanted it. And Laurel wasn't ready to hear it. She could keep quiet about it, for now. "But I want to see you again. This isn't a one-time thing for me."

"I'm glad," Laurel whispered.

Andy kissed her. "So, you ready again?"

Laurel laughed and pushed her shoulder. "I need a little more than five minutes' recovery. It's an age thing."

Andy rolled her eyes. "Bull."

"Listen, when I was your age I could come every other second too, but now, I need a breath—or a thousand or so—in between orgasms." Laurel kissed Andy's throat and eased her hand down between Andy's legs. "But some things don't need any recovery, and I know exactly what you'd like right now."

Andy gritted her teeth. Laurel's lightly stroking fingers tightened her like a spring deep inside. "Damn."

"Mm," Laurel murmured with a hum of complete satisfaction. Kissing Andy's throat, she picked up her pace, long firm strokes, her thumb at just the right angle to push Andy right to the edge.

"Son of a…if you don't stop…"

"You'll do what? Hmm?" Laurel found the spot she'd discovered earlier that sent Andy off after a few strokes. She loved making her come. She'd be happy to do that all night long. Sleep be damned.

Andy threw her head back and groaned through her teeth. "Fuck."

Laurel buried her face in Andy's neck as Andy came all over her hand, hot and fast and hard. When Laurel released her, Andy fell onto her back with a long groan.

"Damn. I could stand to do that a thousand or so times."

Laurel snuggled up against her. "How about we go again in an hour or two."

Andy chuckled. "I'll be ready."

❖

Reese sat up, wide awake. The bed beside her was empty. Tory stood silhouetted in moonlight before the window that overlooked the harbor. "Tor, are you all right?"

A second later, Tory slid back into bed with a sigh. "Yes, sorry. I couldn't sleep, and the longer I lay there, the more I had to pee. It's a vicious cycle."

"Want me to adjust the AC?"

Tory stroked her arm and kissed the point of her shoulder. "No. I'm okay. Just a lot going on, I guess. Makes me restless. My mind won't turn off."

"Back rub?"

"Mm. Are you bucking for sainthood?"

"Brownie points for when I skip the two a.m. feedings."

Tory traced a line down Reese's middle, lingering on all the spots that made her crazy. "You'll need an awful lot of brownie points."

"I'll earn them," Reese said. "Any way you want."

Laughing, Tory leaned over her own prodigious middle to kiss her properly. "You're right—you will. For now, though, a shoulder rub would be great."

"What do I get if I'm really, really good at it?" Reese teased, settling both hands on Tory's shoulders.

"A very special reward."

Reese kissed the back of her neck. "Prepare to be transported."

Smiling, Tory closed her eyes and tried to ignore the jittery tension slowly invading her mind and body.

❖

"Andy?" Laurel asked her when she opened her eyes in the dark and found the bed beside her empty. The room was dark now. Laurel vaguely remembered Andy getting up to use the bathroom and turning off the lights sometime before she'd fallen into a dead sleep. Or maybe coma.

"Shh," Andy said from across the room. "Do you have a flashlight?"

"Yes," Laurel said, immediately alert. Something in Andy's voice had changed. An edge of tension, sharply focused. "What is it?"

"Someone in the yard."

"The flashlight is in the top drawer next to the refrigerator." Andy rummaged quietly, and Laurel eased from beneath the covers, listening hard for any sounds. She didn't hear anything. "Maybe it's one of the owners coming home?"

"If it is, why are they hanging around in the yard in the dark in the middle of the night instead of using the front entrance?"

"I don't know, forgot their keys maybe?"

"Maybe."

Laurel'd adjusted to the darkened room now. Andy, fully dressed, flashlight in hand, reached for the door.

"Andy—" she whispered.

"Call 9-1-1. Tell them my name and that I believe there is a prowler, possibly a B and E in progress. Don't forget to tell them your address."

"All right." Laurel didn't protest, although her stomach twisted into knots. This was what Andy did. She trusted her. She was already punching in 911 when Andy eased her way outside. The words *be careful* fell on a silent room.

Phone in one hand, she dragged on her pants and searched for her shirt. Gone, God only knew where. She yanked a T-shirt off a folded pile in her laundry basket.

"Provincetown police," a male voice said.

Laurel paused, shirt in hand, and explained the situation.

He said, brisk and official, "I'll have someone there in four minutes. Is Champlain armed?"

"I don't think so."

"Did Champlain say anything about seeing a weapon?"

"No, nothing."

Through the window a light flickered and arced, then a shout and a wild barrage of lights slashing back and forth, as if someone was whipping a strobe around on the end of a rope.

"I think there's a fight of some kind," Laurel cried.

A siren sounded, drowning out the noise of her pulse pounding in her head.

"Keep the line open," the man said steadily. "Do not go outside."

"But if Andy—"

"The best way to keep everyone safe is to wait where you are."

The light was no longer moving, and all Laurel heard was the steadily advancing siren. Help would be there in just a minute. Was that too long? Too late? Her heart thundered in her chest. Another set of lights, brighter this time, the beams shooting through her front window, lighting up the interior of her small cottage as a vehicle careened down the alley.

The siren wailed.

Muffled shouts.

"The other officers are here. I'm going outside."

"Wait—"

Laurel yanked open her door and bolted outside. The backyard with its carefully tended flower beds and trimmed shrubs was bathed in the harsh glare from the police car, unnaturally bright. How many hundreds of times had she waited outside the ER for a police car or EMT ambulance to bring her a critically injured patient? How many times had it been too late?

Andy and a uniformed officer stood over a figure lying facedown in the grass, squirming fitfully. Andy cradled her right forearm, and in the strobing red light from the cruiser, the blood on her hand appeared black.

"Andy?" Laurel ran forward. "What happened? How badly are you hurt?"

"I'm okay," Andy said. Sweat gleamed on her face. "It's a scratch."

The male officer said, "You need to get it looked at."

"Let's get this guy to the station first," Andy said.

"If you're injured, the only place you're going is to the clinic," Laurel said flatly.

The male officer, whose name tag said Smith, grinned.

The back porch light of the main house came on, and a barefoot man in sweats stepped out. "What's going on?"

"Provincetown police," Smith called. "Everything is under control. I'll come talk to you in a minute."

A Jeep pulled up behind the cruiser, and Reese Conlon, in jeans and a white T-shirt, her holstered weapon on her hip, got out.

"What have you got?" Conlon said when she jogged over.

"Champlain caught this guy casing the house," Smith said. "He put up a little fight. Champlain stopped a knife blade with her arm."

Reese motioned with her thumb toward the vehicles. "Let's get over to the clinic. Smith, wait for Parker, and you can wrap up here."

"Sure," Smith said.

Andy said, "I can—"

"No, you can't," Laurel said. "We are going to the clinic where I can see what kind of damage you've done this time."

Andy sighed and took the pressure pack Reese passed her from a field kit she'd retrieved from her Jeep. She pressed it to her arm and winced. "Yeah, okay."

Reese strode toward the Jeep, and Laurel put her hand on Andy's back.

Andy muttered, "Sorry."

"For what?" *Rushing out with nothing but a flashlight in your hand? What if he'd had a gun?* The image made Laurel's stomach churn, but she kept silent. Not her place to say.

"Well, you know," Andy said, "it's going to be obvious we were… you know. Together tonight."

"I don't care about that." Laurel waited while Andy carefully climbed into the rear of the Jeep and followed her in.

Reese turned in the front seat to look back at Laurel. "How fast do we need to get there?"

"I think you can forgo the siren," Laurel said. "She's walking under her own power."

"I'm good, Chief," Andy added.

"Let's let Laurel decide that," Reese said and pulled out into the street with lights flashing.

Chapter Twenty-two

Lights shone from the clinic windows when Reese turned into the parking lot. Nita's was the only car in the lot.

"Nita must be here to see a patient coming in with some kind of emergency," Laurel said, frowning. "I wonder why she didn't call me."

Reese stopped by the front entrance and cut the engine. "Are you on call?"

"No, but..."

Reese got out of the car, waiting by the back door as Andy climbed out. "You steady?"

"I'm fine, Chief," Andy muttered again. This was like some kind of nightmare *Groundhog Day* sequel—ending up here with the chief babysitting her and Laurel taking care of her. Laurel hadn't said anything on the ride over, and she hadn't looked her in the eye either. Couldn't tell if she was worried, which she didn't need to be—or pissed, which was worse. Tonight wasn't like the last time—she'd been careful, she'd called it in, and she'd judged—rightly—that she couldn't wait until her backup was actually on the scene. The perp would have been in the house by then, and they'd have had a much more serious situation to deal with.

So what was the problem?

Laurel came around the car to join them, and they walked toward the front entrance. Still not looking at Andy.

"I'm not on call," Laurel said, "but usually the most junior member of the team gets the emergencies. I would've come in."

Reese tried the door, found it locked, and sorted through her keychain until she found the one she wanted. She opened the door and pushed it wide. "Well, I'm pretty sure things don't work that way here. Everybody pulls an equal load, so if you're off, you're off. 'Course, since Tory is now officially *not* on call and the CDC *is*, I guess the schedule is shot."

Laurel laughed. "Yeah. There's that."

"Hello?" Nita called, coming down the hall.

"It's us, Nita," Reese called back. "Got a little more business to take care of."

Nita appeared in the reception area, her gaze moving quickly between the three of them. Honing in on the bandage Andy had pressed to her forearm, she said, "What happened?"

Reese settled her hand on Andy's shoulder. "My officer here is bucking for Rookie of the Month. Maybe a little too hard."

"I was just minding my own business," Andy said. "In fact, I was fast asleep when—" She stopped abruptly. Maybe announcing her personal business with Laurel to the chief and Laurel's boss wasn't a good idea.

Nita shot a glance in Laurel's direction and raised an eyebrow.

Laurel smiled back.

At least someone was getting a smile. Andy's arm stung like she'd been branded, and she was feeling just a little peevish. Maybe if Laurel smiled at *her*, she'd feel better.

"I need to take her back and get this cleaned up," Laurel said. "What are you doing here? Do you need any help?"

"I was just picking up the last of our masks and gowns. Kerri Sanchez called, and she's back at the ship. They've had more than a dozen new patients show up in the last few hours, and they're worried there might be more. Word about the seriousness of the situation has obviously gotten around. We might be looking at the beginning of the peak right now. I'm going back out to lend a hand. I'll probably be out there until morning—or later."

"I can come out after I finish here," Laurel said. "We'll have to call Randy and reschedule our regulars."

Nita shook her head. "No, we need you on land to cover any clinic emergencies and to start the contact tracing with Harley's team in the morning. We should have it covered out there."

"What about transport?" Reese said.

"I should know within the hour, but I think we ought to alert the local EMTs. From what Kerri said, there are at least a few patients who look too sick to be managed on board."

"This is starting to sound bad," Reese said.

"It's not good," Nita said. "I'll call you as soon as I know anything."

Reese said, "Fine. I'll take care of calling the EMTs."

"Thanks," Nita said.

"I'll hang out here and make some calls," Reese said, turning to Andy and Laurel, "and drive you both back when you're finished."

"That sounds good, thanks," Laurel said. "Come on back, Andy."

Andy followed, and once in the treatment room, Laurel pointed to the examining table. "Hop up while I get gloved."

"I don't think it's anything," Andy said. "Doesn't hurt much now."

"Uh-huh." Laurel lifted a tablet from a rack by the door, swiped, and tapped. "I really hope you're not going to be a regular here."

"Probably nothing else will happen for twenty years," Andy said.

"Somehow, I doubt that," Laurel said quietly. She set the tablet aside, opened an instrument tray next to the exam table, scrubbed up in the sink for a minute, and pulled on gloves. "Let's have a look. Go ahead and take the pad away."

Laurel elbowed on the wall switch for the overhead light, bumped the handle with her arm until she got it pointed on Andy's forearm, and gently patted the blood from the surface of her arm with a wet gauze. A laceration, six or seven inches long, angled from just below her elbow across the widest portion of her forearm, ending just above her wrist. Dried blood obscured the depth of the wound.

"Can you extend your fingers," Laurel said, "and hold them up when I try to press them down."

Andy lifted her arm and held her spread fingers out in front of Laurel while Laurel carefully tried to push them down.

"Good strength and all the tendons are intact. How about sensation?" She lightly touched the top of each of Andy's fingers. "Normal feeling? Any tingling, numbness, or decrease in sensation?"

"Feels normal," Andy said.

"Good." Laurel stepped back, a rush of relief erasing some of the tightness in her shoulders. "From the looks of the laceration, your flexors should be fine, but make a fist for me anyhow, slowly."

Andy did, and as her muscles flexed, fresh blood oozed from the knife wound.

"Okay, that's enough." Laurel stripped off her gloves and filled a basin with saline and dilute Betadine. "I'm going to flush it out, which is probably going to make it sting, but we not only need to clean it, I have to get a good look before I suture it."

"Are you sure you have to suture it?" Andy said. "Maybe a few butterflies?"

"That would take an entire kaleidoscope of butterflies," Laurel said, shaking her head. "You'll heal faster and scar better if we get it closed properly now."

"Okay, you're the boss."

Laurel smiled for just an instant, thinking how many times she'd heard that during the past night—a night that seemed a long time ago now. The wall clock read just after two a.m., so she'd probably gotten more sleep than she realized, considering she'd been worn out by seven and couldn't remember anything past eight. Somehow, she'd managed to fall asleep despite everything she thought she knew about herself getting turned upside down.

With a mental shake, she focused on Andy's arm. As she expected from the exam, the wound was shallow, and after she finished irrigating and injecting with local anesthetic, the suturing took only fifteen minutes. As she wrapped Andy's forearm, Reese rapped on the door and said, "Okay to come in?"

"Yes, we're just about done," Laurel said, taping the loose end of the gauze bandage.

"How's it looking?" Reese said.

"It's superficial, but a long laceration," Laurel said. "Infection is probably the only risk factor now. When was your last tetanus shot, Andy?"

"When I started at the academy," Andy said, "so that would be... eighteen months ago."

Laurel nodded. "Good. Any drug allergies?"

"No, nothing. No illnesses, no meds. Healthy as can be."

"I'd like to see you keep it that way," Reese said.

"I didn't want to risk him getting inside, Chief, and he sure looked like he was headed in that direction. There might've been civilians inside."

"There were," Reese said. "Smith just called me. It's definitely our B and E boy, so it's a good collar, Champlain. I just don't like my officers getting injured."

Andy straightened, her eyes brightening. "We got him? Excellent."

"So is she out of commission?" Reese asked Laurel.

"I think we can manage the pain with nonnarcotic pain meds, and if the plan is for her to be part of the contact tracing team, I think she can work," Laurel said. "I wouldn't put her back on the street for at least a week, assuming the wound heals as expected."

Andy sucked in a breath, her eyes on Reese.

"Let's go day-to-day, then. That means daily med checks, Champlain."

"Yes, Chief."

"All right. Finish up, and I'll give you two a ride."

Laurel cleaned up quickly, turned out the lights, and Reese locked up.

"Where to?" Reese said as they walked toward the Jeep.

Andy glanced at Laurel, hoping their night wasn't over. After the incredible time they'd spent together, she didn't want to just say good night like tonight wasn't the most life-changing experience she'd ever had. But she waited for Laurel to make the call.

Laurel didn't look at her. "You can drop me off first, Chief. I'm closest."

"Okay then."

Two minutes later, Reese pulled up to the small alleyway leading down to Laurel's cottage.

"I'll see you at the station in the morning, then," Laurel said, "when the team meets at six thirty."

"Right," Andy said flatly.

Laurel closed the Jeep door and headed down the alleyway, listening to the Jeep's engine fade away as she walked toward her cottage. Nothing that had happened in the last eight hours had been what she'd expected—not Andy, not sex like she'd never imagined it could be, not the sheer heart-stopping panic of Andy in danger, and certainly not the fear that lingered. What a fool she'd been to think light and casual would be simple. Or even possible.

❖

At the station, Reese checked with Smith that the prisoner had been processed and the appropriate public defender notified, called the mayor—who'd insisted upon being read in to even the slightest occurrence that might affect the tourist trade and thus business—with an update on the cruise ship situation, and arranged for the duty officer to pull in another team of officers to assist in the event evacuations became necessary. On her way home, she detoured to the pier to see for herself what was going on. Bri's cruiser angled across the entrance to the pier, the light bar circling. She'd set up a couple of portable barricades to prevent anyone from driving down.

"Any news?" Reese asked.

"Not yet," she said.

"Lopez and Lombardi will be available if things get busy."

"Great," Bri said, turning as headlights flashed from a vehicle turning off Bradford.

An EMT rig pulled up in front of the barricade, and Bri jogged over to move it aside. As the driver idled, waiting for passage down the pier, Reese leaned in the open window on the passenger side. Reverend Flynn Edwards, who also happened to be an EMT, was at the wheel with a new medic Reese didn't know in the passenger seat. The scattering of colorful beads in her dreads caught the reflection of light from Bri's cruiser and shimmered like small diamonds.

"What's the word?" Reese asked.

"Nita just called and said they have four to transfer. We've got another rig rolling right behind us."

"Okay—go ahead down." Reese's phone rang and she stepped back as Flynn pulled away. "Conlon."

Nita said, "We have a few to transfer, but the local EMTs ought to be able to handle it. I've already called ahead to the hospitals up Cape, so we're all set."

"You can do without a chopper?"

"Yes, most of the patients are sick but not critical and can be handled here," she said. "We've still got quite a few to evaluate, but the serious ones have been seen."

"Let me know if anything changes. I'll be home." To Bri, she said, "Let's keep this whole area clear and only let essential personnel through."

"You got it, Chief."

Satisfied the situation was in order, Reese climbed back into the Jeep. Five minutes later she pulled in behind the house and made her way as quietly as she could through the first floor and upstairs to the bedroom. The room was dark except for the moonlight providing just enough light for her to move around without risking waking Tory.

"Everything all right?" Tory asked from the bed.

So much for not waking her up. Reese stripped and left everything on a chair in case she needed to get dressed again before morning. "Everything's fine. Did you sleep at all?"

"Not really. Still restless. Just one of those nights."

"You want me to sleep downstairs?"

"No," Tory said, "I want you to sleep where you belong."

"Let me shower, and I'll be right there."

When Reese crawled under the sheets a few minutes later, naked and her skin cooling from the shower, Tory eased back against her. Reese curled around her and slipped an arm around her waist. "Bedtime story?"

Tory laughed. "I think just you being here will be enough to help me relax."

Reese kissed her neck. "You don't have to go to sleep, but you *do* need to close your eyes. Give you and everyone else some downtime."

Tory snuggled a little closer. "I can do that."

Reese lay awake, feeling the babies tumbling around in what felt like some kind of wrestling match. After a few minutes, Tory relaxed and her breathing deepened into sleep.

CHAPTER TWENTY-THREE

Laurel slept fitfully and woke a half hour before her alarm. After a quick shower, she pulled on light joggers, a short-sleeved, pale green V-neck workout shirt, and running shoes and left for her pre-coffee, fast-walk half-jog. She timed her route to arrive at Joe's at 6:05. As she crossed the stone patio fronting the coffee shop, Andy walked out the door with coffee cups in her hands. Laurel's heart somersaulted, an automatic response that had nothing to do with what her brain might tell her was the smart thing to do. Chemistry. Hormones. And something more, an undeniable rightness in her soul.

"Hi," Andy said quietly. "Thought you might need this."

"How'd you know I'd be here?" Laurel asked.

"I didn't." Andy shrugged, gave a wry half smile. "Just hoped."

Laurel blew out a breath and took the coffee. Most of the wrought iron tables scattered around the patio were still empty, and she motioned to one in the far corner with a view across the road to the harbor. "Want to sit down?"

"Just wait one second." Andy hurried back inside and thirty seconds later reemerged with two paper napkins, one cradling a croissant, and the other a cinnamon roll. She put the croissant in front of Laurel. "Spinach and cheese, right?"

Laurel frowned. "How did you know that?"

"I asked the barista. I think she was a little disappointed that you didn't come in, though. She said to say hi."

"Oh, I guess I really am a regular."

"I think it was more than that." Andy brushed a stray lock of hair from Laurel's cheek with a fingertip. "You're hard to forget."

"Andy," Laurel said gently. "I was hoping this wouldn't have to be hard."

Andy settled back in her chair and met Laurel's gaze. "Me too."

"I haven't had a serious relationship, a *real* relationship, for a very, very long time. You probably weren't even in high school."

"Let's not go there again, okay?"

Laurel nodded. "Fair enough. But that doesn't change the truth of it. I feel like I've been searching around my whole adult life trying to figure out what works for me. What I really want. And I always seem to be missing the mark."

Andy winced. "Are you going to tell me that last night was a mistake?"

"No, I can't do that because I don't feel that way. Last night was…" Laurel waved a hand, annoyed at herself for being so damn uncertain. The last thing she wanted to do was hurt Andy, and she knew she could. That scared her more than the thought of being hurt herself. "You were wonderful. The night was…magical. Well, most of it. And maybe that's part of the problem."

Andy picked up her coffee, took a sip, and steadied her temper. Whatever this was about, she couldn't blow it. She knew better than anyone, maybe, that some things couldn't be taken back. Some words, some wounds, lasted forever. The pain might get submerged, buried beneath denial and resistance and self-control, but the hurt and the anger and the betrayal never went away. She wouldn't let impatience or ego or frustrated desire become a wound between them.

She leaned forward, let Laurel see in her eyes what she felt. "Here's the thing, Laurel. We started out admitting that we had no rules, and you know why? Because there *aren't* any rules. Rules work for the middle ground, for imposing order, for making things with lots of moving parts safe and effective. Like laws for the greater good. But what happens between two people? That's different. Relationships aren't about rules—they're about *feelings*, about connections, about what makes you happy and satisfied. I've got a lot of those feelings where you're concerned. So how fast or slow we go doesn't make any difference. Age, experience, past mistakes, they might make you and me who we are today, but they don't make *us*. *We* make us. And I want to make us."

Laurel bit her lip. "You're the most amazing person I've ever met."

"I promise I'll keep trying to be that person, because I want to be that person for you."

"I was scared last night," Laurel said. "I was afraid that you'd be hurt, and you were. And you know what I felt besides terrified panic?"

Andy shook her head.

"Desperate. Like I was about to lose something that I would never be able to replace."

Andy sucked in a breath. "I'm a good cop, and I'm learning to be a better one. You don't have to worry about me."

"I believe you, and I will still worry."

"Are you saying that's a problem?"

Laurel shook her head. "No, I'm just saying there are a lot of things I have to think about. And I—I don't want to lose you while I do that."

"That's not going to happen."

"There's a lot going on right now, and it might be a good time to just slow down a little." Laurel grabbed Andy's hand. "In two months the season will end, and you'll be leaving. I probably will be too. I…I'm not sure I'll be able to just walk away as if this was all a summer fling."

Andy's spirit lifted. As if she hadn't thought of that already. If Laurel let her in, if Laurel felt what she felt, no way would she walk away. "If you need slow, then we'll do that," Andy said, "but just so you know, when I'm not busy working, I don't think about anything except you. And every time I'm around you, what I want is to be back in bed with you. And I'm not having a fling."

Laurel caught her breath. Andy was habit-forming, a good habit, the kind that made you feel alive, like the endorphin rush after an exciting, adrenaline-fueled emergency where you won against all odds. The look in her eyes, dark and a little smoldering, turned her on like a light suddenly switched on in a pitch-dark room. So bright and blinding, tears formed before the world snapped into brilliant focus. "You drive me crazy."

Andy grinned. "Good. Let me know when you can't take it anymore. I'll help you out with that."

And Laurel laughed. "God, you're sure of yourself."

"I'm sure of what I feel. I just need you to be."

"I want that too. I want…" Laurel stopped. "There's Kerri and Ralph."

She waved to them, and they came over, Ralph carrying a cardboard tray with three coffees.

"We heard this was the best coffee in town," Ralph said.

"At this end of town at least," Laurel said. "Were you up all night?"

"We wrapped up about four," Kerri said. "We're meeting Harley at the station."

Andy and Laurel rose to walk over with them. Nita pulled into the lot just as the four of them arrived. Harley came down the street from the opposite direction, walking with a young guy in cutoff jeans, a tank top, and flip-flops. They paused for a second on the sidewalk where he said something, his head bent close to Harley's. Harley laughed and jogged over to join them. "Do I see coffee?"

Ralph held out the cardboard container, and Harley took the one with an *H* penned on the side. "Thought you might need this."

"Thanks," she said reverently.

"New friend?" he asked in a teasing tone.

"Oh, they're staying at the same place I am. Just getting acquainted." Harley grinned and took her coffee. "If I get a minute for dinner, I might look them up."

"We should get started, but I can't promise anyone will get much of a break later today." Kerri led the way inside, and they trooped back to the conference room. Once everyone was seated, she said, "Quick recap—we saw forty new patients last night, all of whom have been tested. Those will go to the lab today, and we'll hopefully get results soon."

"What about the first batch we sent out?" Nita asked. "Shouldn't we have gotten those back by now?"

Kerri winced. "Should have, yes. I've been on the phone to Roger, who's been on the phone to the National Institute of Infectious Diseases, who've been pushing the labs to prioritize our processing. But gearing up the new protocols takes time. Hopefully, not much more."

"Let's hope not," Nita murmured. "If the case numbers escalate and we don't have test results, we'll have a hard time instituting any kind of tracing."

"Fortunately we have an excellent chance here for containment," Ralph put in. "Angela has been working magic with a computer analytic program that maps the location on the ship of the various individuals who have contracted the virus. We don't have complete results yet, but the preliminary evidence is irrefutable. This is an airborne contagion, with what is probably going to be a fairly high rate of transfer."

Andy said, "What does that mean in layman's terms?"

"It means that while the virus is infectious, transfer requires some reasonable degree of close physical proximity for more than just a few minutes. Touch transfer from contact with inanimate surfaces is possible, but not as likely."

"That actually sounds like we might have an easier time containing it," Laurel said. "Just passing someone on the street probably isn't enough exposure to contract it. Correct?"

"That's true," Ralph said. "And that's why we need to hit the restaurants we know passengers from the ship visited, as soon as possible. The patrons who were there are probably at much less risk than the people who actually work there. If they become infected, then they're going to put their close circle of relatives and acquaintances at risk. The key to contact tracing is to identify these infected individuals as quickly as possible, and then isolate the potentially infected contacts."

"At this point, we'll issue a national alert to all medical professionals," Kerri said, "who will then test and acquire the necessary contact information—if we begin to see general outbreaks elsewhere."

Laurel said, "So right now we need to canvass the establishments in town for any symptomatic individuals and get them tested as quickly as possible, right?"

"That's the plan. I'm emailing you all the updated list of establishments we need to screen," Kerri said, tapping into her phone. "We still have a chance to stop this here, but we have to move quickly."

❖

"Reese," Tory called down from upstairs.

Reese poured milk into her coffee and carried it out to the living room. "In the kitchen…"

"Can you come up here for a minute?"

"Sure."

Reese checked her watch. Twenty minutes before she needed to be at the station. She could stop by and say hi to Reggie, if she left in the next five minutes, and promise to come back to feed her lunch.

Tory, still in bed, said softly, "I need you to do something for me."

"What do you need?" Reese set her coffee on the nightstand and unlocked the top drawer where she kept her service weapon when at home. When Tory didn't answer, she glanced at Tory's face and, heart racing, said, "Is it time? I'll get the Jeep. I'll be right back."

"No," Tory said so emphatically Reese stopped midstep. "Call Nita and tell her I need her over here right now."

"I can have Flynn here with an EMT rig in five minutes, or I'll drive you to the hospital myself. I can get you to the ER in forty-five minutes."

Tory shook her head. "I don't think we have forty-five minutes. I'm not even sure we have twenty minutes. Get Nita. Tell her it's a silent labor and the baby's descended."

"Okay—right. I've got it," Reese said. "Don't move...just...don't do anything."

Tory smiled fleetingly, her face strained, and closed her eyes. "I think I've been in labor since last night. It's just—they're small and it's a second pregnancy, and things are moving fast. Really...fast."

"Fuck," Reese muttered under her breath and punched in Nita's number. "Nita? It's Reese. We need you at the house right now. Tory says the babies are coming. Yes. Here." She disconnected and called the paramedics. "This is Reese Conlon. Is Flynn...get ahold of her. Tell her we need a rig at my house in the next five minutes with whatever she needs for two newborns and my wife. Yes...thanks."

Reese shoved the phone in her pocket. "She's coming, Tor. What can I do?"

"Nita will know what to do. Just, stay right here."

Reese knelt on the floor next to the bed and took Tory's hand. She pressed Tory's hot fingers to her cheek. "I'm right here. I'll be right here every minute for as long as you need."

CHAPTER TWENTY-FOUR

Nita put her phone aside and looked across the small conference room table at Laurel. "When's the last time you delivered a baby?"

Laurel frowned. "Uh, about three months ago in the ER."

"Good." Nita rose, waving her up. "Because Tory is getting ready to deliver."

Laurel jumped up, nearly upsetting her chair, and Nita looked to Kerri. "Sorry, we're going to have to abandon you for a while."

"Go, go," Kerri said. "We can still put two teams on the street now. Call me whenever you get free."

"Andy," Nita said, "we need a fast ride. I can drive, but maybe you can get us there faster."

"Sure can," Andy said on the way to the door. "Meet me outside."

Andy stuck her head out into the hall as Nita and Laurel hurried toward the exit. Sergeant Pinera strolled around the corner on his way to shift change.

"Sarge," Andy called. "I need a squad. The chief's wife is having the babies."

Pinero stopped on the spot. "What, now?"

"Sounds like." Andy backed toward the exit.

"They want an escort to the hospital?"

"I dunno—Dr. Burgoyne says she needs to hurry."

"Yeah, sure. Take unit seven. It's gassed up and ready to go."

"Thanks, Sarge." Andy shoved out the door.

"And call me when you find out what's going on," he shouted after her.

Andy jogged across the lot and motioned Nita and Laurel to the cruiser. She jumped behind the wheel, flipped the back door locks, and Laurel and Nita climbed into the rear.

"So what's happening, exactly?" Andy said as she wheeled out of the station lot, lights flashing and sirens blaring.

"From the sound of it," Nita said, "Tory's been in labor all night, and things are moving along quickly now."

"Did anything unexpected happen?" Laurel asked, worried that they were looking at an obstetrical emergency during a home delivery with precious little backup. Someone with Tory's experience, with a second pregnancy and twins, wouldn't delay getting to the hospital in plenty of time.

"I didn't get much history," Nita replied, one hand braced on the door as Andy sped up. With not much in the way of early-morning traffic, Andy blasted through town. "Reese said Tory thought it was a silent labor. It happens sometimes, two or three percent of the time. That's why women end up in the emergency room ready to deliver without even realizing they're in labor. Tory had a precipitous delivery the first time, and this presentation was so much different, she may not have recognized what was happening."

"Well, that's scary," Laurel said. "What's the plan here? Are we going to try to slow the labor?"

"Doesn't sound like we can," Nita replied.

Andy announced, "Two minutes."

Nita said, "We're going to have three patients very quickly. Once the babies are delivered, you're in charge of them. I'll see to Tory."

Laurel blew out a breath. "How far along is she? Are we looking at immature lungs?"

"They're almost term." Nita ignored the tangle of knots in her stomach. Right now, Tory had to be just another patient, which meant Nita needed focus, clarity of thinking, and confidence. "They're probably two weeks shy of term."

"That's good, then," Laurel said. "Short of some other complication, they won't need intubation. What about Tory's last pregnancy? You said there were problems?"

"She had an abruption."

"That's all we need," Laurel muttered. Uncontrollable bleeding was one thing they weren't going to be able to manage during a home delivery.

"I've got an emergency vehicle coming up behind us," Andy said.

Laurel shifted, looked out the rear window. An EMT rig. "Backup."

"Have them set up inside with all their pediatric and adult resuscitation equipment ready to go," Nita said to Laurel as Andy swerved into the drive and stopped the cruiser in a shower of gravel.

"Got it," Laurel said.

Nita already had the door open, and Laurel jumped out after her.

"Good luck," Andy called, pulling the cruiser around to make way for the EMTs.

Laurel followed Nita up an outside set of wooden stairs to a side door. Nita tried the door, and it opened. She pushed through, Laurel on her heels, and crossed through the open-plan living area to a set of stairs.

"Reese, Tory," Nita called, hurrying up the stairs. "It's Nita."

"In the bedroom," Reese called back.

Laurel halted abruptly in the doorway as Nita charged across the room to Tory. Reese Conlon, kneeling by the head of the bed, was pale beneath her summer tan. Tory, her hair damp with sweat, lay propped upright beneath a sheet against several pillows, one hand in Reese's, the other gripping the sheet.

"Where are we, Tor?" Nita drew the sheets down below Tory's abdomen and placed her hand just below her belly button.

A commotion on the stairs signaled the arrival of the EMTs.

"Not too far away," Tory said, taking long breaths between each word. "I finally got some contractions worth the word." She smiled wryly, the muscles in her jaw tightening as she gasped.

"Breathe, baby," Reese murmured, "just breathe."

After a moment Tory let out a shaky breath. "Yeah. Under a minute."

"All right then," Nita said briskly, looking over her shoulder at the sound of rushing footsteps drawing closer. "Laurel, any minute now."

"I've got it," Laurel said, ignoring her pounding heart. She'd been here—or someplace like it—before. She recognized the adrenaline surge, and the sharp edges of nerves. Every image, every sound, crystallized.

A paramedic with wheat-blond hair, crystalline blue eyes, arched cheekbones, and a wide, strong jaw appeared in the doorway. "Hey—I'm Flynn Edwards. What can we do?"

"Laurel Winter," Laurel said. "Twins on the way. We'll set up for the babies over here. We'll need warmers in addition to the usual suction, ET tubes, pedi IV catheters, and nasal catheters ready."

"No problem. I'll handle that," Flynn said, turning to her partner. "Phil, you assist the birth."

"Right." The smaller woman, emergency kit in hand, hustled across the room to Nita's side. "Hi, I'm Phil Ramon. Let me know what you need."

"Let's get an IV into her, and I need gloves."

Phil passed her a set of sterile gloves and set about putting an IV catheter into Tory's left arm. Nita tore the package open and pulled on the sterile gloves. Leaning over the bed, she parted Tory's thighs and checked the baby's position.

"I've got a head," she said calmly. "Presentation's normal. Phil, pass me a sterile pad."

Nita laid the pad below the point the baby's face would emerge. "Next contraction, go ahead and push, Tor."

A few seconds later, Tory bore down, her rasping pants rough and loud in the quiet room.

Nita gently cradled the head in her palm and slid her finger upward, checking around the neck, and felt the cord looped around the neck.

"We've got a nuchal cord," she said quietly to Phil. "Grab two hemostats and scissors and be ready to pass them to me if I have to cut it free."

Phil rummaged in the instrument pack. Nita caught the cord around her finger, tugged on it, and felt the length of it loosen. Teasing it free, she maneuvered it over the baby's head. "Cord's clear."

"I have to push," Tory gasped.

With her other hand, Nita supported the shoulder, applied gentle traction along the axis of the baby's neck to protect the delicate nerves in the shoulders, and said, "Go ahead, Tor, this one's on its way."

Seconds later, the other shoulder eased free and the baby delivered into Nita's hands. A second later it took its first breath and let out a small but hearty cry.

"Clamp the cord and cut it, Phil," Nita said calmly, "five inches from the belly button. Yes, right there. Good."

With the cord cut and clamped, Nita lifted the baby and held it up for Reese and Tory to see. "Here's your son, you two." And then over her shoulder, "Laurel?"

"Right here," Laurel said from beside Nita, holding out a warm receiving pad. Nita gently deposited the baby into Laurel's hands and turned back to Tory. "All right, Tory, one to go."

"Can you feel the other one?" Tory said, her voice weak but steady. "I'm not feeling much in the way of contractions now."

"Not yet."

"Bleeding?" Tory muttered.

"Not much bleeding. You're doing great. Let me do the doctoring for now—you just work on the mother part for a minute."

Gently, Nita palpated Tory's abdomen, felt the uterine contractions, not as strong as she would've liked. They had one more baby to deliver, and the uterus, like any other muscle in the body, was flagging.

"Let's give her a dose of oxytocin. Phil, do you have it?"

"Yes," Phil said, pulling a vial out of her kit, drawing up the medication, and injecting it into the IV line.

A minute later, the uterus contracted vigorously, and Nita said, "Here we go. Round two."

This time, the baby took its time making its way into the world, but three minutes later, the head and shoulders appeared, and with just the slightest bit of traction, she slipped out. The newborn instantly announced her presence with a loud and irritated wail.

"Laughing," Nita announced. "This one's got attitude."

After the cord was cut and the baby passed off, Nita gently massaged Tory's uterus through her abdomen, coaxing the muscle to contract so the bleeding would slow. "All right, now, let's get these placentas delivered."

Tory, her voice stronger now, called, "How are they?"

Laurel reported from across the room, "One minute Apgars are nine and ten. They're great."

Tory closed her eyes. "Good."

"You did *great*, baby," Reese said, resting her forehead against Tory's. "I feel like I just ran an ultramarathon, and you did all the work. I love you. They're gorgeous."

"Go see them for me," Tory said. "Make sure everything's all right."

Reese glanced at Nita. "She's all right?"

"She's doing great," Nita said. "Go ahead."

Reese got up from her knees, her legs shaking. She'd never been as terrified and exulted all at the same time in her life. She crossed carefully to the other side of the room and peered down at the newborns, swaddled in warm blankets so only their faces were showing. Red, wrinkled, absolutely amazingly beautiful faces.

"Which is which?" she said.

"This one's your son," Laurel said, touching the one on the left, "and this one's your daughter. Heart and lungs sound perfect. The physical exams are normal."

"Okay then. So, yeah." Reese grinned what she figured was a goofy grin, but she didn't have any words to express the wonder. "You'll look after them, right? Because I want to get back to Tory."

"Of course," Laurel said, understanding in that moment that as much as Reese Conlon loved the babies, she adored her wife. "I'll ride with them all the way in."

Reese eased onto the bed next to Tory and slid an arm around her shoulder. "They're beautiful—you did a great job."

"Everything checks out?" Tory said. "Heart and lungs and neuro?"

"Laurel says they're perfect, and they sound pretty damn healthy to me."

"The placenta's delivering," Nita said. "We're almost done."

This was the last tricky part. If all of the placenta didn't expel, if a fragment remained behind, Tory would continue to bleed, perhaps copiously. Carefully, Nita caught the expelled placentas, saw the two cords, carefully checked all the surfaces and edges to make sure that no fragments had been left behind, and passed it over to Phil. "Bag this and make sure it goes with you. The pathologist will need to take a look at it."

"I've got it," Phil said.

"Okay then, let's get everybody ready to go," Nita said, straightening for the first time in what felt like a week. Every muscle in her body hurt, the aftereffects of the tension that had held her frozen in one place while every atom had been focused on Tory and the babies. She took a deep breath. "Do we have two ambulances?"

"Right outside," Flynn said. "We're ready to transport when you are."

Nita leaned over Tory. "I'm going with you. Laurel will ride with the babies."

"Are you sure?" Tory said. "What if there's a problem?"

"Flynn's the best, and Laurel will be there too," Nita said. "If there's any problem at all en route, they'll let us know, but the worst is over."

"What if..." Tory swallowed. "We have to monitor them for infection. We still don't know if I'm—"

"We'll go over all that with the peds and infectious disease people when we get there." Nita smiled. "They're perfect. What are we calling them?"

"We almost had it narrowed down," Reese said, "but not quite." She glanced at Tory. "Go ahead, baby. You choose."

Tory reached for Reese's hand and said, "Benjamin and Sarah."

CHAPTER TWENTY-FIVE

Laurel and Nita grabbed a ride back to Provincetown with Flynn and Phil. No one had much to say after the initial euphoria of handling a challenging case and coming out on top had worn off. This time the stakes had been personal for all of them. Back at her cottage, Laurel took a few minutes to grab a quick shower, a change of clothes, and a slice of cold pizza. She was used to going without much sleep, and she figured she had a solid twelve hours still left in her, but she needed fuel. She'd burned up a lot more than physical calories over the course of the morning. The emotional turmoil of any difficult case always left her feeling drained, but this was one of those special circumstances where the personal investment went far beyond professional responsibility. She doubted she'd ever forget a minute of being in that room and hearing Nita's cool, steady voice, or Reese's soothing words of encouragement, or Tory's incredible strength. And the babies. She smiled thinking of their dramatic entrance and the way Tory, wrapped in Reese's embrace, had held them for a minute before they readied for transport. She'd watched Tory glowing with contentment, but Reese had been the one who captivated her. Reese covered Tory's hand with hers as Tory held the babies, but her gaze never left Tory's face. Her love was so raw and so intense, Laurel had to look away.

On the ride back in the silent ambulance, she'd thought about love. And she'd thought about what she wanted. What she wanted to give, and what she wanted to have.

As soon as Laurel finished the hasty lunch, she texted Andy.
I'm back. Where are you?
Andy: *West End of town. With Harley. Everyone OK?*

Babies and Mom doing great
Andy: *Alright!*
Where are you going next - will meet you
Andy: *Cottage Inn and Grill*
cu there

When she left to walk into town, anticipation rose like a brisk morning breeze off the ocean, promising a bright new day and untold adventures. Time in its practical sense meant nothing. It might've been dawn or dusk or midnight, and she still would've felt the same excitement. She was about to see Andy.

She could think about it, analyze it, categorize it, and attempt to explain why or why not, but she couldn't deny what she felt. Exhilaration, arousal, joy.

Harley and Andy walked out of the Cottage Grill just as Laurel arrived. She waited for them on the sidewalk as they hurried down the flagstone path. Andy looked trim and tight in her crisp uniform, and Laurel would've taken a moment to enjoy the image even if she hadn't seen the intoxicating fire in Andy's eyes as Andy's gaze met hers. The anticipation that had begun when Laurel left her cottage flared into something far more powerful, and she looked away. She had hours of work ahead, and somehow she was going to have to spend those hours with Andy without immolating from the need to touch her.

"Hi," Andy said, drawing closer. "How'd everything go with the chief's family?"

"Amazing. Not what I'd want to do every day, but still... incredible," Laurel said. "How's it going with the screening?"

Harley said, "Slow. Some of the owners are reluctant to provide us info on their staff, and trying to explain why it's important *and* that at this point it's just a precaution takes some doing."

"Have you found anyone who might be symptomatic?" Laurel said as they walked east to their next destination.

"Two possibles," Andy said. "A bartender at one of the hotels called in sick with what he thought might be food poisoning, and a hostess at the Manor House, complaining of a summer cold."

"They'll need to be tested," Laurel said. "Do you want me to do that?"

Harley said, "We notified Kerri, and her team will follow up there and get further points of contact. We're the first line, and then as the pyramid grows—if it grows—they'll take the next level."

"Okay. I'll stick with you, then?"

Harley paused, brought up a list on her tablet, and said, "I'm texting you the next four locations. We might as well split up and cover more ground. Anyone you can't reach goes on the follow-up list. Anyone you can't clear or who might be potentially infected gets kicked up to Kerri and Ralph."

"All right," Laurel said after a few seconds. "I've got it." She glanced at Andy. "Talk to you later."

"I'll find you."

As she turned toward the street, the red Porsche pulled up alongside them. Winchester got out, looking fresh and energetic with her flawless makeup and thousand-dollar outfit that was supposed to look summer-casual—and might have, in the Hamptons. She left the Porsche idling as she walked over to them. "How's the contact tracing going? How many people do you need to reach? Any symptomatic?"

Harley held out her hand. "Gillian McIntyre. We didn't get formally introduced out on the pier."

"You're…?"

"Oh, CDC. Just one of the grunts."

Winchester's eyebrow arched up. "I don't think you'd be here if that was true."

"There's always grunt work to be done." Harley grinned and something in Winchester's eyes sparked.

"Well, Dr. McIntyre, is it? Can I have a statement for the record? How many establishments will you be visiting—how far has the infection already spread? Do you plan on setting up a mobile testing site?"

"Those are rather informed questions," Harley said conversationally. "You must have very good researchers at your paper."

Winchester's cool smile and piercing gaze never changed. "I'm a reporter. Research is part of my job."

"I'll bet. Well, as we aren't keeping it a secret that we are contact tracing, I can tell you that it's going fine. Anything further than that, you'll need an official statement from Dr. Sanchez." Harley looked at the chronometer on her wrist. "And I believe a statement will be forthcoming to the national health agencies within the hour. So I'm sure you'll get all the information you're interested in from that."

Winchester glanced at Andy. "I take it you're detached to the CDC team. Any news through channels when the cruise ship will be allowed to depart?"

Andy smiled. "My chief would be the one to talk to about that."

Winchester scowled. "All right, but off the record, how serious is this situation? Also, off the record, the governor's cousin is on board the ship. Naturally, the information blackout is a problem, and anything we can provide in the way of updates would be much appreciated at higher levels."

"I can give you this, for the record," Harley said.

"Anything you can provide would be much appreciated." Winchester's smile warmed a few degrees, perhaps genuinely. "*Personally* appreciated."

Harley shrugged. "You'll get this in an hour from a national bulletin from the Institutes of Health. We're monitoring the situation here closely, and thus far feel containment is likely. The president has been advised, and authorities are being alerted at ports of entry, including airports, of the possibility of screening incoming passengers."

"That is not much information."

"It's what I've got. Have a nice day."

"Thanks." Winchester strode to her car, her phone to her ear, and drove off.

"Think that will satisfy her?" Laurel asked as they resumed walking.

"Oh, I doubt it," Harley said. "But it never hurts to smooth things over with the press. Now that we're openly contact tracing, there's no reason not to admit it. Everyone we've talked to knows what we're doing and is probably already sharing that information. Plus now, Winchester can get a few minutes' jump on the television stations with an update to their digital platforms." She shrugged. "Again, nothing that won't be public in less than an hour."

"And," Andy said with just a hint of a smirk, "you've made a friend."

Harley grinned. "That never hurts either."

Laurel left them to head up to Bradford to her first destination.

The afternoon progressed at a slow pace as she recited the same explanations over and over again in each establishment, talking to staff, when present, and calling others when the business owners were cooperative and provided their contact information. At six, she called Kerri to update her. "I've gone through my list, and I still have fifteen people from various places to track down. Two more possibles."

"Good, who are they?"

Laurel gave her the information. "Should I try to reach the others tonight?"

"Why don't you grab Andy and get some dinner, and after that, make a circuit of the places where you've missed some of the staff who weren't on duty yet. Now that we know how many we have to track, I've got more tracers from the county health offices coming in tonight. Harley will take them, and we'll close up the rest of the gaps tomorrow."

"How's it looking?" Laurel said.

"About as good as we could hope. I just got the first batch of tests back—finally—and the transmission rate thus far looks manageable—more than seasonal influenza, but if we can prevent community spread, we can stop it."

"How long do you think it will take to complete all the follow-ups?"

"Another week possibly if we don't see further signs of the outbreak escalating. Then retesting to be sure."

"So it's working." Laurel let out a breath. "Thank goodness Tory called you as soon as we saw what was happening on the ship."

"That and the fact that President Powell and the National Institutes of Health put together a national response plan. If we do see multiple points of outbreak, we'll be ready. This could all be over in a month."

Laurel said, "I'll call Andy and let her know the plan."

"Good. Thanks," Kerri said.

"Hey," Laurel said when Andy answered. "I just talked to Kerri. She wants us to hit some of the establishments after dinner to see if we can catch the night staff that we missed during the day."

"Sounds good. I'm starving. How do you feel about grabbing something and eating out on the pier?"

"Sure. Meet you at Town Hall?"

"Yeah. Harley is going to meet up with Kerri and Ralph. So just you and me."

Laurel flushed at the husky invitation in Andy's voice. "That sounds perfect."

CHAPTER TWENTY-SIX

When Tory woke in the hospital, the late afternoon sun slanted into the room, the golden light reflecting the inner glow of total contentment that suffused her. She turned her head and smiled, the happiness expanding into an uncontainable fusion of joy and wonder. Reese slept in a recliner next to the bed, her head cocked at what had to be an uncomfortable angle, but she somehow managed to look breathtaking even in sleep.

"Hey," Tory called softly.

Reese's eyes flew open and she sat upright, all vestiges of somnolence gone. Her gaze flicked around the room quickly, as if assessing danger, and then settled on Tory's face. The wariness dissolved into the look Tory counted on seeing, day after day. One of tenderness and desire.

"Sorry," Reese said, her voice just the slightest bit rusty. "Fell asleep there."

"It's all right, you know, for you to take a break," Tory said. "You're not on guard duty."

Reese's dark brows winged up over those incredibly piercing blue eyes, the eyes Tory loved beyond all others.

"Oh, really?" Reese said.

"All right, yes, you are here to make sure we're all all right. And we are. In fact, according to my internal clock, the babies should be showing up any minute for the next round."

Reese grinned. "They're hungry little items, aren't they."

"Hungry is healthy, so I can't complain. Plus, I'm more than happy to offload all the nutrition they're interested in."

"I wish there was some way I could help out."

"Right now all they really want is to be warm, dry, and fed."

Reese made a face. "I could handle the dry part okay. The other… all yours."

Tory laughed and held out a hand. "Believe me, you provide everything that's necessary."

Reese sat on the edge of the bed and took Tory's hand. "Whatever you need, whenever you need it. You just say."

Tory tugged her down and kissed her. "I know. And I will."

Tory's phone vibrated on the tray table next to the bed, and Reese picked it up and handed it to her.

Tory glanced at it. "Kerri. I should probably take this."

"You're not really supposed to be working," Reese said without any conviction whatsoever. As if anything was going to get in the way of Tory doing what she felt needed to be done. Now that the worst seemed to be over, at least in terms of terror and pain, Reese was content to let Tory decide what Tory could handle.

"This is Tory…hi, Kerri." She listened a moment and, after a few seconds, pulled her lower lip between her teeth and nodded silently. Not Tory's usual reaction to any kind of crisis.

Instantly alert, Reese began marshaling her forces for whatever the upcoming battle might be.

"I understand," Tory said. "Yes, of course. Absolutely. How is everything there?" Tory nodded a few more times and finally said, "Thanks. I appreciate it. More than you know."

She set the phone aside, her expression so vulnerable, and so unusual, Reese's spine tingled. "*What? What is it?*"

"My viral test came back negative. I'm not infected. The babies should be clear."

Reese hadn't realized until that instant how tightly the fear had held her in its grip. Her muscles turned to soup, and she dropped her head, shuddering. Tory tugged on her hand, and Reese leaned her head to Tory's breast.

"It's all right, baby," Tory murmured, stroking the back of her neck. She kissed Reese's cheek, the corner of her mouth, and lifted her head to kiss her mouth. "I'm all right. We are all all right."

Reese kept her eyes closed for a few more seconds until she

gathered the reins of her control. "I know." She kissed Tory's throat and straightened as the door behind them opened.

"Here we are," announced a cheery voice, and two nurses trundled in, pushing bassinets. Reese got out of the way as the nurses propelled the infants over to the bedside.

A middle-aged matronly nurse in navy scrubs with smiling brown eyes said, "Ben is still a little sleepy."

"But," the younger of the two with a colorful dragon tattoo on her left forearm and a ring through her right eyebrow added, "Sarah is awake and ready."

Tory laughed. "Something tells me that's going to be a pattern."

"It's funny, isn't it," the older nurse said as the younger one slid Sarah into Tory's arms, "how babies seem to declare their personalities right from the start."

"Well, these two have plenty of that," Tory said, settling Sarah down for her feeding.

The older nurse lifted Ben out of his bassinet and said to Reese, "You want to hold this one while your wife does the first round?"

"Sure," Reese said, gathering him up and sliding onto the bed next to Tory. "I might as well be good for something."

The nurse gave Reese a cheeky smirk. "Oh, I bet you're probably good for a thing or two."

Reese cocked a brow and grinned.

Tory laughed.

❖

At a little before midnight, Andy and Laurel left the Boatslip, the last place on their list.

"I wonder how many more we'll have to check out tomorrow," Andy said as they walked east toward the center of town.

"There's got to be fewer than we had today," Laurel said, "since we started with the contact list for more than a hundred people, and now, hopefully, we're looking at a tenth of that."

"We're going to be at it for a while, though," Andy said, "until we don't turn up any more with symptoms."

"The testing will help, now that the lab is cranking the results out faster." Laurel pressed closer to Andy as a clutch of scantily clad men tumbled out onto the street from a bar. Laurel smiled as they passed by in a boisterous cloud of alcohol and laughter. "Kerri is bringing in teams from the local public health groups, so we might be back to our regular scheduled programming before long."

"I won't mind that," Andy said, "except for the part where I won't be working with you every day."

"I know," Laurel said. "It's work, but it's kind of nice too."

The night was warm and the streets crowded, like every other summer night, but Andy was off duty, and the lightness in her chest, the happiness that made the ordinary suddenly extraordinary, filled her. On impulse, she grabbed Laurel's hand. "My place is just up there, past the hardware store sign. You want to come down? I've got cold beer and a great view of the harbor."

"I do," Laurel said without an instant's hesitation.

Andy swung their joined hands. "Good."

A few minutes later, she led Laurel down a narrow walkway between two storefronts to the small building on the edge of the beach. After unlocking her door, she pushed it wide and held it to let Laurel in first. Across from the entrance, the sliding glass doors to her small, private deck let in a view of the dark harbor shimmering with reflections of the moonlight on the water.

"This is a great place," Laurel said.

"Not as cozy as yours, but the view can't be beat." Andy resisted the urge to kiss her right then and there. Going slow was getting harder by the minute. She'd thought it would be easier—why, exactly, she couldn't remember now. Now all she could remember was the softness of Laurel's skin and the heat of her touch and the achingly sweet sound of her pleasure. Slow was pretty much a fantasy now. "Uh, right. Why don't you go ahead out onto the deck. Beer good? Or I've got soda, I think."

"Oh, beer's great."

Andy grabbed the drinks and hurried outside. Laurel leaned against the railing, facing the harbor with her head tilted back just a little and her eyes nearly closed. An ocean breeze lifted her hair from her shoulders, the way it had the first evening when Andy'd seen her standing against the rail out on the deck of the bar, surrounded by women who instantly faded from Andy's awareness. Laurel had been the only one she could see.

"Here you go." Andy handed Laurel the beer and slid an arm around Laurel's waist. Like that first evening, she'd been hyperaware of Laurel for hours all day, walking through town, talking with restaurant and bed-and-breakfast staff, reviewing and comparing notes. Working with her. Just being near her, always sensitive to her scent, the lilt in her voice, the little frown she got between her eyebrows when she was thinking. The low-level arousal that had simmered in the pit of her stomach for the better part of the day flared to life. Waiting was no longer an option.

Andy pulled Laurel a little closer and kissed her neck. "I don't know if I've mentioned it, but you smell great."

Laurel shivered. Andy's lips were warm, somehow warmer than the night air. She turned, placed her bottle on the flat surface of the railing, and draped her arms around Andy's neck. Their bodies almost but not quite touched. "I think it's sunscreen."

Andy grinned. "You should wear it year-round."

"Andy," Laurel said, "I need to say something."

Andy swallowed. "So do I."

"You first."

Wait.

Too late.

Andy framed Laurel's face and kissed her. The kiss was slow, but far from gentle, edged with hunger and maybe a little impatience.

"I just wanted to say that first," Andy said when she drew away, her voice low and husky.

"I like the message." Laurel's breath was coming fast, and she'd forgotten what she wanted to say. She'd known when they'd arrived. Known right up to the moment Andy's lips skimmed her neck. Then whatever had seemed so important just…didn't any longer. The thrill in her body, the lift in her heart—that mattered. Andy mattered.

"There's quite a bit more to the story," Andy said, clasping Laurel's waist just above the flare of her hipbones, her thumbs stroking up and down Laurel's abdomen.

Laurel's thighs quivered as desire pooled low down in her depths. She took a deep breath. "I realized something last night, this morning, maybe even before that, and I don't know why it took me so long to admit it." Laurel raked a hand through her hair. "God, I'm not making any sense."

"Laurel," Andy said, her palm sweeping up to Laurel's middle and almost but not quite reaching her breasts before she stopped. "We might have to talk later. I really need you."

"That's what I wanted to say," Laurel said, the words sounding strained as she pushed them past the wanting that almost closed her throat. "I want you. I want to tell you things—I *have* told you more than anyone, and I trust you. I want you touching me. And I *don't* want that to end when the season does. I don't want a fling."

"Your beer's going to get warm," Andy said, "but I've got more in the refrigerator. Come inside with me now. Please."

Laurel was already moving, Andy's arm around her waist, half pulling, half guiding her back through the sliding glass doors, across the room, and through a doorway into a bedroom. The bed lay misted in moonlight, a signpost in the night, waiting. They'd barely reached it before Andy tugged her shirt out of her pants, fingers tugging at the buttons.

"Let me," Laurel gasped, frantically parting the rest of the material. Andy's hands flew to her waistband and stripped her clothes down her thighs.

"Lie down," Andy said, already tugging at her running shoes.

Laurel fell back, twisting out of her shirt and bra, somehow lifting her legs at the same time as Andy got her naked. Then Andy was above her, still clothed, her thigh between Laurel's, her hands and her mouth everywhere, stroking, kneading, teasing, until Laurel bucked and writhed and came so close to exploding she felt insane with need.

"Andy," Laurel said, "please. Please. I need you to make me come. Please."

With a sound something like a growl, Andy rolled away and onto her knees, bracing herself over Laurel's body on her extended arm, her eyes on Laurel's, her hand gliding down Laurel's abdomen and between her thighs.

"Oh God." Starbursts detonated behind Laurel's eyes. Her hips thrust, open and demanding. "Now, now, now."

Andy kissed her, that hard, commanding, demanding rush of

mouth and tongue, and filled her. Laurel arched, the orgasm an eruption of twisting heat rising, consuming, driving the breath from her body. She clutched at Andy, moaning, "Don't stop, don't stop, don't stop," until her breath left her.

Heart thundering in her chest, Andy stilled, every muscle rigid, her heart brimming with wonder. Gently, she kissed Laurel again. "You're incredible."

"Mm. My line." Laurel's arms came around Andy, pulling her down. "Why aren't you naked?"

"I've been busy," Andy gasped, still a little breathless.

Laurel laughed weakly. "Take your clothes off. As soon as I can move again, I plan to be busy too."

"There's something you need to know," Andy said, cradling Laurel close.

"Is it good?"

"Better than that," Andy said, stroking Laurel's hair as Laurel insistently opened her pants and slid a hand underneath. Andy tensed. "Laurel, baby, wait...I..." She tensed as Laurel's fingers found her. "Oh, damn. Don't wait."

"I'm not going to." Laurel cupped her, squeezed and stroked and teased, and in a few seconds Andy groaned, coming fast and hard. Laurel kept her hand between Andy's legs as she kissed her throat. "I plan on being a lot busier in a few more minutes."

Muscles still trembling, Andy roused herself enough to shed the rest of her clothes and dragged the sheet up to their hips. "I never wanted a fling. From the first time I saw you out on the deck that afternoon, I wanted something more. I didn't know what it was then, but I do now."

"What?" Laurel asked. "What do you want?"

"I want you and everything that means—your smile when I walk in the room, your face in the morning when I open my eyes, your hands on me when I need to be touched. I want to be the only one to please you. I want your secrets, and I want to give you mine. I want *us*. Not for the summer, not for the season, but for the future. Wherever you go, I want to go with you."

"I want you," Laurel said. "I want us. Wherever, whenever, without end. Wherever you go, I'll go."

"We'll decide what comes next when the summer is over." Andy tugged Laurel on top of her, and Laurel cradled her face against Andy's throat. Their hearts slowed and steadied, beating in time, together. "For now, we're here, we're together, and we've got all the time we need."

"There's one more thing I need to say," Laurel whispered. "I love you."

"Say that again," Andy murmured.

"I love you."

"I love you back."

EPILOGUE

Labor Day

"Hi, Andy," Gladys said as Andy came in at the end of her shift. "Chief wants to see you."

"Okay," Andy called on her way back to the chief's office. Her door was partly open as usual, and Andy rapped on it as she stuck her head in. "Hey, Chief, you wanted to see me?"

"Come on in and close the door," Reese said.

Andy slipped in, closed the door behind her, and strode toward the desk. The three-day holiday weekend had been hectic, the last gasp of the summer season before things abruptly changed, temperature-wise and with the disappearance of the tourist population. She had a feeling she knew what was coming—the exit interview—and although she expected it, a faint ache settled in her midsection. She'd gotten used to being part of this team, this town, and more than that, she and Laurel seemed to fit here, each in their own way. She squared her shoulders.

Reese raised an eyebrow at her posture and waved her toward the chair. "Sit, Champlain. Relax."

Andy sat, more relaxed than she'd been in the same position a few months before, but she'd probably never be completely relaxed in any situation where she wasn't sure what was coming next. Still, the wary need to protect herself was gone, and that felt just fine. She knew why too. This place, this job, had been good for her, and even more than that, Laurel was good for her. Pretty much all the good things in her life had happened that summer.

"So, next week we'll see a pretty big change around here," Reese said. "The population will drop by eighty percent, and by Columbus Day, even further than that. Things can get pretty cold and quiet here in the winter."

"I grew up on the Jersey Shore, Chief, and I know what you mean. During the summer, it's nonstop action. Then September hits, the tourists leave, the summer people with seasonal homes head back to the cities, and only the year-rounders remain. Fall and winter it's dark, early nights, and cold mornings."

Reese laughed. "You got that right. Still, we've got a pretty fair population here year-round, and crime still happens. We can always use good officers. How do you feel about staying on?"

Andy blinked. "Staying on—until winter?"

"No, not winter, permanently. I've got an opening, and I want you to fill it."

"Jeez, yes, I mean, I'm honored…" Andy hesitated. "Except…"

"Except?"

"I have to talk to Laurel. I'm not sure she'll want to stay, and I'm not staying without her."

"Ah, I understand. Right. You should talk to her."

"Can I let you know tonight?" Andy asked.

Reese smiled. "Tomorrow would be fine."

"All right. Thanks, Chief. I…uh…working here has been the best thing I've ever experienced. I know I'm lucky."

"You earned it, so no thanks are necessary."

As soon as Andy signed out, she walked outside and called Laurel. "Where are you?"

"At the clinic, listen—"

"I have to talk to you. It's really important."

"Listen, I need to talk to you too," Laurel said in a rush.

Andy's chest squeezed tight. They'd had no positive viral tests come back for over two weeks, but she still worried that somehow Laurel would be unknowingly exposed at the clinic. "Is everything all right? Are you okay?"

"Yes, I'm great. At least…" Laurel hesitated. "I think so. Maybe."

"What's going on, then?" Andy said, walking toward the center of town and the apartment she'd need to vacate at the end of the month. "Can you tell me now?"

"If this doesn't work, it's fine," Laurel said, her words still rushed, "and we can talk about some other options, but Nita and Tory offered me a full-time position here, but if you—"

"The chief just offered me the same thing."

Laurel laughed. "Really? What did you say?"

"I said yes, if it was all right with you. What did you say?"

"I said yes, if it was all right with you."

"I guess we're going to have to find someplace permanent to live, then." As soon as Andy got the words out, she could have slapped herself in the head. "Okay—that's not how I meant to say that."

"You're right, though." Laurel's tone had taken on the low husky edge that always turned Andy on in a heartbeat. "We *are* going to need a bigger place—for the two of us."

"You good with that?"

"I'm great with that."

Andy let out a long breath. "You know something? I love you."

"I love you back."

❖

Reese eased the back door open and slipped into the living room, hoping not to wake the babies if they were by some miracle asleep.

Tory stood at the breakfast bar, Reggie perched on her hip, eating a piece of toast. She smiled as Reese practically tiptoed across the room. "You're not supposed to be here until lunchtime."

"I just wanted to sneak home for a minute. Are they"—she pointed to the ceiling and whispered—"asleep?"

"They are. And *we* are having a snack." Tory bounced Reggie on her hip. "Aren't we, baby?"

Reggie held out her toast and peanut butter to Reese. "Bite?"

Reese leaned down, took a bite, and made *mm, good* sounds. "Any more of that around?"

"Mm-hmm." Tory pointed to a loaf of bread, a jar of peanut butter, and the toaster with her own toast before taking another bite.

Laughing, Reese set about making her toast.

"Did you talk to Andy?" Tory asked.

"Yeah. Did you and Nita talk to Laurel?"

"We did."

Reese leaned against the counter, waiting for the toaster to finish. "So we ought to have new hires."

"I suspect so."

Tory set Reggie down and murmured, "Why don't you play Bugs and Buttons until Grandmom comes."

"'K." Reggie made a beeline for the couch where her tablet rested on the seat.

Tory said, "Kate called to ask when she was going to start babysitting the whole pack."

"What did you tell her?" Reese asked.

Tory threaded her arms around Reese's waist and leaned against her. "That I'm ready, and they are too, I think. They're taking to the bottle just fine."

"What do you hear from Kerri?"

"We videoconferenced this morning. They're still putting out a few fires here and there, but they haven't had any significant outbreaks, and we've been clear here for three weeks. All the repeat tests have come back negative." Tory cupped Reese's cheek. "I won't be at risk if I go back to work."

Reese pulled Tory closer and kissed her again. "I'm fine with whatever you want. After this summer, a little normal will suit me fine."

"I'm ready for lots of ordinary too," Tory whispered. "We've earned a nice quiet off-season."

"Not sure I'd go that far." Reese laughed. "Something tells me that life will never be quiet again."

Tory rested her cheek against Reese's shoulder and closed her eyes. "That's okay too. We've got everything we need, no matter what the future brings."

About the Author

Radclyffe has written over sixty romance and romantic intrigue novels as well as a paranormal romance series, The Midnight Hunters, as L.L. Raand.

She is a three-time Lambda Literary Award winner in romance and erotica and received the Dr. James Duggins Outstanding Mid-Career Novelist Award by the Lambda Literary Foundation. A member of the Saints and Sinners Literary Hall of Fame, she is also an RWA/FF&P Prism Award winner for *Secrets in the Stone*, an RWA FTHRW Lories and RWA HODRW winner for *Firestorm*, an RWA Bean Pot winner for *Crossroads*, an RWA Laurel Wreath winner for *Blood Hunt*, and a Book Buyers Best award winner for *Price of Honor* and *Secret Hearts*. She is also a featured author in the 2015 documentary film *Love Between the Covers*, from Blueberry Hill Productions. In 2019 she was recognized as a "Trailblazer of Romance" by the Romance Writers of America.

In 2004 she founded Bold Strokes Books, one of the world's largest independent LGBTQ publishing companies, and is the current president and publisher.

Find her at facebook.com/Radclyffe.BSB, follow her on Twitter @RadclyffeBSB, and visit her website at Radfic.com.

Books Available From Bold Strokes Books

Aurora by Emma L McGeown. After a traumatic accident, Elena Ricci is stricken with amnesia, leaving her with no recollection of the last eight years, including her wife and son. (978-1-63555-824-1)

Avenging Avery by Sheri Lewis Wohl. Revenge against a vengeful vampire unites Isa Meyer and Jeni Denton, but it's love that heals them. (978-1-63555-622-3)

Bulletproof by Maggie Cummings. For Dylan Prescott and Briana Logan, the complicated NYC criminal justice system doesn't leave room for love, but where the heart is concerned, no one is bulletproof. (978-1-63555-771-8)

Her Lady to Love by Jane Walsh. A shy wallflower joins forces with the most popular woman in Regency London on a quest to catch a husband, only to discover a wild passion for each other that far eclipses their interest for the Marriage Mart. (978-1-63555-809-8)

No Regrets by Joy Argento. For Jodi and Beth, the possibility of losing their future will force them to decide what is really important. (978-1-63555-751-0)

The Holiday Treatment by Elle Spencer. Who doesn't want a gay Christmas movie? Holly Hudson asks herself that question and discovers that happy endings aren't only for the movies. (978-1-63555-660-5)

Too Good to be True by Leigh Hays. Can the promise of love survive the realities of life for Madison and Jen, or is it too good to be true? (978-1-63555-715-2)

Treacherous Seas by Radclyffe. When the choice comes down to the lives of her officers against the promise she made to her wife, Reese Conlon puts everything she cares about on the line. (978-1-63555-778-7)

Two to Tangle by Melissa Brayden. Ryan Jacks has been a player all her life, but the new chef at Tangle Valley Vineyard changes everything. If only she wasn't off the menu. (978-1-63555-747-3)

When Sparks Fly by Annie McDonald. Will the devastating incident that first brought Dr. Daniella Waveny and hockey coach Luca McCaffrey together on frozen ice now force them apart, or will their secrets and fears thaw enough for them to create sparks? (978-1-63555-782-4)

Best Practice by Carsen Taite. When attorney Grace Maldonado agrees to mentor her best friend's little sister, she's prepared to confront Perry's rebellious nature, but she isn't prepared to fall in love. Legal Affairs: one law firm, three best friends, three chances to fall in love. (978-1-63555-361-1)

Home by Kris Bryant. Natalie and Sarah discover that anything is possible when love takes the long way home. (978-1-63555-853-1)

Keeper by Sydney Quinne. With a new charge under her reluctant wing—feisty, highly intelligent math wizard Isabelle Templeton—Keeper Andy Bouchard has to prevent a murder or die trying. (978-1-63555-852-4)

One More Chance by Ali Vali. Harry Basantes planned a future with Desi Thompson until the day Desi disappeared without a word, only to walk back into her life sixteen years later. (978-1-63555-536-3)

Renegade's War by Gun Brooke. Freedom fighter Aurelia DeCallum regrets saving the woman called Blue. She fears it will jeopardize her mission, and secretly, Blue might end up breaking Aurelia's heart. (978-1-63555-484-7)

The Other Women by Erin Zak. What happens in Vegas should stay in Vegas, but what do you do when the love you find in Vegas changes your life forever? (978-1-63555-741-1)

The Sea Within by Missouri Vaun. Time is running out for Dr. Elle Graham to convince Captain Jackson Drake that the only thing that can save future Earth resides in the past, and rescue her broken heart in the process. (978-1-63555-568-4)

To Sleep With Reindeer Justine Saracen. In Norway under Nazi occupation, Maarit, an Indigenous woman, and Kirsten, a Norwegian resister, join forces to stop the development of an atomic weapon. (978-1-63555-735-0)

Twice Shy by Aurora Rey. Having an ex with benefits isn't all it's cracked up to be. Will Amanda Russo learn that lesson in time to take a chance on love with Quinn Sullivan? (978-1-63555-737-4)

Z-Town by Eden Darry. Forced to work together to stay alive, Meg and Lane must find the centuries-old treasure before the zombies find them first. (978-1-63555-743-5)

Bet Against Me by Fiona Riley. In the high-stakes luxury real estate market, everything has a price, and as rival Realtors Trina Lee and Kendall Yates find out, that means their hearts and souls, too. (978-1-63555-729-9)

Broken Reign by Sam Ledel. Together on an epic journey in search of a mysterious cure, a princess and a village outcast must overcome life-threatening challenges and their own prejudice if they want to survive. (978-1-63555-739-8)

Just One Taste by CJ Birch. For Lauren, it only took one taste to start trusting in love again. (978-1-63555-772-5)

Lady of Stone by Barbara Ann Wright. Sparks fly as a magical emergency forces a noble embarrassed by her ability to submit to a low-born teacher who resents everything about her. (978-1-63555-607-0)

Last Resort by Angie Williams. Katie and Rhys are about to find out what happens when you meet the girl of your dreams but you aren't looking for a happily ever after. (978-1-63555-774-9)

Longing for You by Jenny Frame. When Debrek housekeeper Katie Brekman is attacked amid a burgeoning vampire-witch war, Alexis Villiers must go against everything her clan believes in to save her. (978-1-63555-658-2)

Money Creek by Anne Laughlin. Clare Lehane is a troubled lawyer from Chicago who tries to make her way in a rural town full of secrets and deceptions. (978-1-63555-795-4)

Passion's Sweet Surrender by Ronica Black. Cam and Blake are unable to deny their passion for each other, but surrendering to love is a whole different matter. (978-1-63555-703-9)

The Holiday Detour by Jane Kolven. It will take everything going wrong to make Dana and Charlie see how right they are for each other. (978-1-63555-720-6)

A Love that Leads to Home by Ronica Black. For Carla Sims and Janice Carpenter, home isn't about location, it's where your heart is. (978-1-63555-675-9)

Blades of Bluegrass by D. Jackson Leigh. A US Army occupational therapist must rehab a bitter veteran who is a ticking political time bomb the military is desperate to disarm. (978-1-63555-637-7)

Hopeless Romantic by Georgia Beers. Can a jaded wedding planner and an optimistic divorce attorney possibly find a future together? (978-1-63555-650-6)

Hopes and Dreams by PJ Trebelhorn. Movie theater manager Riley Warren is forced to face her high school crush and tormentor, wealthy socialite Victoria Thayer, at their twentieth reunion. (978-1-63555-670-4)

In the Cards by Kimberly Cooper Griffin. Daria and Phaedra are about to discover that love finds a way, especially when powers outside their control are at play. (978-1-63555-717-6)

Moon Fever by Ileandra Young. SPEAR agent Danika Karson must clear her werewolf friend of multiple false charges while teaching her vampire girlfriend to resist the blood mania brought on by a full moon. (978-1-63555-603-2)

Serenity by Jesse J. Thoma. For Kit Marsden, there are many things in life she cannot change. Serenity is in the acceptance. (978-1-63555-713-8)

Sylver and Gold by Michelle Larkin. Working feverishly to find a killer before he strikes again, Boston homicide detective Reid Sylver and rookie cop London Gold are blindsided by their chemistry and developing attraction. (978-1-63555-611-7)